Diving Heart First

Magnolia U #1

Emmy Lewes

Editing by Larissa Antonioni, FictionAlly & J.A. Azez, Juwi's Archives & Erin Larson-Burnett, EKB Book Services

Book Cover by Amanda Weir

1st edition, 2026

ISBN: E-Book 979-8-9942848-1-0

ISBN: Paperback 979-8-9942848-0-3

ISBN: Hardback 979-8-9942848-2-7

ISBN: Audiobook 979-8-9942848-3-4

Library of Congress Control Number: 2025927332

To all the girls who felt like a failure because a boy didn't love them the way they deserved, this one's for you.

Author's Note & Content Warnings

Hi, friends.

First of all, thank you for picking up this book. I hope it leaves you happier than when you started. I'm a firm believer that books that represent parts of our souls or situations we've experienced in our lives are powerful. My prayer is that if you see yourself anywhere in this book, you feel more empowered and loved.

I'm so excited for you to dive in with Maisie and Connor. Before we get there, I wanted to take a moment to mention a few things. While these characters are only eighteen, they do engage in adult intimacy. If you wish to avoid explicit descriptions of this content (or if you are in any way related to me), note these take place in chapters 40, 51, and 55.

Some other things that I'd like to give you a heads up about: the death of a grandparent (off-page) is a strong component of how the plot progresses. There is also a scene in which alcohol is used for coping. Maisie, the main female character, has anxiety and does have a panic attack (on-page; chapter 22). There is a brief reference to cheating (not between the main characters) and death by an automobile accident (not of main characters) as well as death of a parent (not on-page, the FMC's uncle).

There is also some physical violence, emotional manipulation by a parent, profanity, depictions of jealousy, lying, depiction of a painful period, brief reference to possible body dysmorphia (side character), marijuana usage, and physical upset (slamming doors, storming down hall).

Lastly, you will meet a character named Karsen early on in the story. He is not a very nice boyfriend. As a sexual assault survivor, I want to be very clear with what is depicted here. Karsen does pressure Maisie and implies she "owes" him sexually. If you are on a healing journey and unable to read any content of this nature, please feel free to skip chapter 12. He does try to force her hand, very briefly, and does not listen the first time she says no. The scene is quick, Maisie stands up for herself, and he does stop as soon as she puts him in his place. We all know he should have stopped the first time and that no always means no. And that not everyone reacts the way Maisie does—with a strong voice—and that does not make them weak or wrong or that they deserved to be treated like that in any way. Also note, he uses derogatory language later in the book—including the word 'bitch.'

I share this because I care about your mental health first and foremost. Please do whatever you feel is best, even if that means setting the book down. I do also want to reiterate that there is a lot of joy in this book. Diving Heart First has deep friendships and lots of shenanigans, laughs, and romance and Connor and Maisie are old soul goof balls, who I hope you fall in love with.

It was a journey to get this book into your hands—a labor of love if you will. And worth every. single. second. So strap in, and I hope you enjoy.

Xoxo,

Emmy

1

Stroke of Fate

Connor

MY LEADEN ARMS AND legs pump through the water like they have thousands of times before. I've been swimming my entire life. And while I have kept up in the gym the past few months—and while this is one of the finest indoor facilities in the country, the water perfectly temped—nothing could have prepared me for this college-level intensity. First day out of the gate, and I think I might puke. *That'd make an impression.* The only thing making it bearable? Getting to sneak glances toward the diving well—where *she* is—every time I'm not face-down in the water.

My first glance of her was on freshman move-in day. I recall Hunter's Corolla squeaking as it pulled up to the curb. Sweat was already dripping down my brow, but as I hopped out of the car, my eyes landed on her immediately. Her wavy chestnut hair fluttered in the breeze as she hauled more than someone her size should have been able to handle. Her legs were the kind of toned that drew every eye as she walked. But what really captured me was her smile. Cliché, I know, but it was unencumbered, stretching from ear to ear. And the way her eyes lit up? She was the most beautiful woman I'd ever seen.

Unfortunately, my chance of meeting her was diminished because Hunter, my long-time best friend and one of my roommates, reminded me we had to get a move on towing things to our apartment—the apartment my dad was paying for, which still made my chest tighten, but I ignored that feeling and let Hunter direct move-in day. He was solid like that. Always reliable.

When we got back for the next load, she was nowhere in sight. It's a big school, with at least a hundred buildings and double that many majors, and I was worried I wouldn't see her again.

But when I got to practice today, there she was, balanced at the end of the board with the poise of a fucking swan in a cut-out suit that left nearly nothing to my imagination. The sight immediately did things to me—unideal things while in my Speedo at my first swim practice.

It's a stroke of fate. I have to talk to her after practice. No, I *will* talk to her after practice. Grandpa always said he knew the moment he laid eyes on Grandma that she was the one he was going to marry. I always secretly thought that was bullshit, especially after seeing how love could implode, but my racing pulse and yearning to know her don't feel like an accident.

Coach Ken blows the whistle, the sound piercing my ear, and shouts that practice is over. We all pull ourselves out of the water, and I huddle up briefly with the guys. Coach recruited me when I was a sophomore in high school, since I had already won states two years in a row for the 50 and 100 free. And two years later, he snagged Hunter, too. He flew me out again for Hunter's recruiting trip, and that was where we met our other two roommates—Brock and Tyler.

"Antonio's after this?" Brock asks, holding his stomach. "I'm starving."

"Fine with me." Tyler shrugs.

Hunter chimes in, "I'm just gonna go to the dining hall. If we keep eating out, I'll have no money left. I'm still trying to find a campus job."

Brock groans. "But what if I spot you?"

"Nah," Hunter remarks, too nice to accept help.

"Connor, you're in, right?" Brock's expectant brown eyes widen.

"Sorry, guys. I have something I need to do," I say, the muggy air licking up my spine as I try to end this conversation as quickly as possible. I can't miss her.

Brock wiggles his eyebrows. "Something...or someone?"

"Jesus, Brock. Not everyone is looking to get laid every second of the day." Hunter jabs his arm. "Cool it."

He's not entirely off the mark, except I want a lot more than someone to warm my bed. Something about her has me drawn in. I need to know her. We'll start with her name.

My heart leaps when the diving coach announces their practice is over, too.

"Gotta run," I say, stooping down to grab my fins and kickboard. I rush to put them away in the designated bin and slip into the locker room. I'm taking the fastest shower of my life when Hunter's blond hair comes into sight.

"Why are you in such a rush?" he asks.

"Like I said, just have something I need to do." I scrub my body clean, trying to get the scent of chlorine off me—as if that is ever possible.

"*Okay.* Care to share with the class?"

I shut off the water. "It's a girl, okay? I saw her on move-in day, and now she's here. At practice. And I can't explain it, but I need to know her."

"Sounds a little stalker-ish, bro."

"I know what it sounds like. Just shut up. I'll see you at home."

"Fine," he says, turning on the spray of a nearby shower.

"Fine," I say, and rush to change as quickly as I can. When I pop out of the locker room and into Cardum Natatorium's main hallway, lined with Magnolia University green, I balk. There she is. Rolled sweats and a tank top that leaves a sliver of her stomach exposed. I'm walking toward her before I can fully process the movement.

"Hi." The greeting slips off my tongue. That's all that comes out. *Real smooth.* I'm not usually tongue-tied around women, but apparently all my words have run dry.

"Hi," she says, followed by a closed-lipped smile.

"You were amazing today," I manage to get out.

Her cheeks turn a dusty rouge, and it's the most adorable thing I've ever seen. "Umm, thanks," she says, her gaze averting as her delicate hand tucks a lock of hair behind her ear. "Are you a swimmer?" Her eyes come back to mine. She's not running; that has to be a good sign.

"Oh yeah, sorry, I'm Connor." I hold out a hand. Grandpa always taught me it was polite to greet everyone with a handshake, but now it feels a little out of place. I wince.

If she notices, she doesn't let on. "Maisie," she says, teeth showing in her smile now as she takes my hand, eyes softening. Her grip is strong, which is funny since her hand is so small that it isn't even visible when mine is wrapped around it.

I release her hand but hold her gorgeous green gaze. "I was thinking, maybe you'd want to grab dinner?"

Her eyes flare, but before she can respond, a lean dude with bleach-blond hair in our school's soccer jersey approaches, slapping her ass before slinging an arm over her shoulder. She startles, and the soft expression from moments ago vanishes. She looks down at the floor.

"Ready to go, babe?" the dude says, pinning me with a death glare.

Well, shit.

Who the hell is this guy?

2

The Opposite Sex

Maisie

MY HEART RATE KICKS up, anxiety swirling in my gut. Karsen has never been fond of me interacting with the opposite sex, which is ironic considering he practically has a gaggle of women that follows him around. Connor is my teammate, and he was just introducing himself. Karsen doesn't have to go all possessive asshole on him, but he won't see it that way.

I slip out from under Karsen's arm, and Connor tracks the movement. "Karsen, this is Connor. Connor—Karsen, my boyfriend."

Karsen reaches out to shake Connor's hand. When Connor extends his own, Karsen grips it tight, pulling him in so they are eye to eye, although Connor has some height on Karsen. Connor doesn't so much as flinch at the abrupt movement. "Stay away from my girl," Karsen seethes, "or we'll have a problem."

Connor's eyes flick to mine, but I don't know what to say. This is a wild over-reaction on Karsen's part, but no good will come of calling that out right now. He'll only escalate, probably yell. He's always been possessive—I'm starting to admit that to myself—and not in a good way. We've been dating for two years, and I've been forced to let go of several guy friends in my life. In the past, Karsen would say that I don't need guy friends because I have him. And if I did befriend a guy, he'd yell, we'd fight, I'd cry, and it was never worth it going through all that to keep the friendship. Not that Connor and I even got a chance to be friends yet.

Connor's jaw ticks. "I think I'll let *Maisie* decide for herself."

A small sense of relief pulses through me. It's like Connor can read my mind somehow and knows I want all of this nonsense to stop.

Karsen expels a cocky grunt from the back of his throat, then he squeezes Connor's hand one last time before letting go. He turns toward me, eyes ablaze. *Shit. We need to leave before Karsen loses it.* My chest tightens.

Out of the corner of my eye, I see Connor shift toward me.

"Let's go," Karsen says, snapping my attention back to him. No room for argument. I don't particularly want to go with him right now, but it's for the best.

Peeking back at Connor, I see his fists are clenched, and he looks like he's ready to fight Karsen off for me. His eyes are pleading with me, brow furrowed in concern, but I don't know what to say. I give him a disheartened half-smile, then turn to walk with Karsen out of the building.

As we step out into the North Carolina sunshine, Karsen says, "I don't like how that guy was looking at you."

"He wasn't looking at me in any sort of way. He was being friendly."

"Well, stay away from him anyway," he retorts, grabbing my hand as we walk toward the dining hall.

I don't argue with him. There's no point. I'd lose. I always lose when we argue. God forbid he be wrong about something. So, we walk in silence until we reach the dining hall.

We make our way to a table of his party friends. Karsen is big into going out, and as the freshman star soccer player, he's already racked up quite the popularity. We sit, and immediately a blonde with legs that seem to stretch on for miles—the opposite of my short diver legs—walks up to the table.

"Great game this past weekend, Karsen." Her face doesn't mask any of her interest. Her bottom lip is sunk between her teeth, and her manicured hand gently brushes his shoulder. It's like I'm not even here.

"Thank you," he says with a cocky smile. Sure, he doesn't flirt back, but he doesn't do anything to show he's taken, either.

As dinner progresses, this happens a few more times, and each time I wait to see if he'll react differently. He doesn't.

Karsen doesn't say a word to me for the entirety of dinner. He doesn't even look at me. Not once. I might as well be invisible. No one else at the table addresses me, either, too consumed by their totem of popularity. I eat my food and slowly shred one of my napkins for something to do with my hands.

I miss the old Karsen. The one who sent flowers to ask me on a date and bought me a dress and heels, telling me to wear them. Sure, it wasn't exactly my style, but it was the thought that counted. I can't remember the last time he did something for *me*. He didn't even help me on move-in day. He had already been here two weeks ahead of my arrival for soccer, and yet he chose to hang out with his friends instead. Though my mom waved it off, my dad was pissed.

As I'm reaching the crux of my self-pity party, Karsen reaches over and squeezes my knee, which I hadn't realized was bouncing. "Wanna go get ice cream?" he asks, and I light up like a Christmas tree. Ice cream is practically my religion, and the notion reminds me he's not all bad. I was probably overreacting. We've been together a long time. Couples have rough patches, right? Maybe that's all this feeling is. It will pass.

I squeeze Karsen's hand over my knee. "Yes, please."

He pulls me from the table, never mind that I wasn't finished eating, and we head back into the heat of the day to cool off with my favorite thing.

3

Roommates

Maisie

FINALLY, CLASSES AND PRACTICES are over for the week, and we're ringing in the weekend.

"That color is *divine* on you." Angie, my roommate, positively beams at my black skintight dress. "I'm so jealous of your tan," she whines.

I laugh. "Well, I'm jealous of these curls!" I counter, pulling on one of her blonde ringlets.

"Why?" she scoffs. "They are so hard to manage."

"Ummm, 'cause they're beautiful. Just like you." I wink.

Angie has quickly become my best friend at college, and thank god, because I've heard horror stories about freshman roommates. She swims, so we have the same schedule, and even though we could not be more different, we clicked from the very start.

Angie trips over a pile of clothes on her way to the floor-length mirror hanging over one of the closets.

"You're gonna sprain an ankle one of these days if you don't keep your side cleaner," I scold.

"Just because your dad instilled that little neat freak that lives inside of you doesn't mean my mess is wrong." She rolls her eyes, still smiling.

She met my dad on move-in day. Her parents hadn't come to help, so mine instantly adopted her. My dad couldn't help making her bed for her, teaching her his favorite method, and then bouncing a quarter off it. Angie ate it up, but she loves to poke fun at my inner neat freak—which, yes, I got from my dad. For me, though, neatness is less a game and more an expectation. He's often different with others than he is with me.

"Whatever you say. But don't come crying to me when you have to explain to Coach why you're hurt. From what you've said, he's a hard-ass about not doing stupid things."

"Hey!" she squeaks. "I'll clean it up later this weekend. Now, can we *focus* on the party? I've been eyeing up some of the men's team, and I'm hoping to have some fun tonight." She waggles her eyebrows. "If you ditched dirtbag, maybe you could also enjoy yourself tonight."

I'm about to contradict her statement when I see "Mom" flash across my cell. I accept the call, holding up a finger to silence Angie, and brace for a conversation with my mom.

"Hey, Mom, what's up?"

"Hi, honey. Oh, nothing, I just wanted to see what you and Karsen were up to tonight."

She's always loved Karsen. I mean, I get it—he's handsome, comes from a good family, excels at most things—but sometimes, it feels like she likes him even more than me, and that shit hurts. My dad, on the other hand, can't seem to stand him.

My heart pounds at the thought of telling my mom what I've been thinking lately. That I'm not sure Karsen and I are so good together, and that I feel a little...lost. I wish I could talk to her about it, but I know she'd just shove me in Karsen's direction.

"He has plans tonight, actually. Angie and I are going to go to a party with the team."

"Oh," she says, the disappointment in her voice palpable. Exactly why I can't say anything to her when it comes to him. "Well, have fun with the girls."

"Will do. Look, Mom, we're about to head out, so I've gotta go."

"Of course, sweetie. Give my best to Karsen when you see him."

"Will do." I stifle a groan, then hang up.

Angie is still checking her outfit in the mirror. "I, for one, am glad asswipe isn't joining us tonight. Also, I think it's weird how much your mom is obsessed with him. Like, why?"

Her words are like a nail to a scratch-off on my heart. "He's not an asswipe, Ang." I pin her with a glare. *Although sometimes he can be.* "And it's the only thing my mom and I have found common ground on in a while. I'm way more like my dad. I think she was hoping for the perfect little princess she could dress up and show off, but instead she got me, a nerdy athlete. But at least with me having a boyfriend, she can focus on that. I know it's not ideal." I let out a deep breath.

"Whatever you say." Angie swipes a final layer of gloss over her lips, recognizing I'm done with this conversation. "Let's go."

The Swim House—where some of the team's seniors live and which takes on the role of party house for the year—is packed. The theme for the night is the 2000s. I'm not usually one for parties, and being around all these people has my internal temperature rising, but Angie really wanted me to come. Plus, these are my teammates, and I want to get to know them better. I haven't exactly bridged the gap into any sort of social relationship with any of them other than Ang, so now might be the perfect opportunity. I take a deep breath, willing myself to cool.

Miley Cyrus's "Party in the U.S.A." blasts through the speaker system as we make our way past everyone dancing in the middle of the living room and halt in front of the makeshift bar—essentially a table with a giant beverage dispenser with who-knows-what in it and a large stack of red Solo cups. My stomach churns. I've never been a big drinker.

"You're picking at your nails again," Angie says. I hadn't even noticed. "This will help with your nerves." She hands me a cup.

I don't know if she's right or not, but I accept her offering nonetheless and take a sip. I scan the crowd. There are lots of familiar faces, but I don't know everyone's names yet. It's a big team, although our little diving portion only consists of six of us. I continue glossing over the nameless faces until I home in on a familiar one.

Connor.

He's already looking my way, and our eyes lock across the room. Before I can react, he's making his way over to me. He's rocking linen pants and a loose white button-down with the first several buttons undone. For a flash, my eyes dart to his strong chest before quickly returning to his face. He's dressed a step above every other guy at this party, but he's also smart to wear linen. The heat in this room could probably fry an egg—unless it's truly just my anxieties continuing to burn me up.

"Hey, Maisie," he greets me casually when he reaches us.

"Hi, I'm Angie," Angie says, then takes a large gulp of her drink. "Who are you?" She bats her eyelashes, coy smile firmly in place, and the muscles in my stomach tighten. She's on the prowl tonight, and for some reason, I don't want Connor to be her target.

He laughs. "Connor. Nice to meet you, Angie."

Her gaze latches onto something or someone beyond Connor's shoulder. "I'll be right back," she says, eyes still entangled with whatever or whoever they are locked onto. She turns to me briefly. "You okay?"

"Yep, I'll be fine here with Connor. Thanks." My stomach relaxes as she saunters away.

When I look back at Connor, I can't help but notice his eyes. They are a beautiful combination of blue and green with a brown halo around the pupil. Even in the dim light, they are stunning. I think I stare a little too long because he smirks, and my cheeks instantly heat.

"No Karsen tonight?" he asks. His words are casual, but his jaw is clenched. Interesting.

"Not tonight. Roomie night out," I say.

"So Angie's your roommate?"

"Yep." Another lash of pain lances through my stomach at his mention of Angie. What is happening? I take a sip of my drink, hoping it will chill me the fuck out.

My eyes wander to the dance floor involuntarily, and Connor follows my gaze.

"Want to dance?" he asks, holding out a hand.

Do I? Karsen would hate that I'm hanging out with Connor alone, but it's only a dance, and Connor is currently the only sort of friend I've made besides Angie, who is currently god knows where.

"Sure," I say, chugging the rest of my drink for courage before setting the cup down and taking his hand. Then he leads us toward the center of the dancing bodies.

4

Nighttime Breeze

Connor

*S*HE HAS A BOYFRIEND, *dumbass.* No matter how many times I've reminded myself of this little fact over the past week, it has not staunched the incessant pounding in my heart every time I see her. Or, if I'm being honest with myself, sometimes even when I'm not in her vicinity.

Her hand in mine as I lead her into the middle of the fray is like exposed wire. Shocking and dangerous.

I turn to face her, the silver ice cream cone necklace around her neck catching my attention for a moment before returning my gaze to her emerald eyes. They are darting all around as NSYNC's "Bye Bye Bye" surrounds us. I don't want her to be nervous, so I drop her hand to shoot my right arm in front of me, closing my hand to the beat in the signature dance style for this song. Yes, I'm aware of how dorky it is, but my plan works. A laugh bubbles out of her. I tuck it away for safekeeping as I let my own laugh spring free.

She starts to dance. Graceful, fluid motions that make my chunky sway look like an elephant next to a gazelle. But then, when the melody comes back around, we both do the move together, laughter ping-ponging between our glistening bodies. She's so beautiful it hurts.

Friends. We can be friends. I want to get to know her. Just because she's with someone doesn't mean I shouldn't follow this pull I feel toward her, right?

A flash of pain lances through my stomach. I don't want to be anything like my father. I can't be the reason a pair is ripped apart.

As I take a purposeful step back, her movements slow and the corners of her lips fall. She studies me, brow creased as we continue dancing.

"Wanna get some air?" she asks, leaning in so I can hear her. Lavender assaults my senses. She smells divine.

"Sure." I nod, gulping.

As we make our way outside and sit at the base of the house's concrete steps, the sounds of the party fade. The night air has a breeze, which cuts the lingering heat of the day. I take a deep breath. *Friends.*

No harm in getting to know her better. "What are you studying?" I ask.

Her eyes widen for a moment, like she's surprised I'm asking. "I'm pre-occupational therapy," she states, the words devoid of emotion.

"What made you decide that path?" I keep the conversation going.

"My dad, mostly." She sighs. "He's a very successful divorce lawyer, and he's always pushed me toward '*greatness*.'" She accompanies the last word with air quotes. "I don't know. I picked it arbitrarily. Something that pays well for the least amount of higher education. Dad math." She draws her thumb's cuticle into her lush mouth. I reach out to gently remove it, and she startles at my touch.

"Shit. I shouldn't have touched you without your permission," I blurt. "I saw you biting, and I didn't want you to hurt yourself." I run a hand along the back of my neck, my entire body feeling hot with embarrassment.

"No, it's okay. I...I tend to rip apart my fingers. Especially when I'm thinking about my dad's expectations of me. It's good that you stopped me." She shakes her hand like she can shake off the need to pick at her cuticles and turns toward me. "What are you studying?" she asks.

"Business." I pause before continuing. Involuntary tears prick at my eyes, but I don't let them fall. "I want to own my own coffee shop one day. My grandpa..." I let out a breath. "He loved coffee. Straight black. We'd have a cup together every morning. He was always encouraging me to do anything I wanted." I bite my lip.

"Was?" she asks, so softly I almost miss it—lost in a sea of memories.

"Yeah, he passed away this past summer. It was sudden."

Her hand wraps around my forearm. She doesn't say anything, but squeezes, leaning in so the sides of our bodies are completely flush. The gesture is unexpected, but extremely appreciated. My whole body warms. It feels right. When she leans back, she says, "I know you'll have the best coffee shop one day."

She barely knows me, and yet her belief in me is like a rod along my spine. I feel taller, supported. Her eyes find mine, soft and genuine. Butterflies erupt in my stomach. I knew she was special.

Before I can say anything else, the Swim House's front door flings open. Maisie jumps up beside me, and I instinctively follow her, putting a hand to the small of her back. A woman—Angie, I realize—strides through the door like she owns the place and homes in on the point of contact between me and her roommate. I drop my arm.

"There you are," Angie says, much too loud for the quiet permeating the evening.

Maisie sways, and I'm suddenly worried she might be feeling the punch's effects. "Ang!" she exclaims.

"I was looking everywhere for you."

Maisie blushes. "Sorry, we 'cided to grab some air. You know parties aren't my thing, and—" Her stomach rumbles, and she grips it, her eyes pinched shut.

"You okay?" I ask, bending to her eye level, hand finding her back again.

"Maisie?" Angie asks when Maisie doesn't respond. She's now bending over, hands on her knees.

"I think I'm going to be sick," Maisie says, shifting toward the grass in the front yard.

"Shit," Angie and I say in unison.

I gather Maisie's hair away from her face and rub soothing circles over her back while she does just that.

When she's through, she stands back up, wiping the corner of her mouth with her palm. Her cheeks are red and her eyes glassy.

"I can carry her home. I promise I'll get her there safe," I say before thinking about it.

Angie's eyes narrow for a moment. "I don't know…"

"It's okay, Ang," Maisie encourages. "Go back to the party. Have fun."

Angie looks once more between Maisie and me before taking a relenting step back. "Fine, but if you need me, I'm a text away, okay? I can be home in five minutes."

"I know," Maisie says, reaching out to squeeze Angie's hand. The motion nearly knocks her off balance, and I steady her by the elbow. Maisie's eyes find mine again, and she tries for a smile, but it comes out a bit of a grimace. I need to get her home.

"Is it okay if I pick you up now?" I ask.

"You really don't have to—"

"I'm not letting you walk when you feel so terrible," I say.

"Okay." She nods.

"I can pick you up now?"

"Yes." The corners of her lips curl. I reach down and scoop her up, one arm supporting her back and the other under the crooks of her knees. Her arm naturally finds its way around my neck. "Thanks," she whispers.

"You'll feel better after some sleep," Angie says. "Let me know if you need *anything*." She looks at me. "I'm trusting you with her. Don't make me regret it."

"Wouldn't dream of it," I say. "Where do you guys live?"

"Right over there." Angie points toward a series of clustered buildings. "Building 203. The tallest."

"The one that looks like a middle finger," Maisie adds, chuckling to herself.

Her goofiness during this time of distress throws me off guard, but it also makes her all the cuter.

"Middle finger, 203, got it," I say and turn to head toward the building.

Maisie's head slowly makes its way toward my shoulder. When it lands, my skin burns at the contact. I'm very reactive to her, but I contain it, not wanting to jostle her too much, so she doesn't get sick again.

When we reach her building, I walk through the—thankfully—automatic sliding glass doors. When I peek down at Maisie, I realize she's asleep. Knowing that she feels comfortable enough with me to not only let me carry her home but also to fall asleep makes the pounding in my chest double. I hate to do it, but I nudge her awake with my nose to her hairline. "Maize, I need your room number." *Maize.* I like the way that sounds.

Groggily, she says, "11B."

I navigate down the hall until we're outside her door. There is a small whiteboard pasted to the front with "Maisie and Angie" written in blue marker. I shift to gently set Maisie down on her feet, but she quickly wraps her arms tighter around my neck. I pull her back into me. "You're okay," I say.

"Sorry about that. I felt like I was falling."

"I should have warned you before I started to set you down," I reassure her.

"That shouldn't be necessary."

"You've had a rough night," I say.

"It hasn't been the worst," she says, cheeks flushing again, and I'm not sure if it's from the alcohol sickness this time.

"Is it okay if I set you down now?" I ask.

"God, yes, sorry."

I set her down, and the absence of her is palpable. I hand her my phone. "Here, save your number, then I'll text you. Just in case you need anything tonight."

"You don't have to do that." She bites her lip, and my attention clings to the movement. One day, we'll have a first kiss. I have to hope that that's true.

Friends, I chastise myself again.

"It's my pleasure," I counter.

"Okay." Her shoulders scrunch up in a shrug, and it's so cute. She takes my phone, entering herself as "Maisie Diver," like I would forget who she was. I immediately change it to "Maize," then text her.

"Thanks for getting me home. I think I can take it from here. They should put a warning label on that jungle juice." She laughs, but there isn't any humor behind it.

"Happens to the best of us," I assure her. "Feel better. Text me if you need anything—I mean it."

"I will, promise." She nods, then puts her key in the lock and opens her door. Over her shoulder, she says, "Good night, Connor. I'm really glad you were there tonight."

"Me too, Maize. Me too."

And then she's gone. I loose a breath and run a hand through my hair.

I'm in deep shit.

5

Grandpa Cereal

Maisie

I AWAKE TO SUNLIGHT spilling in through the window above my bed, and I roll over, grunting against the harshness of it. My sandpaper tongue sticks to the roof of my mouth. *Ugh.* There's a reason I don't typically drink. I'm a lightweight, and it tends to make my anxiety worse. The memory of puking on the grass last night is visceral.

It's softened, however, by strong hands gently holding my hair and rubbing circles on my back. *Connor.* He might be the kindest man I've ever met. Who else takes such good care of someone they practically just met?

I finally stretch out my limbs, sitting up. Rubbing my eyes, I realize Angie isn't in her bed. That's odd. Flipping my phone over, I see it's only 10 AM. She typically sleeps until noon on weekends. I hope she's okay. I'm about to call her when I see a few texts that came in while I was sleeping.

> **Angie:** Won't be home tonight. But still have my phone on if you need me xoxo

I fire off a text back.

> Everything okay?

I wait a minute, but she doesn't respond. Her bed is unmade, and there are clothes strewn about, but none of that is atypical. She could have already been home and left again while I was sleeping, and I'd be none the wiser.

I check my other texts.

> **[Unknown Number]:** Hey it's me. I mean it, text me if you need anything.

> **[Unknown Number]:** Realized you might not know who me is. It's Connor.

I smile at his consideration and save his contact. Right after I do, another text from him comes in.

> **Connor:** Checking in. Do you want me to bring you breakfast? Make sure to drink some water when you wake up

> I promise to drink water soon, and I'm doing okay. Not horrible. Planning to head to the dining hall for some food soon. Thanks for the offer though :)

He texts back immediately.

> **Connor:** Glad to hear it. I'll meet you over there

My stomach swoops. He's truly going above and beyond. I'm not sure I've ever felt so taken care of before. Other than by my cousin, Lauren. She's always been my ride or die, and she's stepped up plenty in my life.

> Okay. See you there

The last texts are from Karsen, from around 2 AM.

> **Karsen:** Need you.

> **Karsen:** Come over.

Karsen: Why aren't you answering?

Karsen: Plenty of girls were flirting with me tonight, but I told them I had a girlfriend. I still do, don't I?

My jaw clenches. I'm glad I was asleep when he texted. I would have felt compelled to go over there because that's what a "good girlfriend" would do. Lately, though, I haven't felt much like hooking up. He isn't big on cuddling, and he doesn't seem to care whether I get off or not. It leaves me feeling used. If I'm being honest with myself, I'm not sure he's ever prioritized me in bed, but he was my first everything. First kiss, first boyfriend, first time. I've given so much of myself to him, and I want things to get better. I'm losing hope they will, though.

Plus, since we got to college, he's been throwing around this bullshit about how many girls flirt with him, always assuring me he didn't do anything—like I should be grateful he has basic human decency—and that I "owe him." I was going to see if he wanted to hang out today, but after reading his texts, I think I'll leave him to his own devices for a while.

I grab a quick shower, change into athletic shorts and a tank, grab my keys, and head to the dining hall. When I arrive, I head straight for the cereal station. My dad always said Frosted Mini-Wheats were the best way to start the day, and I haven't gone a morning without them since. I fill a bowl and make sure to fill a glass with water too before I search the circular-shaped room for Connor.

As I scan, my eyes snag on his large frame at a table against a wall of windows overlooking the Quad—the large grassy area at the center of campus with Adirondack chairs where students like to hang out. Once again, he's already looking at me, and I feel my cheeks heat. He waves me over.

When I reach the table, I set my tray down, claiming the seat across from him.

"How ya doin' after last night's adventures?" he asks, taking a sip of his coffee.

I rub at my temples. "I could be better, but I could also be a lot worse, and I think I owe being better to you. Thank you. I'm sorry about, you know...getting sick." I wince.

"You don't have to apologize for being sick, Maize. That's not how friendship works." He smiles, and I feel it in my chest. He really is a great friend. I'll bet Connor would never treat a woman the way Karsen has been treating me. I wonder if he has a girlfriend. She's lucky, whoever she may be.

I take a bite of my cereal, and Connor's eyebrows shoot up when he sees what's in my bowl. "You like Frosted Mini-Wheats too?" His smile gets impossibly wider.

"Yeah, I eat them every morning," I say, noticing the same cereal is swirling around in his bowl. Only a few pieces left, though, so he must have been here a little while.

"I do, too. My brothers always made fun of me, telling me it's 'grandpa cereal.'"

The memory of him sharing about his grandpa last night knocks through my brain like a pinball machine. I didn't know any of my grandparents, but I lost my Uncle Richard—my cousin Lauren's dad—when I was ten. I know how devastating losing a close family member can be.

"I think being compared to a grandpa is an honor," I say, and his mouth quirks on one side, his gaze swinging to the Quad momentarily. I leave him with his private moment.

"I do, too," he says, eyes finding mine again. "So," he mumbles around a bite of cereal, "where are you from?"

"A little town called Springfield, Ohio. You?"

"No way!" His mouth hangs open for a moment before he continues, "I'm from Columbus."

"Are you serious?" I laugh. "We're practically neighbors."

"Funny how we both ended up in North Carolina for college, both in water sports. It's like we were supposed to meet or something." He winks, and I can't tell if he's joking or flirting with me. I'm sure he's just messing around. He said it himself earlier; we're friends. Plus, I have a boyfriend—I shouldn't want him to be flirting with me.

"Kismet," I say, then down half my water. It's life to my dehydrated body.

His eyes soften. "All right, I officially need to know more about you. Top three movies. Go."

I smile because this is an easy answer. "I'm a die-hard Marvel fan, so my top three would consist of only Marvel, but my favorites tend to switch."

He rubs the back of his neck. "I've never actually seen any Marvel movies," he says as he shrinks back like I'm going to scold him. Which I might.

"How can you have never seen a Marvel movie?" I try to keep my tone even.

"I don't know. Guess I missed the trend, and then felt too far behind to pick it up." He shrugs.

"Well, we're going to have to fix that, won't we? A Marvel movie-cation. I'll bet if we get started soon, we could catch you up before the next one comes to theaters. I'll warn you, though, it's a big commitment. Are you in?"

He salutes. "You have my full cooperation." He laughs again, and I can't help but laugh along. Connor is goofy, and it makes me comfortable letting my goofy side out, too. Karsen tends to get annoyed when I'm too goofy, saying he doesn't want me to embarrass him.

I don't know why I keep comparing the two. I shake my head; I need to stop.

"Wanna watch one after you're finished with your cereal?" He tips his chin toward my breakfast.

I'm about to accept when a disheveled and sandy-looking Angie appears at the side of our table.

"Ang, oh my gosh, are you okay?"

"Can we talk?" Her eyes slide to Connor, then back to me. "Alone?"

Connor grabs his tray and stands. "I'll get out of your way. Text me if you want to meet up later, Maize." Then he walks away.

"Thanks," I say, feeling an emptiness in my chest at the sight of him leaving, but I quickly focus on Angie, who takes his vacated seat.

"Men are the worst," she huffs, sand falling off her arm and accumulating in a small pile on the table. Part of me doesn't disagree with her, but the other part is watching a man who very much doesn't suck walk away.

6

Forever Friends

Connor

I DON'T HEAR FROM Maisie the rest of the day, and I try hard not to let it get me down. Angie did look a mess, so she's probably focused on whatever was happening there. I'm not used to this feeling. This desire to be with someone all the time. I want to know more about her, even if we can only ever be friends. That Karsen guy doesn't deserve her, though, if how he acted the other day is any indication. My fists clench at the memory.

In an attempt at a distraction, I grab pizza from Antonio's as a surprise for my roommates.

"Dinner is served," I shout into the apartment, hoping everyone will hear.

Hunter is playing video games on the couch, but Tyler and Brock are nowhere to be seen. Tyler soon makes his way down the stairs, grabs a slice, then walks back the way he came. He's not one for small talk, but he's a good dude.

Hunter pauses his game and comes into the kitchen to eat at the table with me. "Thanks for the pizza, man," he says around a mouthful.

"No worries," I say, tapping a finger on the table.

He raises an eyebrow. "Something on your mind?"

I'm about to answer when a shirtless Brock storms into the kitchen, his dark mop of hair askew, making me wonder if he has a lady friend waiting for him upstairs.

"Fuck yeah. Pizza!" he says, taking a seat at the table with us. "This is the perfect pick-me-up."

"What do you need to be picked up from?" I ask, hoping that focusing on someone else's problems will distract me from the fact that the woman I can't stop thinking about has a boyfriend.

"This girl from last night. Let's just say things didn't go as planned." He shoves half a slice in his mouth, grabbing a napkin to catch the grease that dribbles down his chin.

Hunter tenses but doesn't say anything. Odd. He's usually one to ask follow-up questions.

"Well, sorry things didn't go your way, man," I offer. "Better luck next time?"

"Yeah, we'll see," he says, devouring the crust, already reaching for the next slice.

"I got salad with chicken too," I say. "Had Coach's voice in my head about balancing every meal with fiber and protein." I laugh and stand to grab a drink from the fridge.

My phone buzzes in my pocket. I fumble for it, hoping it's Maize. My heart sinks when I see it isn't her, then skyrockets when I realize it's from my dad. My temples throb.

> **Dad:** I called today for a report. Your coach says you're meeting all expectations.

I practically crush my phone. This is exactly what I was worried about when I accepted this apartment from him. He doesn't have any right to be talking to my coach about me.

I slam the fridge door so hard that I hear some of the condiments fall off their shelves.

"Whoa, what's going on?" Hunter asks, already moving to stand by me, a hand on my shoulder.

"Nothing," I say, shrugging him off. Hunter knows all about how shitty my dad is. I could talk to him, but I haven't told the other guys, and honestly, I don't feel like hashing it out right now. I take a breath.

"You good?" he asks, eyes narrowing in concern.

I offer him a watery smile. "I'm good. Promise."

"Wanna play some Mario Kart?" He hooks a thumb over his shoulder toward the family room. "I'll let you be Princess Peach. We all know she's the best."

I cackle. He always knows how to get me out of my own head. "You're on," I say.

We head into the family room, getting comfy on the brown leather couch that my dad *also* provided. My chest tightens at the thought, but Hunter gets the game going.

Brock brings the pizza box in and sits on the floor in front of the coffee table. "I play winner," he announces.

We spend the next few hours snacking, racing, and hanging out. Tyler even joins us at some point. When it's time for bed, we each go our separate ways. As I crawl into bed, staring at the ceiling, I can't help but be thankful for my roommates. They're gonna be forever friends.

I plug my phone in, but before I set it on the nightstand, I impulsively fire off a quick text to Maisie.

> Hope everything's okay with Angie and you had a good rest of your day

I wait a minute to see if she'll respond, but when no text comes through, I set it face-down on my nightstand, roll over, and let sleep overtake me.

7

Let's Celebrate!

Maisie

CLASSES ARE GOING PRETTY well for the most part. On Monday afternoon, I'm back in my three-hour chemistry lab, which is giving me the hardest time—the lab specifically, but it's an occupational therapy school requirement. Regardless, I can't seem to get myself to care about why mixing one substance with another and writing ten pages about it is interesting. How is that going to help my future career anyway?

I put away the supplies from today's lab and head over to the sink station to wash off the grime. I always feel gross after messing with chemicals and sweating in my goggles and gloves for hours. Once I'm cleaned up, I cross the room to grab my bag and phone from the section of "clean" tables, meant for non-experiment work only. Picking up my phone, I see I have a voicemail from Lauren and a text from Angie. I open my texts first and see the message from Connor that I decided not to answer. I wasn't quite sure how to respond. Shaking my head, I pull up Angie's thread instead.

Angie: Guess WHAT!

What??

Angie: You're talking to the newest junior reporter at the Magnolia Daily!

Omg Ang! Congratulations!!!! I'm so proud of you!

Angie wants to be a travel journalist after graduation, so this is a great step for her. I'm almost a little jealous she is making such great moves for her future—and only a few weeks into our freshman year—but I'm also beyond happy for her. She's a real go-getter, and her hard work is paying off already.

Angie: We have to celebrate! When do you get home?

I just finished Chem Lab, so I can head home now. What do you have in mind?

Angie: Hmmm, how about that fancy ice cream place that opened over on 3rd? I heard they have romance books too! Something for you and something for me.

I'll never say no to ice cream

Angie: Sweet ;) I'll see you when you get home. Don't detour!

I make my way out of the science building and into the sun. I don't think I'll ever get tired of the weather here. Then I remember I have a voicemail and press *play* before placing the phone to my ear.

"Hey, love! How is school going so far? Just wanted to check in on you. Have practices started yet? Please please please tell me you're doing some fun things too. Anyway, call me back when you can. Love ya, bye!"

I smile as I draw the phone away from my ear. Lauren is one of my favorite people on the planet. I've always thought of her as the big sister I never had. She's four years older than me and went to college in California, so I haven't seen as much of her as I'd like for a few years, but we still call and check in frequently.

She's been my best female friend for as long as I can remember. I'm thankful to get to add Angie to that list now, but Lauren will always be Lauren.

I open her contact and call her. She picks up on the third ring.

"Hey, you! What's crack-a-lackin'?"

"Oh, not much over here. I'm walking home from *chem lab*," I respond, dropping my voice dramatically.

"Uh-oh, I know that voice. What's your beef with your chem lab?"

"Nothing really. It's just boring as hell. I can't find anything interesting about it. It's long and makes me smell weird. I wish I didn't have to take it as a pre-req for occupational therapy school."

"Hmm, well, maybe ride this one out, but if you find yourself not liking your pre-req classes, it *is* okay to switch your major, you know? I know you picked it from a list Uncle Alan gave you, but that's kind of what this whole college thing is about. Figuring out what you want to do."

She doesn't get it. Her mom, my dad's sister, is the most laid-back person in the world. Aunt Kaity works part-time at her local bookstore, is certified to teach yoga, and makes chunky jewelry as a side hustle. Ever since Uncle Richard passed away, Aunt Kaity has lived by the "life is too short" motto. She's always encouraged Lauren to do whatever she wanted in life as long as it made her happy. She and my dad could not be more dissimilar.

"Yep, sure, that's what it's for," I force out.

"I'm serious, Maisie. I know Uncle Alan is intense about stuff, but it doesn't mean his way is the only way. You're eighteen, out of the house and on your own. It's okay to explore and live your life the way *you* want to."

Her words make sense, but they feel like trying to jam a puzzle piece in the wrong spot. Still, I decide I'll let her words marinate.

"I hear you, LoLo, I do," I respond with my silly childhood name for her.

She laughs on the other end before responding with her own nickname for me: "MaiMai, I want you to actually hear what I'm saying, but I also know you need time to process stuff like this, so I'll let it go...for now. How is everything else? Your roommate? Diving? *Karsen*?" She says his name like a curse. She's never liked him and has not been shy about vocalizing it.

At first, I'm not sure how to respond. Do I tell her the truth? I've never *not* opened up to her before. I know she'll tell me to leave him, though, and I don't know if that's what is best. I settle on an in-between.

"Karsen has been pretty busy with soccer. Things have been a bit strained, but I think we just need time to work through it."

"You deserve better," she says.

"Not every relationship is all sunshine and rainbows. We aren't in the honeymoon phase anymore and college has been a big change for both of us. We'll figure it out." I'm not sure I believe that's true, but I love him. That has to be enough, right?

"Fine, but I—"

I don't let her finish. Instead, I continue, "Diving practices have started. You know how much I love my sport, but I'm still not sure this level is the best fit for me. I guess it's too late now—" My stomach drops as I say it out loud. My dad convinced me Division I was achievable, so here I am, even though I never thought I was good enough for D1. Disappointing him feels akin to being chased by a bear. I move on quickly. "But anywayyyyy, my roommate—Angie—is amazing. We've been hanging out a lot, and she's high-energy, but, like, not in an annoying way. I feel comfortable around her, and you know how hard that is for me. I'm actually on my way to meet up with her now, so I have to go in a minute."

"Maize, that's great." I hear the soft pride shining in her words. "I can let you go. Feel free to text any time, and I'll check back in soon, okay?"

"Sounds good, LoLo. I'm glad you called. You know you mean the world to me."

"I know, MaiMai. Back atcha. Love you, talk soon."

"Love you too, bye."

We hang up right as I'm approaching my dorm building. Today might have sucked a little because of lab, but it seems to be turning around. I navigate to our room to grab a shower before Angie and I can go on our celebratory trip to town.

8

Beef Tongue Stew

Connor

I SUCK IN A lungful of the heated chlorine air, then spray the last of my water into my mouth. The break before our last set is almost up, but my eyes are glued to the diving well where Maisie is currently getting an earful from her coach.

"Just try it in pike! What is the worst that is going to happen? You can't compete this in tuck at this level."

My chest constricts. She doesn't need to yell to get her point across.

Maisie's shoulders bunch. She doesn't say anything, just nods as she bites at the skin around her nails. I hate seeing her like this.

My own coach blows the whistle for us to get moving, but as I glide through the water, I'm thinking of ways to turn Maisie's day around. After practice, I shower quickly, hoping to catch her before she leaves, but after waiting outside the women's locker room for what is arguably a creepy amount of time, I give up waiting. But I don't give up on her. I send off a text before walking home.

> Bad day?

> **Maize:** I've had worse. Nothing some beef tongue stew can't fix

> Beef tongue stew?

Maize: It was the most old people food I could think of. Ya know, to go with our old people cereal

Her day must already be turning around if she's joking like this. I smile, then type back.

> How about some liver and onions? That always does it for me.

Maize: Haha that's just gross.

> Grosser than beef tongue stew??

Maize: Alright alright. Both are disgusting. Old people can't have everything right I guess.

> So seriously, you ok?

She doesn't text back right away. I decide to shoot my shot.

> I was thinking maybe a Marvel movie was in order?

The typing dots appear and disappear a few times before her text comes in.

Maize: You know what? I think that's just what the doctor ordered. I'll queue up the movie, you bring the snacks :)

> Pudding cups and applesauce? Don't want you to have to put in your dentures on my account, Betty.

Maize: Haha. Betty?

> Betty White, the crowning glory of all old people.

Maize: But she's dead!

Yea, but no one has taken up her post as the coolest old person alive yet, so it still counts.

Maize: You're such a weirdo lol

Be over soon White ;)

I swing by the campus store to load up on snacks. I think about texting her to see what she wants specifically, but then decide to get a truckload, so she can just pick what she likes. The guys will eat whatever she doesn't want. They're practically human trash cans.

Before I know it, I'm outside her room, and suddenly, my face feels hot. I'm nervous, but I work up the courage to knock. She swings the door open with a dazzling smile, and I am once again struck by how beautiful she is.

"What did you bring me?" She eyes the plastic grocery bag in my hand.

"The better question is, what *didn't* I bring you?" I laugh, then step into the small dorm room. I trip over a pair of shoes, but right myself quickly. That would have been embarrassing.

"Sorry about that," she says. "Angie is a bit of a space disaster. You'll get used to it."

I scratch my chest. She's implying there will be many more visits here. I loose a breath. *Friends,* I remind myself, then add, *Boyfriend,* for good measure, although that makes me grind my teeth.

Maisie, picking up a few things throughout the room, looks back at me, standing here like some sort of oaf. The way she can make me lose all sense is remarkable.

"You okay?" she asks, snagging her bottom lip between her teeth. I want to use my thumb to release it, but that wouldn't be very *friend*-ly of me. Instead, I smile, trying to ease any tension she might feel from the angry vibe I was putting off. Especially after witnessing the way Karsen reacted around her, I don't ever want her to feel unsafe with me.

"I'm dandy," I respond, moving further into the room. "This one yours?" I point to the pristinely made bed.

"How'd you know?" She laughs and pats it like a prized possession.

"Lucky guess." I wink and dump the contents of the bag onto her bed.

Her eyes widen for a moment, but then she gets to sorting. "Wow. You brought—" she points and counts silently in her head "—three bags of chips, two kinds of popcorn, four varieties of soda, six kinds of candy—a mix of chocolate and sour—and two pints of ice cream? Are you planning to feed a small army?"

"Nope, just one girl who I wanted to have choices."

She looks at me then, and her expression is hard to read. Her eyebrows are raised, her eyes soft, but there's a slight frown on her face. Did I do something wrong?

"That was...really thoughtful of you. Thank you, Connor." She hugs herself like she's unsure of what to do with her arms.

I step into her space, hold up my hands by her arms, then look to her for permission. She nods, and I unwrap her arms from her body, lingering for only a second longer than is strictly necessary. Her smooth skin against my hands sends lightning up my arms, straight to my heart.

I eye the snack setup, and her gaze follows. "Anything you like?"

When I look back at her expectantly, she relinquishes a smile that I memorize. A mental picture for later.

"Cool Ranch Doritos and root beer are my favorite. And ice cream. I'm not sure I can express how much I love ice cream." Her cheeks redden, and it's the best damn thing.

"I figured," I say, "since you were wearing an ice cream cone necklace at the party the other night."

"You noticed that?" she asks, fumbling to open the bag of chips.

I reach out, take the bag, open it with one tug, and hand it back. "I did." I'm not sure what else to say. I'm not going to say, *"Hey, I think I might be head over heels for you if the way I can't stop thinking about you and react when I'm around you is any indication."* That would probably freak her out, and I doubt we'd be hanging out anymore after that. I'd rather have her as a friend than nothing at all, so I cool it.

She tucks her hair behind her ear. "Which snacks do you want?"

I pluck up a bag of popcorn, some chocolate, and the ginger ale. She raises an eyebrow at me.

"What?" I ask, moving the rest of the haul to the desk by the window.

She shakes her head. "Ginger ale is such an old-person soda."

"Well, I like it."

"I like that you like it," she says, and her cheeks brighten with color once again. "Grab the laptop while you're over there?"

I bring the laptop over to the bed, which she has already climbed onto and scooted back against the wall it's leaned up against. She pats the spot next to her. Setting the laptop down, I shift my snack haul to the side, then settle in beside her. My heart is pounding, and I'm worried she can hear it. But she seems focused on setting up the movie. When it starts playing, she dips a plastic spoon into her ice cream, flips it over, and curls her kissable lips around it in a smile.

"I can't wait for you to experience this," she says.

"Me either." Because I want to know about everything that she loves. I want to love it too.

As the movie plays, I try to pay attention, but I'm too aware of her, of my own body, of the taut air between us. We're a respectable distance apart, but her lavender scent is wafting my way. She watches me every time she wants to see my reaction to a scene, and she also covers her mouth anytime she's nervous about what will happen next—which I find adorable considering how many times she's told me she's watched this movie. *Fifteen.*

As much as I am aware of the warmth radiating between us, it's just as much comfort as it is attraction. Maisie is kind, passionate, and fun. She's easy to be around, and I'm thankful to be spending time with her.

The movie ends, and she stretches her arms above her head, yawning. "Thanks for this," she says.

"I'm the one who should be thanking you. I would have missed out on this amazing movie if it weren't for you."

She beams, and I slip off the bed, collecting our trash and organizing the unopened snacks on her desk. I'm leaving them here; the guys can fend for themselves.

"Maybe another one soon?" she asks, dragging that lip between her teeth again.

This time, I can't help it. I step closer, reach up, giving her all the time in the world to move, then gently release it.

"Oh," she says and blushes. "Thanks. I guess I pick at more than just my nails." Her eyes flit to the side, one shoulder shrugging.

"I'll keep reminding you if you want," I practically whisper.

"I wouldn't hate that," she says, and we smile at each other.

"I'll get going. And to answer your question, yes. Definitely another one soon. Text me anytime. Have sweet dreams, Betty."

"Thanks, Connor. Good night."

I slip out the door and walk home with a huge grin on my face.

9

Hat Trick

Maisie

KARSEN JUST SCORED HIS second goal of the soccer game, and he's doing a victory dance surrounded by several of his teammates. I clap and let out a small yelp of support, but the sound is drowned out by the throng of women a few rows down from us. They're wearing his jersey and are practically tripping over themselves cheering for him.

I roll my eyes and turn to Angie, who is staring daggers at the women. She decided to come with me today, which was nice of her, considering how much she hates Karsen. Otherwise, I'd be sitting alone.

"I don't like soccer, but I like you," she had said earlier with a playful smile as she packed a bag of snacks for us.

Now, Angie reaches into said bag and hands me a clementine. I peel it as the players on the field reset for kick-off.

"Has he still been playing the *you-should-be-grateful-I-don't-flirt-back* card?" she asks after taking a sip of her seltzer water.

Yes. "Girls have always fawned over him. I get it, he's hot."

"He doesn't have to remind you about it and make you feel like shit, though." Angie has been increasingly vocal about her dislike of Karsen. She's seen him out at parties and has confirmed he never does anything over the line, but I've opened up to her about what it's like when we're together. She has not been shy about telling me how toxic it is.

"I know," is all I say. I toss the clementine skin into the bag and wipe my hands on my jeans.

"If you say so," Angie replies skeptically.

We both return our attention to the game.

The Magnolia Vipers beat the Carolina State Bears 4–0. Karsen scores another goal right before the end of the game, bringing his goal count to three and making it a hat trick. He is impressive as always. The soccer star.

I wait at the front of the parking lot for him. Angie has a date, and she said, as much as she loves me, she wasn't missing a chance for some good dick. I laughed and told her to go on without me.

The sun is in my eyes, but I think I spot Karsen lingering inside the tunnel that leads from the field to a long set of steps down to the parking lot. I use my hand, blocking the light in order to see better. He's surrounded by three women, all wearing jerseys with his number tied up so their stomachs are showing, their shorts leaving little to the imagination. One is touching his arm and moving closer as she says something.

"Karsen! Down here," I call out in a sing-song voice without an ounce of regret.

He startles but quickly moves to extricate himself from the women and jogs down the steps to me. "Hey, babe," he says as he reaches me, bending down to kiss my cheek. "Didn't know you were waiting for me."

My eyes narrow, but I let it go. "Well, I am. Great game, by the way. You were amazing as always. Wanna grab dinner?"

"I'd love to, but Caroline was just telling me about a party at Xi Pi Rho tonight." He uses his thumb to motion to the gaggle of women still gathered at the top of the steps. They're glowering at me.

Awesome. I love being hated for being with the *hot soccer star*.

"Figured I'd run home for a quick shower and then order some takeout while I pre-gamed with the guys. You'll meet me there, though, right?"

"I don't really feel like going to a party tonight, Karsen. You know they drain me. Can't we just hang out? Maybe watch a movie or something?" My eyes search his face for any sign he might care about what I want—*for once.*

"Well, the girls said there was going to be some top-shelf stuff and a band. Can't miss that, right? I'll go by myself and then we can just have some alone time after," he says as he snakes his arm around my waist. The smell of his sweat assaults my senses, and I take a step back, disconnecting his hold.

He's not typically good company after he's been drinking, but he usually ends up persuading me into his bed anyway. Saying no isn't my strong suit. But lately, I think I might be getting a little better at pushing back.

"We'll see," I say cryptically.

"You always say that, but you know you can't resist all this." He waves a hand down his body like it should be worshipped.

"We'll see," I repeat. "I have my period anyway."

His nose scrunches in distaste, but he doesn't add anything else.

I rock back on my heels and say, "I'll see you later, Kar. Great game again."

"Thanks, babe. You know you're my lucky charm." He moves to kiss me, and I let him even though he still stinks.

I wave and start to walk away. He slaps my ass for good measure. My spine locks up. It hurts worse than I'd like to admit. I've told him several times not to do that while I have my period.

I shake my head and keep walking, hoping not to see him later.

10

Shammies and Friends

Maisie

T HE NEXT MONTH OR so of college passes by in the blink of an eye. I've fallen into a routine: class, meals, practice, homework, going to parties with Karsen when I get tired of saying no, Marvel movies with Connor, and roomie nights with Angie. Our first dual meet is this Saturday, and my nerves are through the roof. We're facing off with Mannon University, our biggest and longest-standing rival.

I'm going through the motions of practice, but my temples are throbbing and my palms are sweaty, which makes grabbing my shins while flipping nearly impossible. The fogginess in my head causes me to miss simple skills, and all of my optionals—the name we have for our harder dives—are either being thrown way over or landing severely under the vertical mark, which only fuels the anxiety cycle. I can tell Coach Megan is *not* pleased with my practice today, but I do my best to drown out the noise in my head and run through each of my dives a few times, regardless of their outcome.

Once I'm done, I grab my shammy and head toward the locker room. On my way, I spot Connor standing in the shallow end of one of the lap pools, holding his navy water bottle aloft, squirting water into his mouth. His bicep is flexed, the vein that runs along his forearm on full display. Some of the water misses and dribbles down his jaw, then down his sturdy neck and sculpted chest. My eyes can't help but track its descent until—shit, he sees me. Our eyes meet—mine most likely full of panic and his crinkled from the smile he gives me. He lowers the bottle and waves.

I awkwardly wave back and continue toward my destination. A whistle blows, indicating practice is over for the swim team, too, and before I know it, an all-too-familiar shadow lingers behind me. I turn just as Connor was about to pull on my wet ponytail. I karate chop his arm like I'm some sort of ninja, and he groans, dramatically playing along with our faux-violent scene, his plans thwarted. I smile, content that I can always be my goofy self with him.

Angie sidles up beside me and says, "Wanna do something together tonight?" She looks between Connor and me expectantly. I balk because this is the first time she's ever suggested the three of us hang out. Of course she and I are friends, and Connor and I are friends, and we're all teammates, but...it still feels weird.

"I don't have anything going on after this," Connor replies with a nonchalant shrug. He looks to me.

"Um." I shake the water out of my ear. "Sure. Why not? What did you have in mind?" Might as well, right? Beats my plans to work on my chem lab.

"What about your place?" She points at Connor, lips quirked to the side.

"I'm game. Just have to run it by the guys, but it should be fine." He rubs the back of his neck, looking almost sheepish. Just as he says it, Connor's roommate, Hunter, appears by his side.

"What's this I hear about a get-together?" His smile is confident and his body posture relaxed even after a hard practice.

"Angie and Maize were talking about coming over to our place," Connor responds. "I was just saying I needed to run it by you guys first."

"They should come! Brock never minds the company of beautiful women—" he dips his head in respectable reverence to Angie and me "—and Tyler has had enough alone time this week; he needs to socialize, show proof of life, all that good stuff," he says through a laugh.

"We should probably still ask them—" Connor starts to say, but Angie interrupts.

"Great! See you all there in an hour." She wastes no time bouncing into the locker room.

"See you then." Hunter tips his head in a Southern-gentleman way toward the two of us and saunters off as well.

I haven't moved. Even though my social worlds colliding should be a good thing, it's left me a bit off kilter. Plus, I've never actually been to Connor's place. We always watch movies in my room. Change *also* has not always been my strong suit. When I don't know what to expect, I feel vulnerable, not knowing if things will go okay or what a new environment will be like. If I'll feel comfortable enough to be some semblance of myself. Will this change things between Connor and me?

I must be frowning because Connor boops my nose, asking, "You okay there, Betty?"

"Yeah, I'm fine. I'm fine." I stumble backward and nearly fall into the bin of practice fins along the wall. "I'll, uh, see you at your place then. Bye!" I lift my hand in a haphazard wave goodbye before ducking into the locker room.

I shake my head to clear it as I walk into the shower area, where I find Angie already naked and scrubbing her ringleted hair.

I know I'm way over-reacting, but I can't help it. "What's gotten into you?" I ask with a mildly accusing tone.

She flips her hair over and bends at the waist to rinse the underside. "What? You're friends with him, so why shouldn't I be? Plus, after interacting with Hunter, I *may* want to explore that some more. Did you hear him call me beautiful?" Her words are garbled by the water. Flipping her hair and straightening, she steps back into the spray and smiles fiendishly.

I lather my own hair as I roll my eyes at her. Of course Angie latched onto that little detail. I take a deep breath, as close to accepting the change as I'll get. "Fine. Whatever. But are you sure you want to see..." I let the question linger, knowing she has history with another one of Connor's roommates.

Angie's nostrils flare. "Who cares about Brock? Whether he's there or not makes no difference to me. I want to spend time with you and your *other* best friend. That's all."

"Alrighty then."

"The d-bag," she whispers under her breath.

I pretend not to hear, giving her privacy in her own thoughts, but I smile because I'm pretty sure she's into one of Connor's roommates—and it's not the one she is claiming to have a newfound interest in. It should make for an entertaining evening nonetheless.

11

Messy Apartments & Shitty Situations

Connor

I SHUFFLE AROUND, TRYING to pick up laundry, empty bottles, and all the crap my roommates have left strewn about everywhere. How very male of them to not give a shit about the state of our place. Can't say I blame them. We're all busy with swimming and classes and whatnot, but still. How is a guy supposed to impress a girl in this dump? Not that I'm trying to impress Maisie. I want her to have a good time, *obviously,* because I care about her, as a...friend. Yeah.

The doorbell rings, and I freeze.

"I'll get it," Brock says, racing toward the white painted door.

When he opens it, Angie bellows, "Hey, guys!" as she confidently sidesteps a frozen and slack-mouthed Brock into the living area. She strides past me into the kitchen, golden hair swaying. I hear her opening and closing our oak cabinets. "Whatcha got to drink around here?"

Brock is still standing there, door shut but hand remaining on the handle. Strange.

Then I see her. She's in her rolled university sweats and a plain white tank top. Her hair is still damp from practice, but she left it loose around her shoulders, showcasing its natural waves. Her signature smile—unencumbered, full-mouthed, and gleaming—lights up her face. She's so fucking beautiful.

I briefly register Angie popping a cork and the sound of Hunter's gruff voice as he says, "Can I pour that for you?"

But then Maisie closes the space between the entry and where I'm standing, still embarrassingly holding an armful of random items.

"Hey," she says, biting her lip to keep from laughing, "did you rob a thrift store and haven't dumped your haul yet?"

I blow out an amused, albeit embarrassed breath. "I was trying to pick up a little before you guys got here. These heathens I call roommates don't exactly clean up after themselves."

"Do too!" Hunter calls from the kitchen.

"Nah, he's right—we're slobs," Tyler says as he enters from the stairs.

"You didn't have to pick up on our account." Maisie waves a hand dismissively. "You've seen our dorm room. It's just nice to hang out in an apartment instead of smooshing people—and by people I mean you—into our tiny room." She spins, fully taking in her surroundings. "I never asked, how did you guys snag this place anyway?"

I shuffle back and forth before saying, "Walk with me to dump this stuff in the upstairs closet?"

"Sure," she says, but quirks a brow like I'm being weird—which, to be fair, I am. The answer to her question isn't simple, and I want a little privacy as I try to answer.

When we reach the landing at the top of the darkened stairs, I drop my armful into the first closet on the right and wrangle the door shut. Maisie is standing on the last step, eyes timid and holding one arm like she is eager to head back the way we came.

I need to rip the Band-Aid off and tell her.

"My dad got this apartment for me." I run my hand through my hair and take a deep breath. *You got this, Connor.* "We have a...complicated relationship, if you can even call it that. I don't usually like talking about it."

"Oh." Her face softens, and her body leans toward me instinctually.

"But I want you to know, to understand me better. It's just not easy for me." I let out a puff of air through my lips as I motion for her to join me in sitting on the top step together.

She obliges, releasing a small smile.

"My dad...well, he's kind of a piece of shit."

I'm always worried people will react poorly to me telling them about my dad. Really, only Hunter knows for that reason. But even though her eyes widen marginally, she shows no sign of disgust. In fact, she's still leaning toward me and has an almost painstakingly tender smile on her lips. Like she's hanging onto my every word.

"He, um—he...he ripped our family apart when I was fourteen. He traveled a lot for business. Gone two weeks, home one, that sort of thing. While he was away, he apparently was cheating on my mom...a lot, and one day, my mom called the hotel where he was staying, and a woman answered the phone.

"My mom pretended to be his secretary calling to make arrangements for his flight home. The woman on the other line was furious and confided that she had just found out she was pregnant. That she and my dad had never exchanged phone numbers. Then the woman told my mom that he had left without saying where he was going. She was in a panic, ranting that she needed to get ahold of my dad right away. My mom hung up, refusing to hear any more."

"What? No!" Maisie gasps, covering her mouth in horror. "Connor, I'm...I'm so sorry."

I pick at the carpet on the step below us, not meeting her eyes so I can maintain the courage to get the rest out. "It was horrible. When he got home, my mom had all of his stuff thrown on the sidewalk in front of our house. She told him to leave and never come back. I can still hear the sound of her sobbing in the driveway after he left. She was so broken."

I swallow, then continue, "After that, my brothers and I stepped up to help out. We each got an after-school job, we spent our evenings and weekends doing chores around the house, and none of us heard from Dad for years. The divorce was swift, but it wasn't a fair split, to say the least. Dad had deep pockets from his consulting job, and my mom was a stay-at-home mom. You can guess who was able to afford the best lawyer."

Maisie nods along, listening intently with a line between her brows.

"Thank god for Grandpa. He moved down the street, really helped fill the gaps. Including making sure each of us knew we were loved. He showed up to every school activity and cheered us on without expecting anything in return. He was a much better father figure than my dad ever was." I shut my eyes against the grief for a moment.

Maisie waits patiently for me to continue.

"A few days after my seventeenth birthday, I got a call from an unknown number. It was him—my dad. I knew my older brother Robert had looked him up and reached out at some point after he went off to college, but I didn't expect my dad to initiate contact with me. I answered the phone, and he didn't even have the balls to apologize."

My throat is tight, and I realize I've been slowly raising my voice, so I take a deep breath to calm my temper. I don't want to scare Maize. "He just asked what I was doing with my life. Where I was working. Where I'd be applying to college. He said he had been following my high school swimming career and expected big things from me. I didn't even know what to say. What do you say to someone who abandoned you and your family?

"Long story short, he kept checking in, but only in regards to my progress as a student athlete. Every time I get off the phone with him, I only feel more anger, but for some reason, I keep picking up." My fists are clenched. I focus on my breathing, releasing my curled fingers. "It honestly makes me sick that my dad pays for the apartment—that he has a hand in anything that I do here—but it also felt silly to turn down such an upgrade. Why should I let him ruin anything else, you know?"

I pause and look into her beautiful green eyes. I see my pain reflected in them. She feels sorry for me. Probably thinks I'm pathetic. I shove my head down and look at my feet.

Her strong yet slender hand rests on my forearm a moment later. When I turn to look back up, she reaches in further until her arms are twined around my body. It's awkward because of the way we're sitting on the stairs, but I let out a relieved huff and adjust so I'm wrapped around her too.

She holds me tighter and is quiet for another minute before she says, "I'm so sorry that happened to you, Connor. No one deserves to be treated the way you have. He doesn't deserve you. You're beyond amazing, so compassionate and caring, full of love for your family and friends." Tears start to well in her eyes and trickle down her face. "I'm glad you had your grandpa. You obviously take after him." Her words are stilted, and my chest pulls seeing her cry for me. For my story, my life. "I'm sorry you didn't have both of them like you should have."

She nuzzles into my shoulder, and her tears fall onto my skin. I wipe them away as she continues talking. "You've been a light in my life these past few months, and anyone would be lucky to be in your life. It's your dad's loss for wasting that privilege. And I don't blame you for taking this apartment from him. I just hope he doesn't think it in any way makes up for what he's done."

Her eyes squint and lips purse. The angry look on her stunning face seems wrong. I lift my hand to her brow and rub it smooth.

"I appreciate the sentiment, Betty, but you certainly don't need to be angry on my behalf." I'm angry enough as it is, but something does feel looser having shared all this with her.

Her face softens, but she still eyes me warily. I stand up and hold my hand out to her. She takes it readily, and I pull her to her feet.

"Let's head back downstairs. I'm a little worried about what our friends might be getting up to in our absence."

Her responding laugh filters through my whole body, releasing some of the tension. I like her so much it hurts, and now she has a part of me I don't share freely with others. I'm not sure how much longer I can take being her friend only, but what other choice do I have?

12

Who Am I?

Maisie

I'M ON AUTOPILOT, WALKING to Karsen's dorm room when I catch myself replaying the other night with Connor. He's the sweetest guy. I can't believe he opened up to me like that. His dad sounds absolutely awful. A resurgence of anger courses through me at the thought, and I run a frustrated hand down my face, forgetting I have makeup on. I stop and pull out my compact mirror to assess the damage. A little smudge, but not *too* worse for wear.

I'm not used to wearing makeup. Honestly, what's the point? I'm in the pool one to two times a day, and it's such a hassle to remove it before getting in the water. However, I know Karsen likes it when I put in a little effort.

I round the final corner and step up to his door. I'm assaulted by a familiar skunky smell. I'm not judging his neighbors, but I hate the smell of weed. I lightly tap on his door, and I hear grumbling on the other side. It's a solid minute before the door swings open, and I'm greeted by a hazy-eyed Karsen. Oh—not his neighbors, then.

"Hey, babe." His arm swings out so far, I worry he might dislocate something. Karsen likes to drink and party with his friends, but I've never seen him smoke before. He knows better, what with mandatory screenings for soccer.

"What has you smoking? Something happen?" I ask, trying not to show how concerned I am.

"Nah. Can't a guy just smoke when he wants to? Damn, why are you on my case like this?"

Frozen by his response, I stutter, "I...I'm not on your case, Kar, it was just a question."

"Yeah, okay. And what about all your 'questions' about what I'm doing or where I am, or why I have to drink so much? Are you my mom or my girlfriend? Fuck." He plops down onto a giant bean bag chair and takes another puff. The cloud heads straight for my face, and I cough. He rolls his eyes.

"I'm sorry for caring about you. You're a student athlete—sue me for thinking you should be careful." I can feel my defensive side coming out, and I take a deep breath to shove it back down. I don't want to fight tonight.

"Whatever. Come here." He pats the spot next to him on the bean bag chair. I hesitate but make my way over to join him.

"I'm sorry," I say, because I want us to move past this as quickly as possible. Arguing with him is exhausting and never changes anything.

"I know how you can make it up to me." He moves to snuff out his joint in a nearby mug, then shifts his weight so that his front pushes into my side. His hand reaches up to pull the back of my hair.

This went from zero to sixty, and I'm not sure I'm okay with that. My head jolts forward as I cough again at the lingering smoke in the air. It makes my head hurt from the pull of his grip.

"Can we...not, tonight?" I whisper.

He either doesn't hear me or acts like he doesn't because he starts sloppily kissing up my neck.

"Karsen, wait. Stop."

He grabs my wrist and moves my hand to cover the bulge in his jeans. "Mmm, but I love your hands on me," he mutters.

That's it.

"Quit it! What the hell is wrong with you?! I said stop!"

I stand abruptly and rip out of his grasp. I stare down at him. He looks pathetic—high and out of his mind if he thinks I owe him *anything*. It's like I'm finally fully seeing him for the first time. He's no longer the boy I first loved.

He's not even my friend anymore. I realize my heart let him go months ago. He didn't deserve it in the first place. I don't want to be with him anymore.

"Why you bein' like this? I'm your boyfriend."

Tears pricking at my eyes, I shudder. "That doesn't give you the right to keep going when I say *stop*," I grit out. "My body is my own, not yours. When I say something, it deserves to be respected. No one should be treated like this. I'm leaving!" I barrel for the door, swing it open, and step into the hallway.

He seems to come to and rushes toward me. I flinch back, and he stops. "Where are you going?" he asks, eyes wide.

"We're done, Karsen." I cross my arms.

"Babe, please." He shifts like he's going to grab my arm, and I block it.

"Don't touch me. Don't follow me. Don't text me. I don't ever want to hear from you again."

I slam the door in his face, and it sounds like his hand makes contact with it a moment later. I jump at the noise, but then I'm shrouded in eerie quiet. I take a moment to gather myself. My heart is pounding, my hands are shaking, and I'm dreading the possibility of this turning into a panic attack. But then, I'm walking with purpose away from this place, away from *him*.

I make it out of the building. I don't know where I'm going, but I keep walking. I don't stop until I find myself in the middle of the Quad. For a moment, I think about texting Connor, but I can't be with anyone right now. I plop down into one of the Adirondack chairs that they leave out year-round and let the tears spill out. They keep coming, harder and faster, letting the weight of it all fall out of me. Not for losing Karsen, but for losing myself. For trusting him with not only my body, but my heart, too. Neither of which he was ever worthy of, even on his best day, but especially not after the shit he pulled tonight.

I feel like I don't know myself. I'm not even sure who that person was who was with him for so long. How am I only fully seeing this now?

These ruminations last a few more hours, and the moon is bright in the sky when I finally gather myself enough to navigate home. Angie is already asleep when I get in, so I quietly maneuver around the darkened room until I make it to my bed. I don't bother taking off my clothes or shoes; I just crawl on top of the covers and let sleep overtake me.

13

Science 101

Connor

PROFESSOR GARTH'S CLASS IS in the Liberty Science Center in a large multi-tiered room, big enough to house at least a hundred other students. So far, Professor Garth has been living up to the reviews I read on the rating-professors site. He keeps things interesting and doesn't try to ding us with petty questions on tests.

As I look around the room, my eyes snag on Karsen a few rows over. My mind wanders back to that day outside of practice. What a tool. I can't believe Maize is with him. He doesn't deserve her in the *slightest*, but I haven't said or done anything because it would only hurt Maisie. And that's the last thing I want.

"That's it for today. Remember, your papers are due on the thirtieth of this month, and if you're smart, you'll start studying for the next exam. I won't be grading on a curve. See you Friday."

Professor Garth waves his hands in a shooing motion, encouraging us to exit class as quickly as possible. Can't say I blame him. I wouldn't want to linger for a class filled with a bunch of freshmen who are only there to cross off a requirement, either.

I gather up my book and supplies and make my way down the tiered steps and through the heavy double doors. I pause to hold the door for a few people behind me, and I hear Karsen's voice echoing from down the hall. My spine stiffens as I home in on what he's saying.

"Man, I ended it with my girlfriend last night. She was being a bitch just 'cause I was smoking a little weed in my dorm. Like, damn, it's college, babe. Plus, I was so sick of her hardly ever putting out. I have plenty of cleat chasers interested—why waste all this on someone who doesn't appreciate it, am I right?"

I see red. I practically rip the door off its hinges as I turn. His friends are cackling and high-fiving in agreement like dipshits. My legs are moving toward him—it feels like I'm not in control of my own body.

When I'm a few paces away, Karsen turns to face me. My arm is already wound up, and the crack of my fist meeting this asshole's face echoes through the hall. Karsen is forcibly knocked sideways. From his hunched position, he slowly looks up at me as he wipes a trickle of blood from his now-crooked nose, rage blowing out his pupils. He moves fast, coming at me with his full force, letting loose a disgruntled battle cry. I dodge. His body dips after missing mine. He quickly catches his balance, and then we're circling each other, the air smelling of sweat and iron from his still-bleeding nose.

"What's your problem?!" he spits out.

"My *problem* is how you were talking about Maisie! You piece of shit!"

"She's not worth it, man." He claws a hand out, and I dodge. We continue in our standoff.

"You don't deserve her. You never deserved her!"

"Oh, and you think you do?" He steps forward, fist cocked.

I shove him back. "Get out of my face before I end you."

"I'd love to see you try," he responds with an arrogant smirk.

I take a deep breath, channeling my ire. I'm gonna wipe that look right off his smug asshole face.

I drop my shoulder and lunge, catching him in the gut. He flies backward and slams into the ground. I scramble to keep him down with a bent leg pinning both of his. I loom over him, about to get another hit in, when suddenly I'm being pulled away. No, I'm not done with him.

"Don't you ever come near her again, you hear me?" I shout as someone manhandles me down the hall.

When we round the corner, I realize I'm being dragged along by two campus police officers. That can't be good.

"I hope it was worth it, son," one of the men—Darius, according to his blurry nametag—says.

"We're going to the dean's office. Now," the other interjects with a lot more hostility to his tone.

Shit. I shift, and the officers let me stand but don't give me any more room than is strictly necessary. I lift my arms placatingly to show I will come with them willingly.

"I'm sorry," I say. "I'm calm, promise."

They let go of me but stay less than an arm's reach away, like I'm some kind of criminal. I know my fate is not looking good, but I can't bring myself to regret what I did. I just hope Maisie is okay.

14

Alexa, Play Frankie Valli

Connor

So do you want the bad news or the worse news?

Betty: What do you mean? Are you okay? What's going on?

Bad news is, I'm suspended for the next four meets and the Vimer Invitational. The worse news is, Karsen is getting off with a warning.

Betty: A warning? What the hell does Karsen have to do with this? Why are you SUSPENDED? What happened? :'(

Want to come over? Probably better to talk about this one in person.

Betty: On my way right now!

I'm pacing, flexing and unflexing my hands. I don't know how Maisie's going to react to me punching the shit out of her boyfriend—or, I suppose...ex-boyfriend? I can't get my hopes up on that one yet.

God, what was I thinking? I don't care about the punishment, although it sucks all the same. I need this *not* to ruin our friendship. That would kill me. Even though I want more, these past few months with her have been a true gift. I would rather have anything Maisie is willing to give me than nothing at all.

It seems like both a few seconds and a year before I hear the apartment's front door creak open, then slam shut. My palms are sweating.

Next thing I know, Maisie is bursting through my bedroom door. Her hair is in a short ponytail, but it's frayed in a way it usually wouldn't be. She's also wearing pajama pants and socks with sandals.

"Maize, are you okay?" I reach for her, but drop my hand before it makes contact.

Her cheeks are flushed. "Am I okay? What do you mean? Are *you* okay? Why are you suspended?" Her voice pitches higher with each question.

"Karsen. That fucking son of a bitch. He said he broke up with you." I run a hand through my hair. I need to know she's all right. "We can talk about me in a second. Please. Are you okay?" My eyes scan her again, and this time, I see more detail. Her eyes are puffy and her lips are chapped. "I just...I need to know if you're okay before we talk about anything else."

Her eyes soften as she steps all the way into my room. "You're sweet. I'm not sure I'm okay necessarily, but I'm the one who broke up with him, so in that sense I am."

She dumped *him*. Why did she dump him? Did it have anything to do with me? That's ridiculous. Right?

"Now, what happened?" she asks.

I look away, letting out a breath to calm myself at the memory.

"Connor, tell me what happened. Please." She shifts her weight anxiously.

"Okay, but before I do, I just want to tell you that your friendship means everything to me, and I feel very protective of you. He was saying...he was...this is all coming out wrong. I have Science 101 with Professor Garth."

"Yeah, I know. We've shared our schedules, Connor—what does that have to do with anything?" She crosses her arms, and it looks like an emotional shield. I'm so worried my reaction to that asshole will be the end for us.

"Well, Karsen and I both have that class."

"Uh-huh." She looks at me like I'm losing it. Maybe I am.

"Well, after class, he...he was running his mouth, and I...I might have...hit him?"

"You *what*?!"

"You didn't hear him. I just couldn't stand it. You deserve so much better." I hang my head shamefully. I'm not ashamed of how I reacted because it was pure instinct to defend her, but I'm ashamed she has to know what happened at all.

"Did he fight back?" Her question throws me off guard.

"Uh, yeah, he did, but it's safe to say I won." I turn a sheepish grin her way, but she's not smiling. She looks...worried. Her eyes are glassy, her brows scrunched, and her posture bent, almost defeated.

"What did he say?" she asks hesitantly.

"I really don't want to repeat it."

"I need to know."

I sigh, once again rubbing a hand through my hair. I don't want to hurt her. She shouldn't have to even be dealing with this. "He basically said you don't put out, so he broke up with you to be with someone who would. 'Cleat chasers' were his exact words. And something about weed, but honestly, I was so upset I don't know if I heard it all."

Her hands ball into fists, and the sight of her anger, her hurt, nearly destroys me. "What an asshole. Connor, I'm so sorry. You shouldn't have hit him. He's...he's not worth it." She stares at the floor like it personally offended her, tears lining her lower lids. The sight breaks my heart.

"Maize—" I take a careful step toward her until her sheened eyes lock with mine "—first of all, stop apologizing for things that aren't your fault. Second, *you* are worth it. No matter what trash he spews. It's you. I couldn't...I feel...I don't know if I can put it into words."

Her hands fall limply to her sides as she takes a deep breath, but then she moves a step closer. She tentatively reaches both hands up until they are around my shoulders, the heat of her hands through my shirt like a brand. I gather her waist in my arms to pull her in for a hug. Her body goes loose against mine, and she sighs. I like having her here, in my arms, where I can protect her. I wish we could stay like this forever.

"So, you're suspended? And they didn't give Karsen a punishment?"

I wince. "Yeah, they didn't give him one."

She tenses in my arms but remains. "Well, that's just...great," she says sarcastically, voice muffled in my shirt as she drops her head to my chest.

I squeeze her a little tighter.

"You can't go hitting people who make you mad. That's not healthy—but it's done. And we're good. I'm sorry you're suspended. For four whole meets *and* the Vimer Invitational?"

My hands glide up and down her muscled back in a soothing motion, like they have a mind of their own. "As long as there isn't another incident, yeah."

Her arms drop from my neck, and she puts a little space between us. My hands linger at her waist because I can't seem to let go yet.

"That's a huge chunk of the season. You might not even have enough times to qualify for Nationals. You...I'm...gosh, I'm so sorry, Connor."

I shake my head side to side and crouch down so our eyes are level. "Look at me. Stop apologizing. I'm okay. I don't want you to worry about me."

Swimming is the last thing on my mind right now.

Her head is in her hands now, like she's the one who should be ashamed. And fuck *that*.

I slide my arm firmly around her back with my right hand and gently extricate her left hand from her face to drape it over my right shoulder.

"What are you doing?" Her eyes flare as she startles.

I pull her ever so slightly closer and whisper in her ear, "Dancing with you."

At that, she relents.

"Alexa, play 'Can't Take My Eyes Off You' by Frankie Valli."

I interlock our other hands, stretching them out to smoothly guide us around the room in a mock ballroom dance.

"This is an old-people song!" A laugh bubbles out of her.

"Then it's perfect for us," I reply, gently dipping her.

The beat picks up, and the rest of the lyrics play out. By the end, we're basically performing a dramatic interpretive dance. I pull her in and out and twirl her. She kicks her leg high in the sky and falls into me gracefully. *Divers.* We end with her nearly tripping over a pile of dirty laundry on my floor and me lunging to catch her, inadvertently redirecting the fall so we both end up tumbling onto my bed in a lazy, joyous haze.

"How do you do that?" she asks.

"Do what?" I say while scooching so my back is pressed against the head-board.

"Turn even the shittiest situation around. You're like if all the good in life was wrapped into one person. We should tap you like a tree and sell your happy sap. We'd make a fortune." She laughs while crossing her legs, now facing me.

"First of all, ew. Weird analogy, Betty. Second, I'm not always happy or something. I have a lot of stuff I deal with, as you now know." I gesture vaguely with my hand, as though that will encompass all the crap I've let her in on recently. "But you bring out the best in me. I like the man I am when I'm with you, and making you happy is one of my favorite things. So, I do what I can to make that happen, but I don't know if it works on other people or anything. You're special that way, I guess." I punctuate my statement by poking her in the leg.

She rolls her eyes like she isn't the most important person to me.

"Uh-uh." I wag my finger. "No rolling your eyes. Accept it. It's true." I boop her nose, and she scrunches it. We laugh.

"It does." She tucks a piece of hair behind her ear. "Work on other people, I mean. I've seen you work your old-guy charm on your friends and, honestly, even strangers. I think you want people to be happy, so you move through life with that in mind. It's one of my favorite things about you." She shifts her face away, feigning interest in my white walls, but not before I catch a hint of a blush on her beautiful, tanned cheeks.

My phone buzzes on my nightstand, breaking us out of the moment. I look over and notice the time. 4 PM. Crap. "You need to head to practice."

Her eyes flare, but her face falls. "It won't be the same without you," she practically whispers, but she slowly moves to get up.

"Do you want me to come watch from the bleachers?"

"That wouldn't be hard for you?"

"Nah, it'll be nice actually. I never get to watch you dive as much as I want because I'm always face-down in the pool for one of Coach's crazy drills. I usually only catch glimpses here and there between sets."

Her eyes light up, and I love it. "Okay! If you're sure, I mean. That would be great."

And wouldn't you know, she blushes again.

15

We Go on Three

Maisie

I'M POISED AT THE end of the platform, my back to the water thirty-three and a half feet below, arms out to the sides. *We go on three,* I chant to myself. One, two...*three.* I hurl my body up and back, tucking my knees to my chest as I grab on to my lower shins, and I make it through the first spin, the second, and finally round the third. I kick out with all my might to stop the rotation and shoot my hands up to break the surface of the water. I hit too quickly. A sting splays across my shoulders from landing so short on one of my worst dives: a back-three-and-a-half tuck, or 207C as it's referred to in competition.

When I resurface, Coach is already yelling about knowing where I am, using my spots, pulling harder for my entry. All stuff I know but can't seem to get my body to implement. I've been working hard on my strength in the gym, but I still can't get this dive. If I keep at it like this, I'm not sure I'll maintain my spot on the team. I shiver thinking about having to relay *that* news to my dad.

I walk out of the water via the steps below the platforms and look around for my shammy. On my way to grab it, my eyes ping up to where Connor is sitting in the stands. He shoots me a double thumbs-up, his smile infectious.

I wonder what he really thinks about his suspension. He seemed so casual about it. Shouldn't he be worried? If it were me, I would be taking it to the athletic director. His punishment seems pretty steep, considering they let Karsen off with a warning. I need to let it drop from my mind for the remainder of practice. If I start thinking too hard about Karsen, it won't end well for me.

My teammates, Lola, Jamey, Finn, Dublin, and Janique, are all practicing various skills on different apparatuses. Dublin and Finn are at the three-meter boards working on their synchro. Lola is after me on ten-meter, and Janique will follow her. Jamey is over on the trampoline, working some twisters in the harness. They're all great. Truly. But I can't say I've gotten to know them much outside of practice.

I watch as Lola's long red braid slices through the air, and she rips her dive's entry. She gracefully exits the pool, and Coach Megan showers her with praises. She was recruited from a top club in South Carolina. Both her parents were Olympians, so in other words, she was made for this. It seems as easy as breathing for her.

"Coach was pretty worked up about that last one of yours, huh?" she asks when she reaches me, her mouth quirked to the side.

"If by worked up you mean she basically thinks I'm pathetic and won't ever get enough points to make that dive worth even trying in my competition list, then yes."

She flinches. "It wasn't that bad. Short, yeah, but keep working on the mechanics and your strength, and you'll have it in no time. You'll see."

She's a sophomore and already team captain. I don't think she understands that I'm barely supposed to be here—or, worse, she does and she's just placating me. I grimace at the thought.

Seemingly unaware of my internal turmoil, she pats my shoulder, then starts climbing the tower again before I can say any more. I head to the one-meter platform to overthrow some back somersaults, hoping the practiced motion will help me when I'm up thirty feet higher.

When my eyes wander over to Connor again, he's looking toward the swimmer's pool. What has his attention?

Oh. It's not a *what* he's looking at, but a *who*. She's gorgeous, of course, with a tall, athletically curvy body. Her plump lips are drawn into a toothy smile, and even with her swim cap and goggles blocking her face, I can tell she has that make-men-dumb kind of beauty. She waves at Connor and, when she knows she has his attention, cups her hands around her mouth and shouts, "You comin' to the party tonight, Connie?"

Connie? What is that about?

"Probably not tonight, but thanks for asking, Veronica!" He shakes his head for emphasis, but he seems mighty chipper about the attention from *Veronica*, in my opinion.

Something pulls tight in my chest. Before I let another thing contribute to my already anxious body, I launch myself and fly backwards through the air again, cutting my feet through the water. While still submerged, I let out a scream no one will hear.

I feel like a blanket with threads fraying at the seams. Why am I the way I am? Why can't I get my dives in order? Why am I reacting to a girl smiling at Connor? I don't know, I don't know, I don't know!

When I re-emerge, Coach Megan blows her whistle, informing us that's time for the day.

"See you all at Dryland bright and early tomorrow. Don't be late!" She punctuates the order with a set of claps.

I climb out of the water and head straight for the locker rooms. I don't look back to check who Connor might be looking at now.

16

I Could Go for Some Shrimp Scampi

Connor

I WAIT OUTSIDE THE women's locker room for nearly forty minutes after practice, but Maisie never shows. Worried, I pull out my phone to text her.

> You solving world hunger in there or something?

> **Betty:** I already left, sorry, figured you'd be busy after practice anyway.

That stings, considering the whole reason I came to practice was to watch her, but I type back.

> Oh, well I didn't know if you wanted to talk some more, since we kind of got cut off by practice

> **Betty:** I'm good, thanks.

> Okay..are you hungry? Was thinking we could grab Antonio's for dinner?

Betty: I think I'm just gonna heat something up in my microwave at home

Why is she acting weird? Why is she pushing me away?

> Alright, well, I'll text you tomorrow, Betty. Have a good rest of your night

I'm worried about what I did to cause this shift in her demeanor, but I know there isn't really anything to do about it right now if she doesn't want to see or talk to me. She's probably tired after a hard practice. If Coach Megan's reaction was any indication, some of her dives weren't going well. I thought she did great, of course, but what do I know?

I pull up the text thread with my roommates to see if anyone else is up for Antonio's.

Swim-ply the Best Roomies

> Anyone up for Antonio's? I could go for some shrimp scampi

Brock: I'm down. I need the carbs after that practice. Where the hell were you today, bro? Coach had us doing the bamboo stick drill. My shoulders are gonna be stiff for a week

Hunter: I'm in. I'm starving. And didn't you see him in the stands?

Tyler: Sure, I'll meet you guys there

Tyler always drives separately in case he feels like leaving at a different time than the rest of us.

Brock: In the stands? What were you doing there?

I'll catch you guys up at dinner

Brock: Sounds ominous, but alright. Meet you guys at the house and we'll head over

Hunter: I'm driving. I don't trust you after last time Brock

Brock: What did I do??

Hunter: The fact that you're asking that says everything

*Tyler adds double exclamation marks to Hunter's text

Brock: What're you all ganging up on me for? I got out of that ticket with my top-notch flirting ;)

Yea, after you purposefully ran a red light because you said it only counts if you don't get caught. Well...ya got caught buddy

Brock: Doesn't count since I didn't get a ticket. That police chick was hot too. Sad she wouldn't give me her number though. Would have liked to see what she had going on under the uniform too if ya know what I mean

Hunter: We know what you mean dipshit. Stop talking about women like this. You're better than that

> **Brock:** Debatable

> *Tyler adds double exclamation marks to Brock's text

> Brock, shut up. Hunter, you're driving. See you idiots soon

We all slide in around a half-circular booth table. Antonio's is the best Italian restaurant in town. Luckily, it also has college student–friendly prices and large serving sizes. Our waitress is setting our waters on the table when Brock blatantly checks her out. She scrunches her turned-up nose in distaste but pulls out her pen and order pad.

"You boys know what you'd like?" She looks no more than five years older than us.

"I'd *like* to say you look damn fine today," Brock says with a wink, side-stepping the poor waitress's question to interject his cringy play on words. "What time do you get off?"

I palm my face. Why is he like this?

She smiles sarcastically before saying, "What are you, fourteen? Now order some food, or I'll just bring you whatever has been sitting out the longest and charge you double for it."

He has the good sense to look embarrassed. "I'll have the spaghetti with meatballs, thanks," he mumbles, keeping his eyes averted.

"Shrimp scampi for me," I add.

"Make that two," Hunter says next.

"Three please," Tyler says quietly, finishing out our table's order.

"Got it. I'll bring breadsticks in a minute." She shoots a glare at Brock, then stalks off toward the kitchen.

"Swing and a miss," Brock says playfully, miming the action of hitting a baseball, apparently already bounced back from the sting of her rejection. Must not have cared too much.

"She's working, dipshit. You don't hit on her when she literally has to serve you. Treat her with some respect," Hunter chastises him.

Hunter's moms both work in women's healthcare. One is an OB-GYN and the other works as a women's mental health counselor specializing in domestic violence cases. Needless to say, they made sure their boy knew how to respect women from a young age and to speak up when other men didn't.

Brock rolls his eyes but shifts uncomfortably, like the words landed their blow. Then he says, "So tell us what happened, C-Dawg. Why weren't you suffering with the rest of us at practice today?"

"Well, I—kind of...punched Maisie's ex-boyfriend."

Three pairs of eyes swing to me.

"What do you mean 'kind of'?" Hunter asks tentatively.

"Well, not kind of. I did. In a hallway at Liberty Science Center."

"Why?" Tyler interjects.

"He said he dumped Maisie—which was a lie, by the way. She dumped him. He was saying some vile shit about her to his friends. Next thing I knew, I was hitting him. Couldn't seem to help myself."

The three of them exchange worried glances.

"You have some pretty strong feelings for her, huh?" Hunter questions gently.

"That's...an understatement, but I've resigned myself to being her friend only."

"Well, now that she doesn't have a boyfriend, maybe you can be friends who fuck? Let some of that pent-up energy out," Brock adds, waggling his eyebrows.

Hunter punches his arm.

"Ow! I was kidding, man." He rubs the spot that was hit.

Hunter ignores him.

"I think you should talk to her and tell her how you feel," Tyler says.

Our waitress drops the basket of breadsticks unceremoniously on our table and walks away as quickly as she came.

I reach for a breadstick as I say, "I want to. Before, I didn't want to say anything because I knew she had Karsen, and saying anything would only fuck up our friendship, but now...I don't know. She was acting strange today, pushing me away. I'm not sure she is interested in anything other than friendship with me, and I'm scared that if I push, I won't have anything with her."

"Hmm..." Hunter rubs at the scruff on his chin. "What if you tell her you have a date and see how she reacts?"

Brock lifts both hands in the air dramatically. "And *that's* treating a woman with respect?" he asks incredulously.

"I didn't say it was my best feminist idea, only that it would garner some information," Hunter claps back.

Brock huffs and digs into the basket for his own breadstick.

"It's not the worst idea," Tyler chimes in. "It's not like you actually have to go on a date with someone else if you don't want to, and if she doesn't react, maybe you can start to move on."

I know in my soul there wouldn't be any moving on, but I let them keep talking. We switch gears to talk more about the practice I missed—how my suspension will affect our relay team, and what if I took my situation to the athletic director? We then move on to how Hunter is struggling in German, and how Brock was going to head to Veronica's party after this.

Tyler leaves as soon as he scarfs down his food. The three of us who remain linger a while longer before paying and leaving. I'm sure the waitress is happy to see us go. At Hunter's behest, Brock leaves extra money for a tip and a note apologizing.

Hunter and I drop Brock off at his party and head back to the apartment. We play a few rounds of his latest video game before going our separate ways.

I'm lying in bed, exhausted, but I pull up my text thread with Maisie and re-read our last conversation. The pang of worry jolts through my chest again. Everything will be fine tomorrow.

I fall asleep humming Frankie Valli.

17
We're Gonna Crush Mannon

Maisie

IT'S FRIDAY MORNING, THE day before our first meet, and Coach is working our basics hard at Dryland—what divers call a gym workout, typically involving trampolines, foam pits, harnessed diving over a mat, and usually a solid amount of conditioning. *Point your toes, you're leaving the board too early, deeper in your pike, shoulders back.*

I'm sweating bullets—not just from the hard workout, but from my nerves for tomorrow, too. I'm doing some standard pike jumps on the large trampoline when Dublin saunters over.

"Ready for tomorrow, Maisie Daisy?"

I stop jumping. Not sure when he decided to give me a silly nickname.

"Ready is a relative term," I reply, miming a so-so motion.

A laugh bursts out of him. My brows lift. It really wasn't that funny.

"You crack me up," he says, wiping at the corner of his eye. When he settles, he seems to quickly scan my body. It's so fast, I'm not sure it actually happened. "Hey, would you want to have breakfast with me after this?" His tone holds a sort of swagger that is hard to describe.

Normally, I wouldn't think twice about having breakfast with a teammate, but he's acting strange. Does everyone already know Karsen and I broke up or something? I don't think I'm ready to be hit on. Or when I'll be ready to date. I don't feel like I can trust myself after everything, let alone someone else.

I clear my throat and say, "I'm pretty tired. I was gonna head back to my dorm to nap and eat after I wake up. Maybe another time?" I don't want to fully reject him in case I'm misreading the situation. In general, I'd love more invitations to hang out with my teammates outside of practice.

His expression falls, but he says, "Yeah, sure, some other time. Have a good nap. See you tomorrow. We're gonna crush Mannon." My refusal must not have squashed him too much because he lifts his fist in mock victory and winks at me before heading back to finish his pike-ups at the horizontal bar.

I finish up with a few back one and a quarters on the trampoline in preparation for my back three and a half tomorrow, then grab my water and head to the locker room.

I put in the passcode for my locker and rifle through my bag for my phone. Connor texted. Twice.

Connor: What're you up to today Betty?

Connor: Wanna watch another movie later? I know you're probably a little worried about tomorrow, so figured it might be a good way to relax? I'm free all day after my noon meeting with Dr. Fitz. Let me know.

Dr. Fitz is the senior athletic director, so Connor must be meeting with him to ask for a shorter suspension. My smile kicks up with pride. I'm glad he's doing that. Then I remember how friendly Veronica was with him last night and my insane reaction to it. I have no reason to be jealous. Connor and I are friends. Just friends.

A movie does sound nice, but maybe I should give it a few days before hanging out again—clear my head of these mixed-up feelings and focus on tomorrow's meet.

I don't wait for a reply before dropping my phone back in my bag. I take a deep breath, not sure how I'm feeling exactly—definitely not great, that's for sure. Connor has been there for me since day one. I care about how he feels. Maybe he wanted the movie night because he's sad about missing his first college meet tomorrow. My shoulders slump in defeat, but there isn't anything to do about it right now. I'll wait until he texts later.

I head outside. It's only 8 AM; Dryland is always at the ass-crack of dawn. A yawn overtakes me. It wasn't a lie when I told Dublin I was planning to take a nap. I walk in the direction of my dorm and focus on taking deep breaths of the fresh air, telling myself it's all going to be okay. Maybe if I keep repeating it like a mantra, it'll come true.

18

An Unexpected Mentor

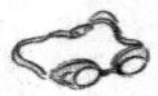

Connor

I AM JUST FINISHING getting changed for the day and am about to text Maisie back, asking her to reconsider a movie night, when my phone rings. "Dad" runs across the screen, and my throat closes up. Really, *now*? I take a deep breath—in for three, out for five—and pick up.

"Hello?"

"Connor. What's this I hear about you being suspended?"

I run a hand down my face, my heart racing. This was a consequence I wish I didn't have to face. "How did you even hear about that?"

"I donate heavily to the school. They keep me apprised. You think they just give away apartments to freshmen? I thought you were smarter than that."

I grind my teeth, an inkling of regret clawing at my chest. "What do you want, Dad?"

"What I want is for you to explain why you won't be competing tomorrow. You're destined for the Olympics. How's it going to look if you can't even make it to your first college meet?"

I hate him. I hate that he has me questioning what I did. I hate that he thinks he has a say or that his money buys him a ticket to knowing what goes on in my life with or without my consent.

"There was an incident. The suspension is my punishment. Unlike you, I take responsibility for my actions." My face burns hotter than the sun.

A long silence echoes on the other end of the line before he says, "Watch your mouth, son."

"I think that's enough for today, *Dad*. I don't know why I picked up anyway."

I'm about to hang up when he says, "I'll make a call."

Then, the line goes dead.

I grab the stress ball on my desk and launch it across my room, letting out a frustrated growl. It bounces off the wall and shoots back at me. I duck out of the way, but it only manages to make me more upset. I storm out of my room, slamming my door, and march down the hall.

Hunter pops his head out of his bedroom, eyes wide as he sees me barreling toward him. He shifts to block my path. "Whoa, whoa." He stops me with a hand on each of my shoulders, but I shrug him off.

"Leave it, man."

"All right." He lets his hands drop to his side. "Tell me what's goin' on."

"Nothing. I mean, fuck—" I pull at the ends of my hair "—my dad called."

His eyes harden in recognition of what that means. "Take a deep breath. Don't let him fuck with your head."

I drop my shoulders and lean back against the wall. Hunter adopts a similar stance opposite me.

"Do you want to talk about it?" he asks.

I take the breath he suggested. "Not really, no."

"That's okay. How about some breakfast? I can make my mom's pancakes?"

"Sure, man, that sounds great, thanks."

"You got it." He strides down the hall and makes it to the top of the staircase before he turns around and says, "For what it's worth, you're one of the best dudes I know despite who your father is. Always have been, always will be. I'm proud of you for not letting your anger toward him poison you. It's okay to be angry. You have every right to be."

"Thanks, Hunter. You're a great friend."

"Back atcha, big guy. I'll get started on those pancakes." He disappears down the stairs.

Continuing to take deep breaths, I try to calm myself down. I hate how reactive I am to my dad. It makes sense considering everything, but still. What if he called and I reacted that way while Maisie was over? I wouldn't want her to ever think she was in danger with me. Especially after seeing how that asshole was around her. I never want to make her uncomfortable.

I need to work on my shit. Running a hand down my face, I push off from the wall. Stretching my arms up and back and then letting them swing forward a few times, I physically allow the tension to leave my body with each throw of my arms. Then, I head down to see if Hunter needs any help making breakfast. I'm sure I'll figure something out.

Dr. Fitz is an imposing man. His office is large, with a whole wall of windows overlooking the O'Donner Memorial Soccer Stadium, space for at least twenty athletes to pile in for a meeting, plants hanging against one wall, and a roaming desk in the middle of the room—but when I walk in, he makes it feel small. His bald head and stern features pale in comparison to his sharp tone.

"Bocelli. Sit."

I obey, taking a seat on the leather stool closest to his desk.

"The dean tells me you're suspended for five meets and an invitational, is that correct?"

"Yes, sir."

"And this punishment is a result of your being physically violent with another student—another athlete, no less?"

"That's correct, sir." My shoulders slump.

"So what brings you in today?" His tone shifts in a way that sounds almost concerned.

"I know what I did was wrong, sir. I know violence is never the answer. And I admit I instigated the situation. It was in defense of a close friend."

"What do you mean by that?" he asks, leaning forward as his hands rest against the desk.

"The student I hit was saying atrocious things about someone I care about deeply—sir," I tack on at the end.

"I see. So this was a skirmish over a girl?"

My eyes widen in alarm. "It wasn't like that. She's a friend. A teammate. She was dating this man until recently, and he was talking very disrespectfully about her. I reacted to his words, but I know that isn't an excuse."

"Hmm," he says as he opens and closes a file on his desk. "Do you react physically often?"

"What?" He's looking at me with intention but no harshness in his features. "No, I...this is the first time anything like this has happened." But then I think back; there was the time some kids were picking on my brother Robert for being a male cheerleader. I shoved them into the lockers, telling them to shut up.

Dr. Fitz seems to see this all play out on my face, because he quirks an eyebrow as if he doesn't believe me. But then he moves on, saying, "Tell you what, I want you to commit to three mandatory sessions with the team psychologist. If you agree, I'll convince the dean to drop your suspension by two meets."

"Mandatory therapy?"

"Yes."

"Is that necessary?" Although I guess this would be working on my shit.

"That's up to you, really, but that's the offer."

"Okay."

"I understand you are Charlie Bocelli's son."

I visibly flinch. "Um, yes, sir."

"He called earlier. It always piques my interest when a large donor makes a call in for their son or daughter. I like to gather more information when that happens."

I stare back at him, my temples throbbing. A loss of feeling overtakes me from the change in conversation to my father.

"I saw in your file. Charlie lost custody rights when you were fourteen. Now, I won't pretend to know what your relationship with the man is like, but as for myself, I had a dad who liked to waltz in and out of my life whenever he felt like it. It doesn't bode well for a child's emotional upbringing." He pauses to rub a hand over his hairless head. "Go see the psychologist, son. I promise it's for the best."

I'm speechless. This beast of a man opened up about his past. He looked into my file instead of simply listening to the words of a man who donated ungodly amounts of money to his department. He offered me a chance, not only at shortening my suspension but at working through some of the pain that ties me in knots. Pain from a father who abandoned me and my family, from a grandfather who was everything I needed until he was gone. From who I am as a person, and this anger that detonates without my full consent.

I nod in agreement. "All right. When's my first appointment?"

A smile tips the right side of his mouth. "I took the liberty of reviewing your schedule as well. How does Monday at 3:30 sound?"

"Sounds perfect." I stand and take the appointment card he hands me. The top of the card lists "Donny Fantil, BCS, BMCP," along with a phone number and email.

"If you need to reschedule for any reason, call that number." Dr. Fitz points toward the card in my hand.

"I will. Thank you, sir."

"Take care, Connor. I hope to see great things from you. Both in and out of the pool."

I blink and mutely nod my head in acknowledgment. Dumbfounded, I exit his office and head for home.

Later that afternoon, I remember Maisie asked me to text her how it went, so I pull up our thread and send off a quick one.

> All good with Fitz. He's going to try convincing the Dean to remove two of my suspended Meets. Just have to do some sessions with the team psychologist. Still no Vimer Invitational though.

I can't quite wrap my head around all of today's events, let alone relay them to her over text, so I resign myself to sending the basics with the intention of talking more after her competition tomorrow.

> Good luck tomorrow, Betty. I'll be in the stands rooting for you. I know you'll do great.

Texting bubbles appear and disappear three times.

> **Betty:** Thanks Connor. Your support means a lot.

> You deserve it. See you tomorrow.

Yeah, we'll sort everything out after she's done competing tomorrow. I'll make sure of it.

19
Muscle Memory

Maisie

As I walk out of the locker room and onto the pool deck, I'm blasted with the familiar warm fog of chlorine. The pool feels like a second home after all these years, which is definitely a comfort—but my new competition suit is a little too tight, my muscles are tense, and my breathing is definitely not at normal cadence. A familiar feeling: the anxiety of meet day.

My teammates are huddled on a group of mats in the corner in various states of dress, stretching, chatting, and visualizing. As I make my way over, I tip my head in acknowledgment to Mannon's divers warming up in a nearby section. They respond with quiet smiles. I recognize some of them from my Junior Olympic competition days. The diving world is small.

Then I look up to the bleachers. Seems Connor isn't here yet, but my eyes snag on two familiar faces. *Oh no.* My parents are here.

Why wouldn't they tell me they were coming? My heart ramps up to double the normal beats per minute, and tension starts to pull at my temple points. I think I might be sick. As if I wasn't nervous enough as it is today. I don't think I can stomach my dad's post-meet report—points I left on the table, where my focus should be, how if I had only been a little better on this or that, I would have won. He says it's to provide helpful feedback, but considering he doesn't even know how to swim, it falls short on the *helpful* aspect and tends to only succeed in making me feel bad about myself. Like a failure for anything less than perfection.

I look away as quickly as I can and close the distance to the mats. Dublin pops up from his forward fold and reaches up a hand, indicating he's waiting for a high-five. I oblige, although not as enthusiastically as I'm sure he was hoping for.

"Ready for the big day?" he says, smiling without a care in the world.

"As I'll ever be," I reply. I shuffle to an open stretching spot and sit down with my legs spread wide. I reach from one side to the other and down the center, feeling the familiar pleasant burn. I breathe through each stretch, praying my body will release some of the stress it's harboring.

The competition starts unceremoniously. We're competing in three-meter first, and I'm third in the rotation. My dives have been decently clean, minimal splash, acceptable scores. I should be thrilled. I'm holding my own at my first collegiate meet, but my stomach is churning. I climb the ladder for my final dive on the board: a back one and a half with one and a half twists, or a 5233D, as the announcer states.

I make it to the end of the board, take my routine deep breath, and start my count of three. I take off and enter the water before I can think too hard. Luckily, this dive typically goes off without a hitch thanks to muscle memory. Although Coach wants to add an additional twist soon. I push away the intrusive thought as I break the surface of the water. There are whoops and cheers from my teammates, the crowd, and even some of the swimmers who have made their way to the dive well to watch.

I spit some water from my mouth as I let a smile overtake my face. I did it. I made it through the 3m. No failed dives. No major embarrassment. Even Coach Megan gives me a stilted nod of approval as I exit the water and head over to stand under the spray of the on-deck shower.

Maybe I do belong here. I've always loved diving, and I always knew I wanted to compete in college, but knowing I did it—passing my first major test as a Division I diver—means the world.

My eyes scan the crowd again. I allow them to gloss over my parents and home in on who I'm really looking for—Connor. He's decked out in school colors and even painted half his face green. He has a foam finger like he's at a football game and is cheering extra loud.

A laugh bursts out of me, and about four sets of eyes turn to see why I'm having some sort of conniption. A sheepish smile creeps out, but even the mild embarrassment doesn't squelch the joy. The tension I'd been holding all day slowly seeps out of me. Sure, I have another set of dives to compete on 10m—one of those being the dreaded back three and a half—but for now, I'll soak in the happiness. It can feel hard to come by at times, so might as well revel in it while it's here.

Lola wins the women's 3m event by a landslide. Janique places second for a solid Magnolia one-two lead. I place fifth, which isn't last, so I keep my head held high. Dublin and Finn also take one-two for the guys, and Jamey snags a respectable fourth place. Magnolia is holding strong against Mannon after the first round of the day.

As we all start warming up on 10m, I sneak one more peek at the stands. Connor's goofy grin spreads when my eyes find his, and he sticks his tongue out at me while squishing his face into funny positions. I'm glad his presence isn't distracting—rather, it's helping. I think I may have overanalyzed hanging out last night.

I laugh again and blow him a dramatized kiss before I can think twice about it. He doesn't hesitate; he pretends to catch it and plants it on his cheek before holding his hands over his heart in mimed admiration. My cheeks warm, but I play it off as best I can and start the climb up the tower for warmups.

20

The 10-Meter

Connor

I THOUGHT I WOULD feel sad that I wasn't competing today, but honestly, it's been a blast. I decided at the last minute to go hard and paint my face, knowing it would bring a smile to Maisie's beautiful face. There isn't a whole lot I wouldn't do to see her smile. I'm still worried about why she's pushing me away, but I ignore it for now. I'm here to support her.

I've also caught the races of my teammates, of course. Ethan, another freshman who was on the same recruiting trip as Brock, Tyler, Hunter, and me, took my spot in our relay, and they finished second. Tyler won first in the 100-yard backstroke, and Brock took third in the 200-yard breaststroke. That one was surprising; I would have thought he'd have snagged a first or second. Even Angie was having a great start to the day, having won her first butterfly event.

All in all, Magnolia was putting in a strong showing against our rivals. It made me proud to be part of the team. Sure, I wish I could participate and help out, but there is something special about showing support from afar without the pressure of worrying about my own races.

Maisie is up next on the 10m platform. I've been a bundle of nerves since this part of the competition started. How anyone can launch themselves off a platform that high is beyond me. So far, she's been doing well, though. Her teammate, Lola, is in the lead, but Maisie is really holding her own. I'm so proud of her. I know she's had a hard time mentally since joining the team, and I hope today helps her accept how amazing she truly is.

I hold my breath as she perches backward at the end of the platform. She launches, spinning through the air so fast, I can't keep track of how many times she goes around. She's about to enter the water when…she doesn't quite make it out of her balled-up form. She smacks the water. Hard.

I'm on my feet in an instant, moving toward the pool deck, my eyes never leaving her.

She isn't moving. Why isn't she moving?

My heart rate kicks up another notch. A whistle blows and a lifeguard jumps into the water. A double beep sounds in the distance, and the announcer states, "Failed dive." Who the fuck cares if she failed it? Why isn't she swimming to the surface?

Panic claws at my sternum. The lifeguard has Maisie tucked securely against his flotation device, and they are almost to the stairs.

My body moves of its own accord, and I somehow make it over the bleachers' railing and jump down to the deck from the stands. I run to her as they pull her out of the water. A whistle blows, but I don't give a damn about the rules right now. All I need is to get to her. When I drop to my knees beside her, she's awake and groaning, and a tempered relief floods my system. I let loose a shaky breath.

"Maize? Maize, you okay?"

"Sir, please move," the voice of an emergency personnel member bellows from the other side of Maisie.

I shuffle back a step but refuse to give them any more space than that. My whole body is on alert, tension coursing through my stomach and limbs. Maisie's coach and teammates are crowded around the outskirts, waiting. The trainer pokes and prods and asks her a series of questions. When he's done and announces she only had the wind knocked out of her and may have some bruising, she sits up. Her sheened eyes meet mine, and I instinctually grab her hand, saying, "You're all right. Everything's gonna be fine."

"I failed," she states plainly. As if that is the worst part about the last ten minutes. Tears fall full-force down her cheeks.

"Hey, shh, it's okay," I soothe and move to gather her in a hug, her body chilled against me urging me to wrap my arms tighter. "Everyone fails a dive now and then. We're all just happy you're okay. *That's* what matters, you hear me?"

She nods dumbly into my shoulder, but I know her—I know she's struggling to believe me. I adjust to gently assist her to stand. A small round of applause comes from the crowd, but other than that, things in the natatorium have continued as if nothing happened. Swimming races are still proceeding, and once the divers see she's okay, they begin stretching again to stay loose for the competition.

My whole world was just spun upside down. Adrenaline keeps me stiff as a board. I can't fathom continuing to do anything other than be with her, making sure she's all right.

I release her only enough to look into her emerald eyes. Her tears are drying up, and she says with a sniff, "That was my last dive. I think I'll just go to the locker room. I don't need to see the final scores."

"Okay, but I think someone should go in with you."

"I'll take her after my next dive," Lola says from a few feet to our right.

I shift to wrap my arm around Maisie's waist and respond for her. "I'll walk her over. Meet you there when you're done. And, uh, good luck on your last dive." I can't imagine having to compete after watching something like that.

"Sounds good, and thanks," she says, her shoulders set and posture strong.

"Come on, Maize, let's get you out of here," I say, leading us away from the diving pool. She doesn't say anything, merely starts walking. She looks pale, and I'm worried that maybe they missed something while examining her. We're almost outside the women's locker room when Angie rushes over.

"I was in the middle of a race, but Brock found me immediately after and told me what happened," she says breathlessly, drenched from just being in the pool. "Here, here, I'll take her." She shuffles so her arms are wrapped protectively around Maisie's waist, practically holding all her weight up.

"I'll meet you on the other side," I say as they disappear behind the door. I shift to move toward the men's locker room so I can exit through there when Brock catches up with me.

"She okay?" he asks, wringing his hands, gaze bouncing.

"Yeah, she had the wind knocked out of her, which is why she couldn't move for a moment in the water. The guy said she'd probably be bruised, too, but nothing serious. Thanks for telling Angie."

"Oh, good, I'm so glad. That looked really rough." He poignantly ignores the Angie comment. "I have another race, but text me after if I can help with anything, 'kay?"

"Sure thing, man, thanks."

He claps me on the shoulder and heads back over to where our other teammates are gathered.

I take a deep breath, letting some of the unease seep out of me. Being worked up isn't going to help Maisie right now.

21

How Do You Two Know Each Other?

♥

Maisie

I FAILED. *I FAILED. I failed.* The words loop through my brain on repeat, like being stuck on a roller coaster. I keep going around and around and around, my head dizzy and stomach upset, praying the ride will end so I can get off and throw up. The water from my shower is too hot on my tender back, so I turn it to cold and wash my hair and body as quickly as possible. Angie never leaves my side.

My thoughts calm a bit as I dress, my cozy sweats providing a layer of internal comfort.

Lola rushed in a few minutes ago, carrying my shammy I left on the pool deck and letting out a sigh of relief when she saw I was okay and Angie was with me.

She offered a brief "Shake it off, nothing to be embarrassed about," then made her way back out to the pool deck for the award ceremony.

I gather my things in my pool bag and nod to Angie that I'm okay to leave. We exit into the hallway and are met with two sets of eyes I was hoping to avoid. Mom's brows crease in worry, but Dad's are bowed down in anger.

"What were you thinking trying to compete a dive that was so far from ready?" my dad demands.

"I've been working on it and hitting it at least fifty percent of the time. I've never failed it like that. I must have been too tired from the 3m competition," I say, averting my gaze, unready to meet the look of my father's ire. His words are doing enough.

"Honey, ease up on her. Please," my mother cajoles while moving her manicured hand to unwind my father's crossed forearms. "Also, hi, Angie. Nice to see you again," she addresses my roommate, who hasn't let go of my arm. Angie squeezes it tighter, letting me know she's here for support.

"I'm not going to *ease up* on her, Madeline. She could have been seriously injured. Her career could have been over before it even began."

My career. My injury would affect *my career.* That's apparently the most pressing thing to my father right now.

My mother retreats a step, and her green eyes, the same as mine, fall.

"I'll talk to Coach about removing it," I say placatingly, hoping that if I agree with him, this conversation can end faster.

"See that you do."

Awkward silence envelops us, but then a cough sounds from behind, causing me to jump. I turn to find Connor approaching, his hands tucked into his pockets, and my racing heart eases. Suddenly, I don't feel as small as I did a moment ago.

"Hi there, Mr. and Mrs. Thatcher." He moves forward to join our little group. "I don't mean to interrupt; I just wanted to check on Maisie," he says politely, eyes doing a quick scan of me even though he saw me ten minutes ago.

Angie smiles beside me, happy not to be the only one witnessing this shit show, I'm sure.

"Mom, Dad, this is Connor."

"Hi, Connor." Mom stretches out a hand in greeting. "I saw you rush to my daughter from the stands. How do you two know each other?" Her words are kind, but there is a hint of disapproval buried in her tone.

He meets her hand with his own. "I'm on the team too. I wasn't competing in today's meet, though." Once he drops the handshake, he adjusts his body so he is standing on my left side, our elbows brushing.

"And why not?" my dad interrupts.

Connor stumbles a bit before replying, "I got into some trouble, and unfortunately need to sit out for a few meets, but the situation has been rectified and I'm taking the consequences in stride." His spine straightens as he speaks.

"All right then, good man," Dad says and nods curtly.

A spike lodges in my chest. My dad's quick acceptance of Connor's suspension is like salt in the wound of how he's reacting to my failed dive. But I guess he only expects perfection from me.

"Honey, where is Karsen?" Mom asks me, eyes darting to where Connor and I are connected, clearly unable to refrain from asking any longer.

"He and I are...no longer together, Mom."

She gasps, and her hand comes to cover her lipstick-glossed mouth.

Angie steps forward like she's about to say something, but steps back as my mom demands, "Why not?!"

Dad rolls his eyes.

"I'd rather not get into the details right now. I'm sorry I didn't tell you. I wasn't sure how, to be honest."

"I am sure you are just going through a rough patch. College is a big change. He will forgive you, and all will be well. You will see." She nods along as if she's trying to convince herself, not me.

Why would she assume he needed to forgive me? Of course, it couldn't possibly be him *that did something wrong.*

"No, Mom. We're done. I don't want to be with him anymore."

"That is silly," she says, waving a dismissive hand. "You two are perfect for each other. You have been together for *years*. You do not just throw that away."

Connor tenses beside me but doesn't move from his silently supportive spot. I take a deep breath, searching for patience before replying, "Mom, please. I want you to hear me. We aren't right for each other. I don't want to be with him. It's over."

"We will discuss this later," she huffs and turns to walk down the hall toward the front of the building, presumably to leave.

Dad eyes the three of us one last time, grunts, and takes off after Mom. Before he gets too far, he partially turns to announce, "I'll be checking in with your coach, Maisie. And when I do, I better hear of a change to your competition list."

And then they're both out of sight.

I blow out a lungful of air and feel a heavy weight pooling at the corners of my eyes, heat rushing up my neck.

"Let's get you home," Angie says quickly.

"Yeah, all right," I say on autopilot.

Connor eyes me with concern. "I'll grab dinner and bring it to your room."

"Sure, okay," I say, unable to focus, my vision narrowing.

Angie loops her arm around my waist and places my arm over her shoulder. "We've got you," she whispers, like she's worried my parents could possibly still hear her.

Angie and I start to move as one conjoined person as Connor heads in the opposite direction for the food, and I'm so grateful to have them both. Even through the thankfulness, though, a monster that is my anxiety is rolling inside me—and I'm worried that now that it's woken up, it might be a while until it goes back to sleep.

22

Breathe

Maisie

MY HEART IS BEATING so fast, it feels like it might pop out of my chest, and simultaneously like an elephant is crushing my ribs. I'm having a panic attack. It's far from my first one, but it is particularly bad. My breathing is labored, and the lack of oxygen has my head spinning and vision blurring. Between that and the knots painfully twisting my stomach, crying isn't even an option right now.

We're back in the apartment, thank goodness. I'm curled on our futon. Angie placed a blanket on top of me but now doesn't seem to know what to do, and I can't instruct her in my current state.

"Water. I'll get you some water," she announces, more to herself than to me.

I'm sweating, and I feel disconnected from my own body. I wish I could tell Angie to get this blanket off me.

A knock raps at the door. Angie startles, but rushes over to see who it is.

"Oh, Connor, right, the food," I hear her say.

I close my eyes and try to focus on breathing. I hear something being set on the ground, and next thing I know, I feel a large hand on my forehead, followed by Connor's deep voice: "She's burning up. Let's get this blanket off her."

The relief is immediate, but I can't open my eyes yet.

"Maize. I'm here. You're doing so great. I'm gonna move you so that I can hold you, okay?"

I nod, really not sure of what would be best at the moment.

He lifts and adjusts me like I weigh nothing, so I'm folded over his lap, curled toward his chest as he sits. His arms are wrapped protectively around me, and he moves one hand to put pressure on my sternum, gently moving it from side to side.

"I know today was really hard. It's okay that your body is reacting this way, but I know it's no fun." A tear sneaks out of me. "I want you to try to breathe with me. I'm going to count everything for us, ready?" I don't reply, but he starts: "Inhale, *one, two, three, four.*" He demonstrates by pulling air through his nostrils. I copy as best I can. "Good, hold it for me." Another four count. "Now release. Push it out through your mouth. Good." He counts to four out loud for me as I exhale.

After following that pattern for several more minutes, my body slowly regains some semblance of control. Connor continues to gently coach me while showering me with reassurances in his soothing voice. No one other than Lauren has ever helped me through one of my panic attacks before.

I can tell I need to cry more, but the exhaustion is weighing too heavy. Sleep will need to come first.

Connor, sensing what I need, shifts so he can lift me to my bed. He sets me down gingerly, adjusting the pillows and comforter until I'm comfortable. "You're going to be okay, Betty. You can rest for now. I won't go anywhere."

Feeling a strong sense of comfort at Connor's presence, I close my eyes and drift off to sleep.

Connor

I had been worried about Maisie when we parted at the natatorium, but I didn't expect to find her in such a rough state when I got to her place. It broke my heart to see her struggling so much. Panic attacks can be awful.

"How did you know what to do?" Angie whispers as I shift to sit on the futon.

My mind wanders back to one night after my dad left. I overheard Mom in her room. It sounded like something was seriously wrong, so I went to investigate. When she didn't respond after I knocked on her door, I decided to just go in.

She was curled up in a ball on the bedroom floor, clutching her chest and shaking. I nearly knocked over the hamper trying to get to her. She was breathing, but it was shallow. I was so panicked, but managed to call for Oliver—my older brother, closest to me in age—knowing he was home. When he came rushing in, his eyes widened in panic, but he called 911. When the paramedics arrived, I went with her in the ambulance and told Oliver to wait there with Liam, our youngest brother, who was only eleven at the time. After a full examination in the ER, it was determined that her heart was fine, and she simply had a panic attack. *Simple* wasn't really the way to describe it, though.

She took the medicine the doctors prescribed and had a pretty good handle on it most of the time, but sometimes one would slip through. When that happened, I'd sit with her and hold her through it. Sometimes I worry about what she does now that I'm not living at home.

"My mom has panic attacks," is what I say out loud.

"Oh, I'm sorry to hear that, but glad you knew what to do. I had no idea how to help," Angie says.

"It's okay. It's different for everyone, but in general, staying calm, giving them reassurance, and asking what you can do to help is a good start."

"Thanks. I'll remember that for next time." Her eyes squint in concern as they move over Maisie's form lying in her bed. "Well, hopefully there isn't a next time."

"Hopefully," I offer.

We sit in companionable silence for a while. Angie reclines in her desk chair, watching videos on her phone with the sound off, so I close my eyes and lean back on the futon. But I don't sleep. I just check in with my own body and do a few breathing exercises of my own—ones Mom's doctors had taught us.

When I sit back up, I turn to Angie and whisper, "It's okay if you want to leave. I promise to stay until she wakes up. It honestly might be better to have fewer people here when she does. Not that I'm kicking you out or anything, of course." I punctuate my statement with my hands up, facing toward her, so she knows I'm not trying to order her around or something.

"No, yeah, you're right. It's totally fine. Evie had texted earlier saying there was a party at Swim House tonight to celebrate today's win. I wasn't planning to go because obviously I wasn't going to leave Maisie, but if you think it's better for just you to be here..." She drops off to indicate the question.

"Yeah, go. We'll be fine here. We have food, and I'll make sure she has whatever else she needs."

"Okay, but text me when she wakes up, please? And also, I'll come home in a heartbeat if that's what she wants. I won't even have a drink. Maisie is my top priority. Promise you'll keep me in the loop." She points a stern finger in my face. It wasn't a question, but I have no problem with that. I appreciate how fiercely Angie loves Maisie.

"You have my word," I whisper, making an "x" motion over my heart.

"Okay, good," she says, dropping her finger and moving as silently as she can to grab her bag before making her way to the door. She looks at Maisie one last time before she fully slips out, barely making a sound.

About twenty minutes later, Maisie stirs.

23

Sweet Comfort

Maisie

WAKING WITH ANVILS FOR eyelids, I fight against the heaviness until my eyes open and find Connor's across the room.

"Hey there, how are you feeling?" he asks, shifting to stand and meet me at the bed.

"I've been better, that's for sure." A breathy laugh pushes past my lips, but there is no humor in it.

"I'll bet. Take your time sitting up," he instructs with a hand on my upper back. The contact is both searing and soothing.

I take his advice, checking in with each part of my body as I stretch out and move to put my legs over the side of my bed. My back still aches pretty badly. I'm a little lightheaded, and I feel weighed down from sleep, but I can tell I'm past the worst of it, which is a relief.

Connor is looking at me with slightly furrowed brows, concern etched in his hazel eyes. I hope he doesn't think differently of me now.

"Thank you for helping me." I rub my eyes. "That's happened to me before, but I was struggling to convey what I needed in the moment. What you did was perfect…" I look away.

"Hey." He cups my chin and lifts my face tenderly until our eyes meet. "You didn't need to worry about anything in that moment except breathing. I'm glad

I was here with you. I'm sorry you had to deal with that, but please know it's *nothing* to be embarrassed about."

His words soothe something in my soul. Like gluing a chipped piece back onto handmade pottery, proving its worth by putting in the effort to save it. My shoulders drop, and my cheeks warm at his touch and kind words.

Connor steps between my dangling legs and adjusts his hand to tenderly hold the back of my neck. His other hand comes to rest on my shoulder, and I instinctively reach my hand up to grab his forearm as he does. He sighs and releases a devastating smile, the kind that crinkles the corners of his eyes.

In this sensitive state, I think my mind is finally catching up to what my body has known for some time now: I like Connor. And not just as a friend.

But his friendship is what I need most right now. I'm not ready for a relationship after everything with Karsen anyway—not that Connor would want that either. I don't even know who I am, and trusting myself or anyone else isn't something that I'm capable of at the moment. I won't jeopardize our friendship trying to figure any of this out. We're friends. End of story.

He breaks me out of my thoughts by saying, "Do you want to talk about what happened with your parents?"

Do I? Not really. A small weight reappears in my chest at the thought of all that they said. "No," I admit. "They're not bad people. They just don't always understand me." I sigh. That's all I have in me to share right now.

He scans my face like he's waiting to see if I'll say more. When I don't, the side of his mouth tugs up slightly. Then he says, "Should we watch a movie? Let that beautiful brain have something else to focus on while your body rests some more?"

Did he just call my brain beautiful? My skin prickles with delight at his words, my traitorous body rebelling against the internal decision I just made.

Connor removes his hands and cocks an eyebrow, waiting for my response.

"Uh, yeah, that sounds nice," I stammer out, still reeling from his words and feeling a rush of cold from the loss of his hands on me.

He quirks a smile and grabs my laptop from its usual place on the desk. He sets it in an open position next to me and tells me to pick the movie. Then he shifts to squat down below my bed in search of a blanket and extra pillows, since we always set up a cozy cocoon on my bed for movie nights.

I suck in a breath as my mind registers his position. My legs are still hanging off the side of the bed, spread wide from when his body was between them. He is practically kneeling, head just off to the side of my left leg. My brain involuntarily thinks through what else he could do in this position. How it would feel if he only shifted a little more to the left and if these pesky clothes weren't in the way...

I swallow down the rush of desire and quickly shuffle back so I'm leaning against the wall my bed is pushed against. I can't remember the last time I felt desire like this. Certainly not in any recent memory with Karsen. That all felt out of obligation. It must be the panic attack. It's making me vulnerable, needy. I would probably want this with anyone who was nice to me right now. *No, you wouldn't.* No, not anyone.

When he pops back up with the supplies, I do my best to smile normally, but I'm not sure if I sell it or not.

He sets the pillows and blankets on the bed in a way that ensures maximum coziness—seemingly unaware of my inner turmoil—then walks over to grab the food from where he abandoned it when he first arrived. "I got us burgers and fries from the dining hall, but I grabbed a gallon of ice cream too." He holds up the container triumphantly. "Which do you wanna start with?"

"I think you know the answer to that," I say with a laugh as I will my body to cool down.

He retrieves two spoons from the bag and makes his way back to the bed. He pops the lid off the ice cream carton and hands me my spoon. "Ladies first," he says with a wink.

I don't hesitate. I dip my spoon and take a huge bite, moaning around the sweet comfort of it. Connor blushes and climbs onto my bed, adjusting so he is lying next to me, propped up on one elbow, his legs bent in but still hanging off the side a little. His large swimmer's body wasn't designed to fit on half of a twin-sized bed. He reaches with his own spoon toward the ice cream, but I parry, knocking it out of the way with my own.

"Hey!" He raises his voice teasingly. "This is to share."

"I never said I was good at sharing," I reply, a wide smile breaking around the spoon in my mouth.

He smiles in turn and reaches out to take the spoon from my mouth to place it back in the container. "That's all right," he says, "you don't have to share. As long as you're happy, I'm happy."

He says it so nonchalantly, like it's a self-evident truth. Butterflies rush in my stomach and settle in my core, but they're followed quickly by a pinch in my chest. The events of the day wash through me unbidden.

Failure, my mind whips at me. *You don't deserve more than what Karsen has to offer.* My mom's earlier reaction is already embedded in my subconscious.

My gaze falls, and I move further away from Connor on the bed.

"Ready to start the movie?" I ask, voice devoid of emotion.

Connor's brows pinch as he eyes me, then moves to sit up into a less relaxed position. He looks a bit hurt, but nods. "Sure, let's start," he says.

He doesn't try to eat any more ice cream. We watch in silence, and not even the comfort of a movie I've seen a hundred times can wash away the sticky feeling coating my heart and mind.

24

Friendship Duels

Connor

I DON'T UNDERSTAND WHAT happened. One minute Maisie and I were perfect, our usual friendly selves, but with a little extra flirtation seeping in. Should I not have told her that I'm happy when she's happy? Was it too much? I've said more than that before. *Ugh.*

She looks like a robot watching a film to study it—damn AI—instead of the joyful little Marvel lover I know her to be. She hasn't even looked over to see my reactions. This is a rare form of torture.

The movie ends, and we must paint an awkward picture. We're stiff as boards, but neither one of us makes any effort to move. I decide to take the plunge and slowly slide off the bed, turning to face her.

"When does the next movie come out in theaters?" I ask.

"Oh, um, not until the summer." She's staring at the far wall.

"Well, I can't wait to see a new one with you. Hopefully we'll have watched enough that I'll understand what's going on," I say, infusing hope I don't currently feel into my voice as best I can.

She flicks a hand. "They make, like, little clips for characters to help you remember and prep you to watch the new movies. You'll be fine."

I frown. It's like the spark has gone out of her, and I don't like it one bit.

"Did I do something?" I ask.

Her eyes widen and her head jerks to look at me. "No, of course not, you've been the best part about this day. I'm sorry. Everything else is just really getting to me. The dive, my parents, all of that. Stuff keeps playing over and over in my head and then my brain says mean things to me."

I shift so I'm standing in front of where she's sitting on the bed and brush a piece of fallen hair behind her ear. "Like what?" I ask.

Her chin tucks away from me, and her eyes fall. "Like, that I'm a failure. Not good enough. Don't deserve to compete. Don't deserve good things."

A current of anger swirls in my chest. I hate that anyone or anything has made her feel this way. I take a deep breath and let out a low whistle. "That beautiful brain of yours sounds like quite the bully. Want me to beat it up?" I let my mouth twist to the side and raise my eyebrows playfully in hopes of making her laugh.

"Too soon," she says, but pushes my shoulder teasingly. Her phone buzzes beside her, and she looks down to see who it is.

I hold my breath, praying it isn't someone who will make her feel worse.

She laughs at her phone before turning it around for me to see.

> **Angie:** Just wanted to check in. And wanted to make sure you didn't forget who your real best friend is. Tell Connor I'm prepared to duel for the honor

"Ha! I'd like to see her try. I would be the obvious winner." I shift my right foot forward, bending at the knees. I plunge my imaginary sword into the air in front of me. "I mean, obviously, right?" I ask, standing back up and running a hand through my hair. I puff out my chest for emphasis.

She shrugs noncommittally, but she can't hide her smile. "We'd have to see. Sisters before misters. Feminine rage and all that. Could be a close call."

"Well, I'd gladly duel for you." I bend down so we're eye to eye. I see red run up her dimpled cheeks, and her eyes dart away for a moment.

"Thanks, Connor. I don't know what I would do without you." Her eyes return to mine. "I mean it."

The moment feels heavy, important. My hands inch closer to her hips. "Back at you, Betty."

My tongue is dry. Should I kiss her? No, not after the day she's had. Right? It's still not clear if she even has interest in me as more than a friend. I can't chance it.

The silence drags on for a beat too long.

Maisie rescues us by asking, "Do you have any plans this week?"

She leans back on her hands, and I follow like a moth to a flame. We're so close. She eyes me warily, and it snaps me out of my Maisie-induced trance.

I need to answer her question. I accidentally spit out, "I have a date Wednesday."

Why did I say that?! My stomach bottoms out, regret eating at me instantly. I search her features for any clue as to how she is reacting to this news. About what it could mean for us.

She inhales sharply through her nose, but other than that, she looks fine. Normal, even.

I avert my eyes. Why did I let the guys convince me this was a good idea? Why did I ask about it now? After the day she's had, I don't think she would mask her reaction, so I guess that makes her feelings pretty damn clear. I didn't really want this information.

"I see..." she says. "So no movie Wednesday, but how about another night this week?" Her voice pitches up.

I don't think I'm doing a good job of hiding the tension pulsing through me. I can hear my heartbeat in my ears. Can she hear it too?

I'm going to need a moment to get a handle on the news that she doesn't return my feelings. A break from seeing her. I know it's shitty, but I respond, "I'll have to see. I start my mandatory therapy this week. Not sure when my sessions will be. Plus, I have that big project due for business fundamentals."

It's a lame excuse. I know it, and it looks like she knows it too, because her casual smile drops, and she replies, "Oh, okay, well then, I guess just text me when you know your schedule." Her icy tone is a punch to the gut. How did I fuck this up so bad?

I reach for her arm, but she slides out of the way.

"I think I'm gonna call Angie to come home. I'm tired and wanna sleep but probably shouldn't be alone just yet."

"I'm happy to stay until—"

"No, it's fine. I can tell Angie wants to come home. She said something about you kicking her out?" She raises an eyebrow, trying to be goofy, but her demeanor is still off.

"I didn't kick her out," I scoff, placing a hand to my chest dramatically, praying for one more smile out of her to tide me over before not being able to see her for a while. "I said it would probably be better for you to have fewer people here when you woke up. I never said she *had* to leave."

She rolls her eyes. "Poh-tay-toe, poh-tah-toe."

"Well, I can at least stay until she gets back..."

I'm grasping at straws. I don't know how to rectify this situation. I can't lose Maisie, but I also know I can't just be the friend she wants. The friend she *needs* right now. I want so much more, and knowing she doesn't seem to want the same? My head spins and my chest constricts. It feels worse than when I get a call from my dad. I can tell she's upset that I didn't want to make a plan to hang out this week, but I need some time. I need to learn how to accept this somehow. If there is a way...

Maisie yawns and stretches her arms high above her head. "Thanks for everything today. You can have the burgers and fries you brought." She walks over and bends at the waist to retrieve the bag of food from the ground. Her ass is on full display, and I can't help that my eyes linger for a moment. I'll never get over her athletic curves.

She straightens and turns to hand me the bag, careful that our fingers don't brush. Then she opens her bedroom door and leans against the side of it, arms crossed.

"Night, Connor. See you sometime."

It's pointed. The lack of plans. The ambiguity of it all. I feel awful, but I don't know what else to do.

"Night, Maize. I hope you have a good sleep and feel better in the morning." I instinctually move to hug her but pull back before I can really initiate the motion. I'm sure she doesn't want that right now. I give an awkward half-smile before dragging myself out the door. She closes it behind me, and I hear the lock shift into place.

I heave a sigh and close my eyes. This was not how I planned for today to go. And I definitely didn't want to make her day worse after everything she's been through. I need to sort through my shit.

I take my time walking home. The more I ruminate on what just happened, the more frazzled I become. By the time I walk through our apartment door, I must look as good as I feel because Hunter's first words to me are, "What the hell happened to you?"

25

He Cares About Me, Right?

Maisie

THE NEXT WEEK DRAGS on agonizingly slowly. Connor is definitely avoiding me, and I don't know why. Fine, he had a date, but how does that equate to us not doing our normal friend things? How can he be helping me through a panic attack one minute, and the next not wanting to make any plans? *Oh gosh, does he not want to have to take care of me after everything he saw?* No, he wouldn't be like that. He cares about me. Right?

My chest tightens. I thought Karsen cared about me, but that was clearly not quite the case. What if Connor's care fizzles out, too?

I shake my head; that's a ridiculous thought.

I want to know how his first therapy session went. I *don't* want to know how his date went. It was probably with Veronica. Just remembering the way his face lit up when they spoke at practice the other day makes my stomach twist.

He and I are friends—and I guess that's all we'll ever be—but if we're friends, then *why* isn't he texting me back?

Ugh. I practically throw my phone into my bag and huff out an exasperated sigh.

"Everything okay over there?" Lola asks. She's a few lockers down from me as we get ready for practice.

"Fine. Well, not fine, but fine. Ya know?"

"No, I don't know. That's why I asked." Her lips curl into an amused smile.

"A friend of mine isn't talking to me at the moment, and I don't know what I did. It's frustrating." I shut my locker gently, the conversation pulling me out of my immediate anger.

"Have you tried apologizing? Sometimes we hurt people unintentionally."

She sounds like she's talking from experience. Doing the unintentional hurting or being on the receiving end—I can't quite tell.

"How can I apologize when he won't even talk to me?" I ask.

"Hmm." She drums her fingers on her chin. "Do you know his schedule? Maybe stop by someplace you know he'll be. Then you can say your piece, and he can choose what he does from there."

"Wow. That's really wise, Lola."

"Why do you sound so surprised?" She laughs.

"I don't know. I guess I don't know you that well. I'd like to change that if you're game, though. Wanna grab dinner together after practice?"

Her eyes widen in surprise, but she smiles tentatively. "Sure, sounds good, thanks."

We finish getting ready and head out onto the pool deck. The others are already out there, stretching and doing other forms of warm-ups. I smile. Things might be shit between Connor and me right now, but at least I'm branching out and making friends with my teammates. That's a step in the right direction.

As practice progresses, however, I don't attempt my back three and a half. At the practice after my failed dive last weekend, Coach and I agreed we'd cut it for now and see if I can work up to it. I called my dad after, and he was happy to hear I took his advice. Well, happy might be a stretch. More like he was pleased I had listened to him—but I could also hear the disappointment he tried to hide in his voice. I know he wants what's best for me; he's always pushed me to be the best I can be. But sometimes, I twirl around the idea of telling him his words have the power to crush me. That they can do more damage than good, and my confidence cracks when he speaks his mind. But I'm scared I'll sound ungrateful. I make a mental note to talk to Lauren about it and focus my mind back on practice.

We have an away meet tomorrow. Luckily, it is only an hour's drive away, so no overnight stays. Not like it would be that different if we did spend the night—Angie and I would still room together like we do at home—but there is nothing like sleeping in your own bed. Plus, it feels wrong to leave when Connor isn't coming with us.

My mind wanders back to him and the psychologist. Did Dr. Fitz convince the dean to remove the suspension by two meets?

I need to get a grip. This will all work out. Connor typically works at the coffee shop on Sunday mornings. I'll go visit toward the end of his shift. We'll talk; everything will be fine. Plus, we had been talking about going as Ant-Man and the Wasp for Halloween next week. He wouldn't cancel our plans just because he went out with someone once, would he? My stomach drops, and my hands feel clammy. Maybe he would.

I try to focus back on practice, but the confidence I started out with has faded. My entries are splashing, my pike is weak, and I don't feel great about competing tomorrow. Tension starts to pull at my temples, and I have to excuse myself to the locker room for some breathing exercises.

Lola finds me lying on a bench in the middle of the locker room. Practice has apparently ended. "I told Coach you weren't feeling well. I wasn't sure what was going on." She stands a healthy distance away from me, like my failure might be contagious.

"Headache," I say by way of explanation.

"Oh, well, we can reschedule dinner if you want..." She trails off, sounding disappointed.

"Might be for the best tonight. I'm sorry. Rain check?"

"For sure," she says softly and moves toward the shower area around the corner before I can say anything more.

I let out a defeated sigh, but I peel myself off the bench, change, and head for home. At least there, I can wallow with some ice cream.

26

Your Tea Isn't Ready!

Connor

IT'S BEEN EIGHT DAYS since I left Maisie's room. Eight days since I've responded to any of her texts. Eight days since I've tried to close off part of my heart in hopes of somehow moving forward. Which has been...less than successful.

I'm nearing the end of my shift at the coffee shop. Letting the smell of coffee soothe my worries, I grab a medium-sized cup from the stack and write the latest order with a black marker. I'm starting to measure the beans when I hear the bell ding in the doorway. Once I start the grinder, I turn to greet the latest customer and almost jump out of my skin. It's Maisie.

What is she doing here? She doesn't drink coffee because of her anxiety, so she never comes into the campus coffee shop. Her gaze bounces around nervously until it lands on me. She tips the corner of her mouth in a sad smile but doesn't move toward the counter.

I swallow, unsure of how to proceed. More students make their way through the door, and Maisie shuffles out of the way. I help each of them as quickly as I can, anxious to see what she is going to say or do.

Once I call out that the last order is ready, I venture a look around. She's sitting at a high-top table in the corner, leg bouncing on the raised bar, biting at a cuticle on her left thumb. As if sensing my attention, she looks up and our eyes meet. Her hand drops from her mouth, and she hesitantly stands. As she makes her way to the checkout counter, I take a protective step back. Her face falls.

"Hi," she says. Her voice is so quiet, I have to watch the shape of her mouth rather than actually hear her say it.

"Hey," I respond as casually as I can muster. "Can I get you anything?"

"Oh, no, I, uh..." Her eyes widen, like I asked her something other than if she wanted a hot beverage.

"I know you don't drink coffee, but we have herbal tea," I interrupt her stuttering.

Her cheeks pink, but she quickly shakes her head and looks down at her shoes. "I, um, didn't come here for..." She drops the sentence. "I wanted to see if you could...talk after your shift?" she says, raising her shoulders, looking almost like a turtle retreating into its shell.

I can't very well say no to her. I've been avoiding her, sure, but I don't think I can flat-out deny her when she's right in front of me. I acquiesce with a shoulder shrug. "Sure," I say. "Shift switches in about fifteen minutes. Do you want that herbal tea while you wait?"

Her hands unclench, and she releases her shoulders a bit. "Yeah, that would be great, thank you." A genuine but timid smile stretches across her face. Even after everything, I long for her smiles. I still want to be the reason she shares them.

"Coming right up." I turn around and start prepping her drink, then hear the bell above the door ding again. This time, when I check to see who arrived, I'm surprised to see it's Veronica. She usually comes in earlier on Sundays with her boyfriend—they make a date out of it—but she's alone today.

"Hey, V," I greet her. "You want the usual?"

She strides confidently up to the counter and shows off her whitened smile. Maisie steps off to the side to make room for her.

"Sounds great. Thanks, Connie," she says as she leans forward onto the counter.

I'm about to ask where Owen is when Maisie takes off toward the door.

My body follows her on instinct, and I call out, "Maize, where are you going? Your tea isn't ready!"

But she's out the door before I can reach her, and it's not like I can go after her while I'm still on my shift. I swipe a hand through my hair, and my gut tightens. What just happened?

A disappointed exhale leaves me as I make my way back behind the counter to finish up Veronica's order. She lifts a curious brow but graciously doesn't say anything else. After she takes her drink and sits down in the seating area, I dunk the herbal tea bag into the hot water that was meant for Maisie. I let it cool and take a sip, allowing the comforting warmth to wash through me.

I guess it's for the best. Maybe if she avoids me, too, one day, this agonizing ache in my chest will go away. Somehow, I doubt it.

27

Telepathic Pseudo - Sister Senses

Maisie

STUPID. STUPID. STUPID. How could I be so stupid? Connor looked stricken when I first arrived, like my presence offended him. Just because he offered me tea doesn't mean he wanted to see or talk to me. He was doing his job. And then, of all people, *Veronica* walked in. He called her "V." They acted so familiar with one another. Which hurts. But why should it hurt? He and I have only ever been friends, and it appears he's *more* with her.

He's obviously been avoiding me for a reason. Is she that reason? Has she asked him not to hang out with me? If so, I have to say, that's a little controlling for how new their relationship is. Or what if it isn't new at all? Has he been dating her this whole time, and I've just never known?

Before I can spiral even further, my phone rings. My heart flutters, thinking it might be Connor, but when I look and see it's Lauren, I pretend I'm not disappointed and answer with a chipper, "Hi, love!"

"MaiMai, my telepathic pseudo-sister senses were tingling for some reason. You doin' okay?"

"Me? Yeah! I mean...okay is a *relative* term, but yeah!"

Silence greets me, and I can tell she sees right through me even though she can't actually see me at all.

I heave a sigh. "Okay, no, I'm not okay." My head hangs. It feels like I'm always the messed-up one, and she has to run and fix me. *Failure.* The word strikes through me unbidden again.

"Wanna talk about it?" she inquires gently.

"Are you sure you don't have something better to do on your Sunday afternoon? You really want to hear about my problems?" I ask.

"Maize." *Uh-oh*; she has her serious voice on. "You're the sister I never had. You mean more to me than I know how to put into words. I always love talking to you, whether you're happy or sad or something in between. We can talk for hours or say nothing as we go about our days. Don't doubt my love for you; it's not conditional. Please. You know me better than that."

My head hangs even lower. I do know that. I think sometimes the relationships in my life feel transactional. Karsen always expected something from me. Even with Mom and Dad...sometimes I worry what would happen if I flunked out of college or decided to stop diving. Would they still love me? Would they be ashamed? I'm already freaking out about how Mom handled the news of my breakup with Karsen. Will we have anything to talk about now that I'm not dating him? Would Angie still like me if I weren't her wingwoman or if we weren't forced together by being roommates? Even my teammates—if I were to get injured and couldn't compete, would they forget all about me? Would anyone even check on me? *Connor would.* Would he, though? Not if Veronica has anything to say about it.

I groan, frustrated with myself. I'm catastrophizing. But it's hard not to when I'm reeling in embarrassment.

Lauren has always and will always be a constant source of love for me. She's proved it time and time again. I can trust her, open up to her about anything, and I feel shitty I made her doubt that I know how much she loves me. Especially since making sure the important people in her life know how much she loves them has been a big deal to her since losing her dad.

My mind swirls back to the first-ever panic attack I had. I was eleven. We were at a family reunion, and some third cousin twice-removed was laughing and pointing at me because I had mud on my butt from falling on the playground. My throat closed up, and it was hard to breathe. Lauren took my hand and swept me into the bathroom as fast as she could.

She held me from behind as we sat on the bathroom floor, telling me I was going to be okay. I had to be okay. We both cried after. It was really scary for both of us. Uncle Richard had just died the year before from a heart attack. Neither of us knew what was happening to me, but we were both beyond relieved when it was over. It was a few years later before the next one happened. That time, I looked it up on the internet and finally had a word for what was happening.

I swallow. "I'm so sorry, LoLo. Of course I know that. I'm just having a bad day and apparently decided pushing you away was easier than trying to talk through my shit. I'd love your advice if you have time to listen."

"Good, hit me with it," she says, and I can hear her settling into her couch on the other end of the line, my pushing her away already forgiven.

"Well, first of all, Karsen and I broke up..." I let that news sink in and hear a gasp on her end.

"Woohoo! Good fucking riddance!" she yells gleefully in response. "Then what?" she says, encouraging me to continue. Guess she doesn't need any more information than that.

"Well, there's this guy, Connor. We've been friends since the second week of school. He's sweet, kind, and on the swim team. We watch Marvel movies together and were even going to dress up together for Halloween next weekend, but..."

"'Were'?" she asks, concerned. "What happened?"

I laugh bitterly. "That's the thing. I have no clue. Last weekend, I failed a dive, and Mom and Dad showed up, and Dad was giving me a hard time, and..."

"They showed up without telling you?" she asks.

"Yeah, and I told Mom about the breakup, and she didn't accept it, and then they both left, but the damage was already done. It triggered a panic attack.

Angie got me home, and Connor came after and did everything right, LoLo. Like how you used to be for me."

"I wish I could be with you for each one you have, but I'm happy to hear someone kind was with you to help you through this one."

"Me too," I say, and the urge to cry is suddenly very strong, but I sniff and hold it in.

"Anyway, that night, I tried making plans with him, and he totally blew me off. Told me he had a date and didn't want to commit to hanging with me."

"He *what*? That doesn't sound right," she adds.

"I know. Then, he hasn't texted me back all week, so I went into the coffee shop he works at, but then...the girl I'm pretty sure he's dating came into the shop, and I just kind of...ran out."

She chuckles softly as she asks, "What do you mean you ran out?"

"I mean, I literally ran out of the campus coffee shop. Didn't even wait for my tea, just up and left." My cheeks burn as I relive it.

"Well, that sounds a little dramatic of you, if I'm being honest, but don't worry; it's not unfixable." She has her problem-solving voice on now—steady and authoritative. "I say give him some time. Maybe something is going on in his life that you're not aware of. Something that made it hard for him to see you in so much pain during your panic attack. You know, like it was for me that first time." Her voice drops to a sadder register.

"I miss Uncle Richard," I say.

"Me too, every day," she says, and I can tell she has her grief smile on. "But anyway, just wait for him to reach out to you. He will when he's ready. He knows you've been trying to contact him. I say give him space."

My shoulders fall, but I know she's right. "Okay," I say. "I'll give him space."

"And in the meantime, make plans with Angie for Halloween so you're not waiting around to see what he'll do," she adds.

Now I really sigh. "Okay, you're right. I'm sure she'll happily dress up with me."

"That's the spirit! You'll be okay, MaiMai. I know interpersonal stuff can be hard, but you're the best. Anyone who knows you knows that. He won't be able to stay away for long."

I smile at her words. She really does always know what to say. "Thanks, LoLo. I think I'll try to see if I can catch up with Angie now, actually. Talk with you later?"

"Sounds like a plan! I'm only a phoneeee call awayyyy," she sings out, imitating that one song from the musical *Annie*.

The first genuine smile I've had in a week pulls at my cheeks. Lauren is the best. I'm so lucky to have her.

"I love you, LoLo."

"Back atcha. Always."

We hang up, and I feel way better than when the conversation started. I take a deep breath. The sun is shining, the breeze is perfect, and I have so much to be thankful for. I take my time walking through campus as I go to find Angie.

28

Sunday Yoga

Connor

I HANG MY APRON in the back room as my shift ends. I give the guy taking over for the afternoon the rundown, grab my tips, and walk out into the sunshine. When I make it to the Quad, I sit in one of the Adirondack chairs. The grass needs trimming, but there are flowers in bloom and freshly shaped bushes lining the walkways. I look up at one of the massive trees that provides shade for the chairs. On my tour of the school last year, the tour guide said some were estimated to be nearly 200 years old.

Looking around, I see some kids throwing a frisbee and others studying or chatting in groups. The Quad is a melting pot of people and activities. It's a good place to sit and think. You have space but don't feel overly alone, which is probably best for my mental state at the moment.

What was Maize going to say to me? It must have been important if she came into the shop, right? That she even remembered my schedule was impressive.

I should probably go check on her, right? She ran out so abruptly. But if I go down that road, I know I'll get scooped back up into the Maisie vortex. She's irresistible. Especially in person. She looked so cute today in her jean cut-offs and graphic T-shirt.

I shake my head. I need to snap out of it—but I'm already getting up from my chair, my body overriding my brain. *Go to Maisie,* it's saying.

I'm about to give in when Tyler appears out of nowhere.

"You just finish your shift at the coffee shop?" he asks.

"Yep. Can you tell 'cause I smell like coffee?" I sniff my shirt, not smelling anything.

"Uhhh, no." He starts stretching one arm at a time. "I just saw it on our shared calendar."

"You going to work out?" I ask, registering his gym outfit.

"Yeah, my flexibility could use some work. I was actually heading to a yoga class."

"Doesn't Lola teach yoga on Sundays?" I ask.

His eyes dart to the side, and he squints, appearing to be looking at something in the distance, the sun flooding his face. "Uh, yeah, I think so," he says casually, then drops into a forward fold. He's a few inches from his toes, but he's trying.

"Mind if I join?" I say with a smile.

"It's a campus class, and you have free will, so have at it." He shifts to the side, crouched down on one knee with the other outstretched.

"All right, maybe I will then, if you don't mind."

"Why would I mind?"

"Because you don't always like to do things with other people?" I say slowly. Like maybe this is news to him somehow.

"It's a community class," he repeats.

"No, yeah, I know, it's just...you know what? Never mind. Yoga sounds great. Thanks for telling me about it."

"No problem," he says with a shrug, moving back into his forward fold. He's a little closer to his toes now.

"All right, well, I guess I'll stop at home to change and see you over there," I say, eyeing him with lingering uncertainty.

"You will," he says and then takes off in a jog. I love the dude, but he is not a man of many words, that's for sure.

Maisie floods back into my mind, but I push her as far from my thoughts as I can. Yoga will be the perfect distraction. Hopefully clear my mind. Maybe I'll sign up for all of the Sunday classes. All that stretching and meditating is bound to help eventually, right?

I march toward my apartment, not stopping until I get there, and decide to believe that's true.

29

How Dare You

Maisie

T HE WEEK SINCE RUNNING out of the coffee shop has been surprisingly uneventful. I haven't run into Connor anywhere, so there wasn't a need to explain my strange behavior. However, I did go to dinner with everyone on the team Wednesday night. Dublin initiated it, and everyone was miraculously free. We went to Antonio's and had the best time. I also think I misread Dublin's intentions when he first asked me to breakfast. That, or he was just testing the waters and didn't feel too strongly about it one way or the other.

He and I have plans to get ice cream together on Monday. His favorite flavor is mint chocolate chip, but I've decided I can look past that. It's honestly nice to make more friends. Angie is my ride or die, but ever since Connor stopped talking to me, I've felt...well, a little like a pariah. I'm glad to know that isn't the case, and my brain was simply being mean to me again.

"Hey, pass me the red lipstick, would ya?" Angie says as she applies another swipe of mascara, her mouth hanging open as she focuses on her reflection in the mirror.

"Sure," I say, passing her the tube. She was kind enough to stick with my originally planned Marvel theme for costumes. It felt weird going as the Wasp without Ant-Man, so I switched it up and decided to go as Gamora, which, now, three containers of green paint later, I'm regretting a bit. She decided to go as Peggy Carter because she said she was manifesting meeting her Captain America—who she claims is arguably the hottest Avenger. I'd choose Bucky Barnes, but that's neither here nor there. Plus, in her words, she already has the perfect hair for pin curls.

"Thanks again for dressing up with me. It's been weird—the radio silence from Connor, I mean."

"Yeah, what in the world is his deal? I have half a mind to march right up to his front door and tell him what a chicken shit he's being!"

"Pleaaaase don't do that." I laugh nervously.

"We'll see," she replies. "He's on my shit list."

"We don't know what's going on with him. I don't think we should jump to conclusions," I protest.

"Mmmm, that's 'cause you're nicer than me." She quirks a red-lipped smile, then caps the tube with a definitive *click*. "Done," she says, turning to show me the finished look.

"You look hot!"

"I do, don't I?" She shimmies a little and pops a heel to prove her point. "Oh, you've got a little something right..." She reaches toward my face, and my spine stiffens, wondering what it could be, but then she gestures toward my whole face in all its green glory and says, "there," with a laugh.

"What, you don't like green?" I run a hand down the length of my body; wearing a black tank top and shorts, my green arms and legs are also on display. "I've heard it's all the rage in the Andromeda Galaxy."

A laugh sputters out of her, and she quickly turns to check if she smudged her lipstick. She shakes her head as she turns back to me. "You're so weird, and I love it."

She lifts her phone to take a selfie of the two of us and airdrops it to me. I pull out my phone and smile upon seeing the two of us decked out in our costumes. Two roommates turned best friends—there's nothing better. I shoot off a quick text to Connor with the picture attached. I write "Happy Halloween" but nothing else.

I slip my phone into my pocket as Angie takes my hand, pulling me toward our front door.

"Now let's go. I'm ready to get my dance on!"

I smile at that and let her pull me toward our night of Halloween-themed frivolity.

We start off at a frat house because Angie had promised some guy she'd stop by. I mostly stand awkwardly at her side as she flirts for a bit. I don't want to drink because I don't know the guy who is pouring, so I swipe through social media and do my duty as wallflower/wingwoman.

Our next stop is the off-campus bar that everyone frequents, Down Home Bar. Angie leads us to the front of the line and even gets the bouncer to waive the cover charge. I swear she's magic.

We each only get water since we don't have fake IDs, but that doesn't stop us from dancing to at least ten straight songs. Sometimes guys make their way over to us. Sometimes we dance with them, sometimes not. Even with my usual trepidation, I manage to have a great time because Angie is with me, leading the way.

In the middle of one of the last songs, Connor's face flashes involuntarily in my mind. I wonder what he might be doing tonight, who he is with, if he is having fun, if he is...thinking about me. But I shake my head—that's a ridiculous notion. He has a girlfriend, or at least I *think* he does. I do my best to filter him out of my mind and go back to dancing with my best friend.

Our last stop of the evening is the Swim House.

"It certainly is Old Faithful," Angie says as we make our way up the stairs.

My heart rate kicks up with worry that I'll run into Connor here, but I take a deep breath and decide that, whether he's here or not, I'm not going to let it ruin my otherwise fun evening.

The music is blasting like always. I do a quick sweep of the living room. No Connor. I let out a shaky breath, but my shoulders don't release their tension, knowing that just because I don't see him yet doesn't mean he's not here.

I spot Tyler in the corner and smile. It's nice to see him out and about. I'm pushing my way through the throng of dancing bodies when my gaze snags on someone else. Veronica. And she has her tongue down another guy's throat. Oh, *hell* no! Before I can think about what I'm doing, I march up to her and grab her by the arm, forcibly disconnecting her from the guy.

"What the hell!" she shouts as she yanks her arm from my grip. Her eyes bore into mine so angrily, I almost lose track of why I came over here. Luckily, I gain my footing quickly.

"How dare you do this to Connor!" I say, pointing at her wide-eyed male companion.

"Excuse me?" Her tone drips venom. "This is my boyfriend, Owen."

I suck in a breath as my eyes widen. *Boyfriend?* My palms start to sweat, and tension immediately pulls at my temples. I take a shaky step back.

"Mm...mm...my bad," I stammer out.

I was doing what any good friend would do. I was coming to Connor's defense. Even if he isn't talking to me right now. This is a horrible misunderstanding. Embarrassment like I haven't felt since everyone saw me pee in the pool in elementary school pulses through my body.

"I have to go...sorry about the confusion!"

I slip away, turn on my heel, and quickly locate Angie. She is chatting with Tyler, but I scoop her by the elbow and hightail it out of there as fast as I can.

Warmth continues to radiate throughout my whole body, and I force myself to breathe the way Connor led me the night of my last panic attack.

Angie reacts quickly this time, pulling me into a hug immediately when we're outside and encouraging me to breathe.

She reminds me, "Everything is going to be okay."

Luckily, the panic doesn't take hold. It was just a spike in anxiety from the absurdity of the situation.

If Connor isn't dating Veronica, then I really have no clue why he isn't talking to me.

I take a seat on the steps outside the house, and Angie joins me. I take a few more deep breaths as I lean my head on her shoulder.

"Tonight was fun, but I'm ready to head home and get in my jammies. You in?"

"Deal," she says.

We stay there for another minute or two before walking home. When we get there, she even spends an hour helping me get all the green paint off. I smile as we each climb into our respective beds after a full night. I can't help but think that even though I don't have any biological siblings, I now have another pseudo-sister.

30

Forgotten Milkshakes

Connor

"DID YOU DO YOUR journaling exercise I assigned last session?" Donny, my therapist, asks as I adjust on the plush red couch in his office until I'm comfortable.

"I did," I reply.

"Would you like to share anything you wrote?" he questions.

Sighing, I reach into my backpack and pull out the pocket-sized black leather-bound notebook I bought at the campus bookstore. You know, one of those stupidly overpriced ones? We discussed at my last session that it may help to have tactilely pleasing objects to ground me when needed. Thus, the notebook. It feels silky in my hands and smells like a bookstore, which reminds me of positive memories with my grandpa—he would take me for a new book every year on my birthday. So, if I start feeling angry, I can stroke my hand over it, focusing on how it feels, smell it, and think of the good memories with Grandpa.

As I open to the first page, my eyes linger on the prompt at the top. *"Where do you feel the anger in your body?"* At first, I didn't know how the fuck to answer this. What did he mean where do I feel it? Sometimes I feel angry—the end. But as I thought back to some of my angriest moments—the other week with my dad, when I decked Karsen, even when I first found out about my dad cheating—I realized there were signs of my anger that manifested physically. My hands often clenched, which made sense, and I also felt tightness in my chest, which I often ignored in the moment because there were more pressing issues. Also, my head tended to feel hot, like all the blood was rushing there at once. I realized that's probably where they get the term "hothead."

I certainly don't think of myself as a hothead, but I also don't like it when I get so angry that I feel out of control.

Donny coughs, and I realize I didn't actually answer his question.

"Sure," I say noncommittally.

As we continue through the session, Donny asks, "What rules do you believe you have to follow in your life? The things that are ingrained in the makeup of who you are as a person? Something you don't even have to think about, you just do."

"Well—" I'm more relaxed and open to sharing now that I'm familiar with Donny's process and I've warmed up this session, but it's still really hard to talk about these things. "My dad always said hard work is the cornerstone of life. You could be bad at something, but if you work hard, it has the power to change anything. So, I did. I do work hard, at pretty much everything. Grades, relationships, swimming. It's confusing because it's a huge part of who I am and most things I have now are a result of that hard work, but when I think about being like him...well, I hate it. I hate *him*."

Donny gives no reaction to my words. He's relaxed in his wingback chair, notebook perched on his right knee, which is crossed over the left. He reaches up to adjust his glasses and brushes a piece of his graying hair off his forehead. He's giving me space in case I want to add anything else. When he sees I'm done, he says, "Two things can be true simultaneously. You can be glad that your dad instilled something in you that has led to success in many areas of your life *and* be angry about what he has put you and your family through. The important thing is to recognize that one is not better or truer than the other. You can observe and feel both emotions without judgment. Acceptance of that and allowing yourself grace in these areas opens the path toward healing."

Two things can be true simultaneously. I mull it over in my mind. Turning it every which way. Such simple but radical words.

There's pressure at the corners of my eyes, but no tears fall. Instead, I take a deep breath, letting everything sink in, and wait for whatever Donny has in store for what's left of our time today.

He ends up leading me in an exercise where he has me tense certain muscle groups and then relax them. It has a very calming effect, and I think I might adopt it into my pre-race routine. He gives me my journal prompt for our next meeting—our last mandated session—and then, just like that, our time is up.

I was so nervous when I first walked into his office a week ago, but Donny has made me feel comfortable quickly. It's been tough work digging up all this old shit, thinking about what I believe and why I believe it, adjusting some negative thought patterns. I have to admit, though, it's been a relief to talk about it.

Mom—even with all of her amazing qualities—was too heartbroken after she kicked Dad out to be able to really work through it with any of us. So, we all kind of pretended like it never happened. Like Dad was never with us. It worked, to a certain extent. But I'm realizing all that time not dealing with it means it is sneaking out in other ways now, like my anger outbursts.

A moment of thankfulness washes through me that Dr. Fitz led me here. I might even continue after the mandatory three sessions. Donny said I could, and in fact encouraged it. I even thought about bringing up my feelings for Maisie today, then decided against it. Maybe next time.

I leave his office feeling both lighter and weighed down with exhaustion. I decide I deserve a sweet treat for my hard work. That, of course, also makes me think of Maisie.

I'm walking toward the creamery when my breath catches. There she is, as if I conjured her myself.

I instinctively duck behind the nearest maple tree. Her laugh rings out above all other sounds, and my chest tightens. I close my eyes, wondering how I got here. I should just tell her. The worst thing that could happen is she rejects me. Sure, it would hurt like hell, but would it hurt worse than not talking at all?

I start moving out from behind the tree, but stop dead in my tracks. She isn't alone. Her teammate—Dublin, I think his name is—is with her. He's eyeing her like she's the sun, and I can't say I blame the guy. She's the ultimate source of light and warmth. I watch as she playfully shoves his arm, and my stomach bottoms out.

I'm too late. She's moved on. She finally broke up with that prick Karsen, and instead of choosing me, she chose this guy.

I wipe a sweaty hand down the front of my face and do the only logical thing. *Run*. In the other direction. And pray she didn't see me.

I'm almost back to the apartment when my phone chimes. It's Maisie.

Betty: Just wanted to say, I hope you're having a good day.

That's it. I scan through all of her unanswered texts above it, including a picture of her and Angie dressed up for Halloween two nights ago. Guilt stabs through me. We were supposed to go together. I'm glad she still went out and had fun, though.

Seeing the visual proof of her care for me in all her texts, I wonder if I had been too hasty when I told her about the fake date. Did her reaction really mean she didn't like me? Does it matter anymore? Has she moved on? Even if she doesn't like me as more than a friend, is it worth not having her in my life?

I shake my head and walk into the apartment building, the creamery milkshake I was planning to consume completely forgotten. *I'll reach out soon.*

31

I'll Give You a Ride

Maisie

ANOTHER WEEK GOES BY with no word from Connor. I'm beginning to worry. I text only occasionally since I never hear anything back. If he had his suspension reduced, today should be his first day back at practice. The first day I'll have seen him in weeks. I change quickly and make my way onto the pool deck. My eyes scan nervously across the swimmer's pool.

There he is.

My hands shake. I'm so relieved, excited, nervous, angry. Our eyes meet for the briefest of moments, but I look away. Apparently, I'm not ready to face all these emotions. I quickly march to the diving well and get wrapped up in a conversation about Janique's history seminar. Her professor is having them do a mockup of the Salem Witch Trials, but modernized to exemplify the injustice of what women endured during that time and how it perpetuates even in today's society.

I sneak peeks over at Connor the entire practice, and once or twice I catch him already looking at me. Each time, I shy away from holding his gaze. I'm a vortex of emotion, but ultimately, I miss him as a friend. No matter what, I need our friendship to be mended. Whatever I did or didn't do that is making him act this way, we can fix it. I know we can.

I placed third at our meet over the weekend, and I think that gave me a false sense of confidence because I'm diving like shit today. I refuse to believe, however, that it's because a certain someone is distracting me. My stomach clenches when I think about how inconsistent I've been since the start of the season. A good diver is a consistent diver. If you can't perform when it counts, then all that work essentially amounts to nothing. Coach Megan has never come right out and said that, but she's alluded to it enough that it's stuck.

I gulp down a breath of air and shuffle quickly to the locker room the *moment* practice ends. I don't bother looking for Connor, hoping to avoid him. I'm not ready to face him, no matter how much I want things to go back to normal.

I'm showered and changed and stepping out into the hall when a call comes in from my mom.

I answer, "Hi, Mom, what's up?"

"Maisie, are you out of practice? Is now a good time to talk?"

"Yep, just finished up actually." I shift my bag higher up on my shoulder as I walk to the front of the building, where there's a section of small tables and chairs.

"I know your father and I said we would be able to pick you up the Saturday before Thanksgiving, but your dad has been selected as a finalist for the Golden Gavel, and the award ceremony is that Saturday. Attendance is mandatory," she adds, punctuating that they really have no other choice and it's not a big deal to go back on a promise they made to pick up their daughter for Thanksgiving.

"So, what do you want me to do? *Not* come home? I obviously don't have a car to drive myself, Mom." I let my frustration seep into my tone, so she knows I'm not pleased about this development.

"I know, sweetie, and we really are sorry, but we figured you could always get a ride with Karsen? I know you two are not seeing eye to eye right now, but surely he would still drive you home. You were together for two years."

At this point, I've made it to the seating area of the natatorium. I slump down into the nearest chair and let my bag fall haphazardly to the ground.

"You want me to *what*? Mom, I'm not asking Karsen for a ride home. He and I *broke up*. Why is that so hard for you to understand?" I ask indignantly.

"I was simply trying to provide a solution to a problem. I figured a ride home would not be a big deal," she says calmly.

I scoff. "Not a big deal? Mom, he...he..."

I don't have the heart to tell her what Karsen has turned into. She always liked him and is good friends with his parents. She doesn't need to know the details, but she does need to understand that riding home with him is absolutely out of the question.

I'm about to reiterate as such when a deep, familiar voice says from behind me, "I'll give you a ride, Betty."

His determined voice runs down my spine like the keys of a piano, and I whirl to look at him. His hazel eyes are darkened, brows furrowed. A shade of scruff marks his jaw that I wasn't able to see when I was sneaking peeks in the pool. He's in a tight shirt and khaki shorts.

My throat tightens. I can't believe he's here and offering to save me from this situation I've found myself in.

I realize my mom is still speaking on the other side of the line.

"Mom, I'll call you back later." And I hang up, slack-jawed and staring at Connor. "Um, hi," I say. *Eloquent, Maize.*

"Hey," he says as he pulls out the chair next to me. "Was that your parents?"

"My mom, yeah," I say, eyeing him as he sinks into the chair, casual as can be, like it's just another Monday and we haven't gone weeks without seeing or talking to one another.

"I didn't mean to eavesdrop, but then I heard you say something about Karsen giving you a ride home for Thanksgiving, and, well..." He doesn't finish his sentence.

"So," I say, "you'll give me a ride?"

"Yep." He pops the *p* as he says it. "We'll have to leave Tuesday, though. I have a class a professor refused to cancel on Monday."

"So we're talking again?" I ask hesitantly.

"Appears so." He shifts back in the seat and spreads his legs to get more comfortable, but his eyes never leave mine. Having his full attention again is almost unsettling.

"All right," I say. "Then, how have you been?"

I'm holding back a barrage of thoughts and questions, afraid of spooking him again. I want to ask where he has been, why we haven't talked, if he needs me to pay for that herbal tea I never drank, how his therapy sessions have gone, how he's feeling about being back at practice—but he'll tell me what he wants.

He answers simply, "Okay." After a moment, he adds, "Gearing towards good, now."

Good because we're talking again? Good because something else good has happened in his life? What does he mean?

Internally, chaos reigns, but I say, "Glad to hear it."

I move to stand, and he stands abruptly with me. Like a gentleman standing when a lady enters a room in those period movies I like.

Not sure what else to do, I pick up my bag and say, "Thank you. I know it's an hour longer than your drive would normally be, so I really appreciate it. I'm not sure I could have made it in a car that long without killing Karsen. I need to go study, but I'll, uh, see you soon?" I raise my eyebrows expectantly.

"Soon," he says, and it sounds like a promise.

My heart flutters, and I try to tell it to take a chill pill. Just because he is swooping in to give me a ride doesn't mean everything is back to normal or that he'll want to go back to being friends again. I'm heeding Lauren's advice and giving him space. Letting him come to me.

I pat him gently on the arm, and it might be my imagination, but his muscle seems to twitch at the contact. My eyes dart up and find his looking at me intensely.

He leaves me with, "Karsen doesn't deserve to breathe the same air as you. Your mom never should have tried to force you in a car with that prick."

My eyes widen, lips popping open, but I nod my head. I slip my hand away and slowly turn to walk toward the exit. I can feel the heat of his stare on my back long after I'm through the door.

32

Your Grace?

Connor

EVEN THOUGH MY SUSPENSION is lifted, and I've seen Maisie at practice regularly these past two weeks, I haven't gone out of my way to see or talk to her *outside* of practice. Seeing her again has been a form of sweet torture. *Two things can be true simultaneously.* I can be absolutely terrified she is going to break my heart *and* miss her so goddamn much that the former doesn't seem to matter. I tried giving it time and space. Didn't seem to take, so I'm onto trying something new now. Doesn't mean I didn't take the past two weeks to ease in, though.

God, just seeing her again was an awakening experience. The smell of her lavender shampoo, her legs in those tight sweats, and then when I overheard her phone call? Well, apparently my protective instincts toward her are still very much intact. Let's get real: there is no easing in with Maisie. She's sunshine incarnate and beams into your life without warning. Even though I'd been hiding from her light for the past month or so, it doesn't mean her essence hasn't slipped through the cracks of my heart.

And now here I am, standing outside her room, holding an herbal tea for her in one hand and my coffee in the other, working up the nerve to knock. Turns out, I don't need to make the decision, because her door swings open, and I'm greeted with a mop of blonde curls. I pitch my eyes downward and meet Angie's raging sea-colored ones.

"Uh, hey, Ang. I'm here to pick up Maize," I say.

"I know what you're doing here, *Connor*. What I need *you* to know is that I have my eye on you." She hits me with the "I'm watching you" motion.

An awkward chuckle slips out. I don't know what to do with that, so I just say, "And I'll have *my* eye on the road. Betty, you ready in there?" I raise my voice around Angie, hoping to wrap up this awkward interaction pronto.

"I'm ready, I'm ready," Maisie says in a huff, lugging a big red suitcase. The handle is holding on by a thread, and the color is faded. That thing certainly has seen better days. She makes it up to where Angie is currently blocking the door.

Maisie turns to her friend, and they embrace tightly. Seems these two have gotten even closer in my absence.

"Call me as soon as you land, promise?" Maisie says to Angie.

"Pinky swear, double, triple, slap back."

They do some kind of handshake thing to accompany all of that, and I stand there patiently until they're done.

Maisie squeezes Angie's hand one more time and then steps out into the hallway, rolling her monstrosity alongside her. I hand her the tea and then quickly swoop down and lift her suitcase by the precarious handle. Maisie's eyes widen in surprise, but then I'm met with one of her smiles. My chest loosens. There is very little one of her smiles couldn't fix.

Maisie starts walking, and Angie hits me with one more nonverbal "I'm watching you" warning. I salute in return, then shuffle to catch up with Maisie as we make our way to the front of her building.

"Where are you parked?" she asks as we step out into the sunshine. I swear, there hasn't been a cloudy day since we got here.

"Just over there." I motion toward my ten-year-old silver Honda Civic.

Grandpa bought it for me when I turned sixteen. He had been helping to drive me to and from work, so he said it was an investment in his sanity. Even though my brothers and I worked hard, Grandpa spoiled us every now and then. I smile at the memory.

We finish the walk to the car in silence. I pop the trunk and haul in the elephant-sized bag. My black duffel looks like a dwarf in comparison, but it's a good thing because there's little room for much else with her bag in there. When I make my way to the driver's side, Maisie is already in her seat, seat belt on, shoes off, tea in the cupholder, and the car's music cord plugged into her phone.

The backpack she was wearing sits comfortably at her feet—a benefit of being short, I suppose. She starts to pull out a mini pillow, blanket, and her water bottle. I smirk.

When she gets settled, she turns to me expectantly and says, "Ready!"

"Well, as long as Her Majesty is ready, I guess we better get going."

Her face twists at the remark, and her brow raises. "'Her Majesty'?" she says with an indignant cough.

"Because you seem to have brought your entire castle for this carriage ride," I respond with a laugh.

"Hey!" She *thwaps* my shoulder playfully. "I like to be comfortable for long car rides. Don't make fun of me!" My stomach sinks thinking I might have actually hurt her feelings, but then her grin grows into a full-blown smile, and eventually she offers a laugh and says, "What does that make you? My royal chauffeur?"

"My Queen." I bow as dramatically as sitting in a car will allow.

"On then, sir. Lest we be late," she says in a truly horrible British accent.

I bark out a laugh but start the car per her command. "Yes, milady," I say, reaching behind Maisie's headrest as I back out of the parking spot. I think I hear her suck in a breath, but after I straighten out and look over, she's looking down at her phone, blanket over her legs, nothing amiss.

"What music will you be bestowing upon us, Your Grace?"

"'Your Grace'? So what, now I'm downgraded to a duchess? Do you even watch *Bridgerton*?"

My cheeks flame. I have, and I have to say, it was…stimulating. Luckily, she changes the subject before we get on that topic of conversation. Not that I don't want to have those kinds of conversations with her. It's just that I need to focus on driving. Getting her from point A to point B safely is my number one priority right now—number two being mending our friendship. Number three is agonizingly hoping that there is more to us than just friendship.

I roll down the windows when we stop at the first light that takes us out of town. She puts on Taylor Swift—her debut album, Maisie informs me, and we let the words to "Tim McGraw" wash over us as we start our journey home. And hopefully, a bigger journey together.

33

If You're Ever Ready

Maisie

W E'RE TWO HOURS INTO our road trip, and Connor hasn't talked about anything of importance. I still don't know why he didn't talk to me for three weeks, or why even after he agreed to drive me home we haven't hung out outside of practice. I don't know what he thought about me running out of his place of work, or if he has heard anything about my...outburst to Veronica. We have, however, made it through several Taylor Swift albums with one intermission for some Disney movie song belting. Connor does a mean Aladdin in "A Whole New World." I'm definitely storing that knowledge for karaoke later.

I take the leap to make real conversation. "Sooooooo..." I say, "how are classes going?"

He sneaks a peek over at me and purses his lips. "They're good," he says. "I've refrained from punching Karsen after all of Garth's classes, so I guess that's progress."

Why is he deflecting? He's making light of a serious thing that happened.

"Are you happy to be back at practice?" I press.

"Sure, although I was definitely out of shape from the time off. My times probably won't be what they should be at this point in the season, but Coach doesn't seem too worried."

"That's good. Are you excited to compete in your first collegiate meet?" I pick at my leggings and look out my passenger-side window at the large stretch of farmland flying by.

"Mmm, maybe not excited, but ready," he says simply.

Why does it feel like I'm pulling teeth?

"Why not excited? Are you nervous?"

"No, I don't really get nervous."

My head involuntarily swings toward him, my mouth popping open. As an overly anxious girly, I simply cannot comprehend not being at least a little nervous for a meet.

"I might get tense—" he smirks, like he knows exactly what I was thinking, "but not nervous. I think…I don't always care about the outcome. I know that makes me kind of a bad teammate, but I just—" He shakes his head. "I don't know. I've been swimming for so long. Each race kind of blends into the next. It sometimes feels a little…pointless? Do you know what I mean?"

I do *not* know what he means. Diving is a part of me. Lifeblood. Even though it makes me more anxious than anything else sometimes. It's something tangible that I work toward and see the results, even if they don't always go my way. I care deeply about my teammates, and I would never want to think about a competition the way Connor is describing. I'm worried something might be wrong.

I respond cautiously, "I've had some really rough practices where quitting seems like a good option in the moment, but I've never not cared about the sport or a competition. I'm sorry, Connor. I'm not sure I can relate. How long have you felt that way?"

He's quiet for a moment. His gaze doesn't leave the front windshield. His hands grip the steering wheel tightly.

"First of all," he starts, a small smile playing at the corner of his lips, "stop saying sorry for things that aren't your fault." He sighs deeply. "And to answer your question, probably shortly after my dad left," he breathes out in a whisper. "He's the one who taught me how to swim. I was four, and he always said I took to it like a fish to water. He got me onto a club team a year or two later, and not to brag or anything, but it was like I was made for it. I won every race. I was winning against nine- and ten-year-olds. And my dad was there for every one of my races. He would brag to all his friends and colleagues that his son was the 'Miracle Swimmer.' The boy who was born to swim."

He laughs, but there is no humor in it. "I don't think I lost a race until I was twelve. And let me tell you, it rocked my world. I didn't like it one bit. But my dad told me that losing was part of life, even for rock stars like me. He said there is always someone out there who works harder, who puts in more work, who will achieve more than me. I think that was the first time I doubted. Why would I work so hard if it was never going to be good enough?"

He shrugs, still firmly holding the steering wheel. "But I persevered anyway because I was taught hard work mattered more than anything else. I kept winning *most* races, and my dad kept supporting me. Until...he didn't."

His hands squeeze the wheel tight. I want to reach out and grab one, but I refrain.

"When he left, I was so lost. I didn't go to practice for weeks. It was like a grieving period, to be honest. And looking back, I guess it was. Although he didn't die. He was just...gone."

His hands slacken once more, and my heart breaks hearing his story. I wish I could take away his pain.

"Hunter came to my house at the two-week mark. He said to grab my bike, that we were going to the community pool. We swam for hours. We slid down the slides and played Marco Polo."

His smile returns, and it makes me so grateful he has a friend like that.

"Afterward, Hunter asked the lifeguards for two applications. He knew I wanted to get a job to help support Mom, and he didn't want me to do it alone. And they hired us. Worrisome decision, really, but who was I to question a good thing?"

A playful smirk graces his beautiful mouth. I'm relieved his tension has melted away so quickly.

"After I was settled into work, I went back to practice. Went back to competing. Went on to win States all four years in high school, and then came here.

But I'm not really sure why I still do it. I just sort of...always have. And the wins stopped meaning as much, and I stopped loving it."

He takes a deep breath and tries to laugh off everything he just admitted. Like it isn't a big deal. It is a big deal, though, and the tears hovering at the edges of my eyes are proof. I wipe at them, determined not to make Connor comfort *me* in this situation. I'm beyond thrilled that he opened up to me again. It means he trusts me. It means friendship. That is a very, very good sign.

"I'm sorry you've lost that spark for your sport, and I'm sorry for the role your dad played in that. You deserve more than what he did to you, Connor. A dad who is there for you, regardless of whether you're a good swimmer. You deserve to be loved for the beautiful, kind, smart, and funny person you are."

A tear hovers under his eye, but it refuses to fall.

"You're so much more than the Miracle Swimmer. You like to dance to old-people music, and you volunteered to drive me eight hours without a second thought. You treat those around you with respect, and you take responsibility for your actions. You make a delicious herbal tea," I say with a laugh. "In fact, you're always bringing people their favorite food or beverage to make them happy.

"You see people and you give them love, no matter what. You come to others' defense; you offer to help when you can. You're a great man, and I'm thankful." I swallow. "I'm truly thankful to have you as a friend." I sit on my hands to stop them from shaking. "We *are* still friends, right?"

This time, his head fully turns away from the road, and his eyes bore into mine.

He quickly realizes his lapse and returns his focus to driving, but he says, "Maize, of course we are still friends. I'm...I'm sorry I've been M.I.A. the past six weeks. I don't really have a good excuse. All I have is an apology. I'm sorry." He reaches out and gently pulls my hand out from under my thigh to hold it in his. My heart rate kicks up, and I'm suddenly worried about palm sweat. "Can you forgive me?" he asks.

I let out a shaky exhale, but I squeeze his hand for emphasis as I say, "I forgive you. I still don't understand what happened, but I don't want to pry. You can talk about it when you're ready. If you're ever ready. And for now, we can move forward. Pretend that little blip never happened."

A smile curves my lips, and I release a breath I didn't realize I was holding. We're going to be okay. I'm not sure what to do with these pesky "I like you" feelings I have toward Connor still, but at least for now, our friendship is back on track.

I add, "And again, I'm sorry you've felt so...apathetic toward swimming. I'll support you no matter what you decide to do. Even if you don't want to swim anymore."

His eyebrows scrunch down like that notion is ridiculous, but he doesn't say anything. I decide to push one more time, even though he has already opened up so much.

"Have you...talked to your therapist about it? I assume you went to your sessions, since you were at practice after our third meet..." I let the question hang as I side-eye him, awaiting his reaction.

He takes a deep breath, his thumb now tracing circles on the back of my hand, which sends sparks flying up the entirety of my arm, and begins to speak.

34

What a Wonderful World

Connor

"Yeah, I did go to therapy." I sit up straighter in my seat and grip the wheel a little tighter with my left hand. My right is still blissfully intertwined with Maisie's. It was instinct to make contact with her. As easy as breathing. I don't want her to ever pull away. "Donny—my therapist—and I have been working on lots of stuff. I'm actually—" I pause even though I know I have nothing to fear where Maisie is concerned. She will support me in this, I know it. "—going to keep going on a weekly basis."

I squint and peek at her out of the corner of my eye, but Maize just smiles and her eyes melt into gentle green pools of kindness, her shoulders dropping.

"I think that's great, Connor."

"You do?" I sound like an insecure fool, but I can't help it. I need the validation right now.

"Of course I do," she says, shifting so her knees are tucked under her and to the side. She keeps one hand interlocked with mine, but uses the other to squeeze up my arm as if reiterating her point with each movement.

Shivers run down my spine. We weren't strangers to a small degree of friendly physical contact before—but this feels different. Intentional.

Her hands are wisps of things, but boy do they have grip. Her ministrations soothe aches in my muscles, and an embarrassing groan sneaks out of me. Her cheeks redden, but she must take it as a sign of approval, because she moves up to my trap and neck. She's so close to me now.

"I think you deserve someone who listens to you and is trained to help you work through all the complicated emotions that come with life. I'm happy you're going. I'm proud of you. And I hope you're proud of yourself too," she whispers close to my ear as she continues massaging my neck.

This is getting distracting, which is not what I need while operating a vehicle moving at sixty miles per hour.

"Maize," I say.

"Hmmm," she hums back.

"You gotta stop, or I'm gonna steer us right into one of the highway dividers."

Her laugh jingles through our small shared space, but she sinks back into her seat and adjusts her feet forward again. Our hands, however, remain connected. I'm glad but also scared of the hope it gives me. She could just mean it as a friendly gesture. Friends hold hands sometimes.

My mind feels like the spinner in Twister—a game my brothers and I played incessantly as kids. Which color will it land on? Friendship blue or Potential Romantic Love red? Or will we get twisted up somewhere in between, like green?

She's back to swiping through her phone, trying to DJ our next song.

"Any preference on the music?" she asks. "I guess I didn't even ask when we started this road trip."

Her smile twists at the corners like that was absolutely on purpose, but she's throwing me a bone by letting me pick the next song.

"How about some—" I'm about to request some Louis Armstrong when her phone starts buzzing in her hand.

"It's my dad," she says, and I hear her concern.

"Answer it," I say as nonchalantly as I can, but I also wonder why he would be calling when we're only a little over two hours into the drive.

"Hello?" she picks up, folding forward to rest an elbow on her knee. I can't hear everything, but I catch the word "snow." Her leg is bouncing, and I guide our joined hands over it, hoping the weight will calm her.

"How bad?" she asks, biting at the same cuticle she always does. "Okay, will do." Her head drops back against the headrest. "Love you too, bye."

"What is it?" I ask. My gaze darts between her and the road. Everything in me screams to comfort the wonderful but worried woman sitting beside me.

"They said there is a huge blizzard coming their way, and it's supposed to stretch across where we would pass through in West Virginia." She takes a deep breath and closes her eyes. "They want us to find a place to stay the night. They said they'd pay for it."

I know I should sound disappointed, and it looks like the unexpected situation is making Maize nervous—which I don't like—but I can't help but be a little excited at the prospect of staying somewhere overnight together. Even if we're in separate rooms and nothing happens, maybe we'll get in our pajamas and crawl into bed to watch a movie. Maybe she'll get so cozy, she doesn't want to go back to her own room. It's a chance to be away from school, in a new place, just the two of us. Anything could happen.

"It's gonna be okay, Maize." I shake off my excitement to make comforting her my first priority. "There's a rest stop not too far ahead. Let's stop there and look up hotels an hour closer to home. That way, we can still get a little more driving in, and we'll be closer when the snow clears. Sound good?"

Her eyes are dim, missing their usual sparkle, but she nods.

"Good. Now, put on some Louis Armstrong for me. This old-people-music lover needs a fix." I wiggle my eyebrows like a dork, hoping to make her smile. The corner of her mouth tips, which has me internally jumping for joy.

She plugs her phone back in and tilts her head in my direction. "'What a Wonderful World'?"

"That's the one, Betty." I squeeze her hand again, and it stops shaking. "That's the one. What a wonderful world."

35

Doritos & Root Beer

Maisie

NOTE TO SELF: CONNOR is great in a crisis. Not that this is a crisis, but tell that to my body. It's shaking like a leaf. As Lauren likes to tell me, fear of the unknown is normal, but my nervous system can take it to the extreme sometimes. My body doesn't seem to know the difference between getting chased by a bear and experiencing a change of plans.

When we made it to the gas station, Connor encouraged me to breathe, all while continuing to stroke his thumb over my hand. The soft touch melted tension throughout my body, making me shiver. He waited until my body was calm before popping out to retrieve snacks and fill our gas tank. I missed the contact immediately. What does all this hand-holding mean? Does he *like me* like me? Or is he just being a steady force of a friend? Either way, I'm grateful for the comfort, and I definitely don't mind the way his touch makes me feel.

When he slides back into the driver's seat, he hands me Cool Ranch Doritos and a root beer. A smile tugs at my lips.

He cracks open his can of ginger ale, which only broadens my smile. "I checked for places while I was waiting in line to pay for the snacks. There is a hotel off the highway, exactly an hour from here. It would be the perfect spot to put a little more distance toward home but keep plenty away from the incoming storm. Thoughts?"

My chest feels heavy in a good way. He did all the work and came up with a plan. He waited until I was calm, took care of snackage, *and* researched and formed a plan all on his own? I didn't think guys like him existed, but Connor continues to prove all my previous notions wrong.

I realize I haven't answered him when his brows furrow in confusion.

Putting him out of his misery as quickly as I can, I reassure him, "Thank you. That's wonderful. I really appreciate you taking charge of this situation. It's hard for me to change plans sometimes."

His eyes soften. "I know, Betty. That's okay. I'm happy to help. Plus, I'm determined to make it the best experience we can. I'm thinking room service for sure!"

Those damn butterflies take flight in my stomach again. Unfortunately, it's followed quickly by an unbidden barrage of thoughts. *He's too good to be true. You can't trust your judgment. You don't deserve him. He will hurt you, too.*

I swallow the lump in my throat and look away before Connor can see the tears pooling in my eyes. How would I even explain the sudden shift to him? Sometimes it feels like someone took a shovel and scooped out all my self-confidence. Between letting things go on so long with Karsen, failing a dive in my first meet, and struggling with the *most basic* of my occupational therapy pre-req classes, I occasionally question whether I'm doing anything right. And then Connor, one of the best friends I've made since starting college, stopped talking to me, and I still don't know why.

My mouth finds my cuticle once more. I've always followed the status quo. I got together with Karsen because it seemed fun at the time, but I never re-evaluated, and look where that got me. I came to a D1 school because my dad told me I should, and I didn't voice that I didn't think that was what was best. I went with occupational therapy because my dad said I needed something practical, so I followed that path. But I don't think my heart is in it.

Connor's hand wraps around mine, gently pulling it away from where I was gnawing at the cuticle. He isn't looking at me but rather looking around as he pulls out from our spot in the gas station. Quiet, steady comfort. That's what he's offering me.

He sees me, I know it. I want to trust him—I do—but I can't trust myself.

I lean my head back and close my eyes, thinking I'll just take a minute to collect myself, but when I open them again, we're pulling into the parking lot of the hotel. I sit up abruptly, looking out my window.

Mountains peek up beyond the gray-and-blue four-story hotel. There is nothing else around. No shops or restaurants. Just a hotel seemingly in the middle of nowhere. I fidget in my seat and look over at Connor.

"Morning, sleepyhead," he says with a smirk.

"I'm sorry I fell asleep," I say.

"Don't be. I'm glad you got some rest. I know the body can crash after a spike in anxiety."

"You do?" I ask, turning toward him curiously.

"Yeah, um, my mom gets panic attacks. I've been with her through a lot of them." He says it nonchalantly. Like that isn't a lot for a child to comfort their only remaining parent during such an intense emotional experience.

My heart squeezes.

"It sucks that she deals with them, too. I'm sorry you've had that burden on you."

He eyes me warily, tilting his head in my direction while still focusing enough to park the car. "It isn't a burden to help those I love. I'm beyond thankful for my mom, and I'm happy to help her sometimes. The same goes for you."

Did he just imply that he loves me? My eyes widen, but he shows no change in emotion.

I scramble to say, "I didn't mean to imply that you didn't. I just meant that it's a lot for a kid to care for their parent that way. I know you're a wonderful son and that you love your mom a lot. I'm glad you feel comforted by helping her."

I lean my elbow on the car door, trying to adopt a casual posture, and reach out with my other hand to give his arm a quick squeeze.

The hairs on his arm stand up when I do. Apparently, this conversation is over, though, because he puts the car in park and asks, "Do you want me to go in first to check us in and then come get you, or do you want to come with me?"

God, why is he so perfect? "I'll come with you, but thank you for the offer."

He nods and moves to get out of the car.

"Connor?" I say, and he stops, looking back at me expectantly. "Thank you, again, seriously. For everything."

His lips curve into a smile as he says, "Anything for you, Betty."

He playfully boops my nose as he says it, and my heart skyrockets. Before embarrassment can soak in from my reaction to the smallest of touches, he's out of the car and rounding to my side. He opens my door, offering a hand to help me out.

"Your Majesty," he says dramatically as he dips into a reverent half-bow, "your lodgings await."

We both burst into a fit of laughs, his eyes dancing with mirth, and I push him in the chest like he should cut it out, even though I very, very much don't want him to.

He gathers my hand and tucks it into the crook of his arm like we're a lord and lady, then leads us toward the hotel's lobby. A full-body tingle races down my spine. The anxiety from earlier has flowed into excitement.

I turn to look at Connor's profile. His strong, scruffy jaw is on full display, his nose tipped high in the air, feigning sophistication, but his eyes are crinkled at the edges, trying to keep his laugh in.

Yeah, I'm excited, but only because I'm with him.

We enter through the automatic sliding glass doors, and adventure awaits.

36

I'm Sorry, Sir, There's Only One Room Available

Connor

"I'M SORRY, SIR, THERE is only one room available, and it is one of our singles with a king-sized bed."

Guilt punches me in the gut. I should have called the hotel ahead of time to check availability. I sneak a peek over at Maize, seeing her teeth on that cuticle again. Her poor hands are going to be raw by the end of today.

"There is nothing else? You're sure?" I press.

The man behind the desk, a scrawny middle-aged gentleman who looks like he'd rather be anywhere but here right now, slowly looks back at his computer screen. He presses a few buttons on the keyboard, but I can tell he is only pretending to look to appease us. I run a shaky hand through my hair.

"We're all full with Thanksgiving travelers avoiding the snow. Will you be booking the room or not?" The receptionist smiles, but it's hollow.

"We'll take it," I answer without hesitating this time. We need a place to stay, and the next hotel is another forty-five minutes away. Getting there would put us in danger of the storm, and I'm not risking Maize like that.

I pull out my credit card to hand to the man, but Maisie grabs my wrist and shakes her head. "I have the emergency credit card my dad gave me. They insisted on paying, remember?"

It doesn't feel right to accept money from her parents, but that's probably because I've had to work for everything—excluding when Grandpa would help when he could, of course—since Dad left. Well, until I accepted the apartment, that is.

As she hands over the card, I do a quick scan of her body. Her cheeks are rosy from the cold and her chestnut hair is windswept. She's breathtaking. I'm worried the sleeping version of Connor won't be able to keep his hands to himself. As I'm appreciating, I realize she suddenly looks calm. She's not shaking or biting or anything anymore. *That's peculiar.*

I'm ripped from my thoughts as the receptionist says, "Here's your receipt, ma'am. Room 108. Pool is just down the hall from your room if you're interested, and breakfast is from eight to eleven tomorrow. We also already have emergency services prepped in the event the storm reaches us, so nothing to worry about." He hands her two sets of room keys, and Maisie hands one off to me.

"Thanks," she says, and shuffles away from the desk. She's already heading back outside, presumably to go grab our luggage, but I tug on her lean, muscled arm. She skids to a stop, her eyes swinging to me. "What's wrong?" she asks, the worry I've grown familiar with etching itself across her beautiful face.

"Are you okay with this?" I ask.

Her features soften and her shoulders drop. "Yeah, we're adults. It'll be fine, Connor. We can make a pillow fort between us or something. Why do you seem so worried?" Her eyebrow arches in challenge.

"I...I'm not," I stammer, giving away that my words aren't exactly true. "I was just worried about you. You know, with another change in plans and all... But if you're good, then..." I let my words hang.

"I'm good," she says with a roguish smile.

"Good. That's...good," I say, and she covers a laugh with her hand.

"All right, *good*. Should we get our luggage?" She hooks a thumb over her shoulder in the direction of my worn-down Civic.

"After you, my Queen," I say, stepping back into the make-believe characters we developed upon starting this trip.

She pretends to pinch a make-believe ball gown's skirts and steps off the sidewalk's edge into the parking lot. Her goofy side is my absolute favorite.

Maisie

I was nervous at first when the hotel clerk said there was only one room with one bed left, but then my perspective shifted. A sleepover with my handsome best friend? It sounded fun. The nerves snuck back in when Connor seemed so hesitant, but then chilled again when we moved into a safe, goofy middle ground. He carried our luggage inside, ever the gentleman, and now we're standing outside our room. Nothing left to do but go inside.

I reach out to swipe the key card and open the door. Connor is right behind me, holding the door open over my head. His nearness causes my body to heat. I hope I'm not visibly red. We make our way into the room, and sure enough, there is one king-sized bed in the middle. The room is basic. There isn't even a couch or plush chair. Just the bed, two nightstands, a dresser that the TV is standing on, and a bathroom off to the left of the entryway.

I peek over to see Connor's reaction. He's a little flushed, but that could be from carrying two people's luggage. It's getting dark outside. I hear his stomach grumble.

"Should we order that room service now?" I suggest.

He laughs. "Guess that would be a good idea. Do you, uh, have a side of the bed preference?"

"The side furthest from the door," I say without hesitation.

He quirks a smile, but doesn't say anything else, just shifts to move my bag onto the luggage cart. He sets his own down on the floor.

"I think I might take a quick shower." I point haphazardly toward our shared bathroom. "Do you need to use it before I do?"

Now I know his tinted cheeks are from embarrassment and not physical exertion. "Nope, I'm all good. Have a nice shower," he says, voice pitching up and eyes darting away like I've caught him doing something he shouldn't.

I laugh and step into the bathroom to start the shower. I then remember his gurgling stomach, so I quickly shout through the door, "Order me a burger, please!"

He fires back a garbled "Okay!"

I sigh as steam quickly fills the small space, and I can't help but think of the amazing man just outside the bathroom door as I strip down and step into the warm spray. Part of me wishes he were stepping in with me.

37

Hungry?

Connor

I USE THE PHONE on the nightstand to call in our room service order. A burger and fries for Maize and a club sandwich for me. I ask if they have ice cream too, but they don't. I wonder if I could sneak out and grab her some before the storm hits.

As my mind spins with ideas on how to get Maisie some ice cream, I hear her sigh through the wall to the bathroom. My head turns sharply toward the sound, and my pants become a little too tight, all my senses tuning into that one sound.

What the hell am I going to do? From the moment I first saw her, I was attracted to her, and now that I know her? Know how funny and goofy and brave and kind she is? It feels like my whole body is pulling me toward her all the time, chanting *Maisie! Maisie! Maisie!* I'm not going to be able to hide my desire, but the last thing I want is to make her uncomfortable.

I pace the room, trying to burn off some of this excess energy when I hear the shower turn off. *Her clothes.* She didn't take her clothes with her. She's going to come out here in a towel. Without thinking, I lunge toward the room door to give her some privacy, but then the bathroom door pops open. I turn on instinct. She isn't looking at me, and our paths collide before I can do anything about it.

I feel damp skin pressed along the length of my body from my chest down, but I'm not looking at her. The sensation of her naked body crushed against me, even through my clothes, sends my heart rate into an uncontrollable rhythm.

She squeaks before rushing out, "Shit, Connor, I...I'm..." There's a long pause. "The towel fell," she whispers.

I know the towel fell, damn it. I can *feel* the lack of towel. All of my brain cells are currently working in overdrive to not look down, so I have none left to verbally reply to her. The bulge in my pants is growing involuntarily. I hear her breath hitch. The warmth of it against my chest only adds to the assault on my senses.

Somehow, my brain comes back online, and I manage to say, "I'll close my eyes and turn toward the door. You grab your towel and go get changed."

She gulps, and I feel the sharp pebbling of her nipples against my torso. I squeeze my eyes shut and slowly shift my body away from hers and toward the door. My shirt is wet, and I feel a chill run down my spine, but it's not from the cold. I hear her soft shuffle toward the other side of the room.

Grandma's face mole. Taxes. Soggy bread. I mentally run through anything to get my mind off the feel of her naked body pressed against me. Praying it cools my desire and my, uh, *member* down.

In a moment that feels simultaneously like a lifetime and no time at all, she says, "Okay, you can turn around now."

I can't make myself move. I'm glued to this spot. *RIP Connor. Died from lack of movement from desiring his best friend too damn much.*

I'm ripped from my morbid thoughts when Maisie says, "Connor?"

"Yeah?" I manage to get out. My voice sounds unfamiliar.

"I said you can turn around now." It's her tone that finally makes me move. That nervous energy infused into her regularly honeyed voice. I don't want her to feel embarrassed.

I take a deep breath, slowly turning to face her. I work hard to keep my face neutral, but my jaw clenches. Her being clothed does nothing to stop the burning I feel for her. She pushes a strand of hair behind her ear and looks away, crossing her arms in the process. Hiding from me the best she can in the cramped space.

I take slow, deliberate steps to close the space between us, not wanting to spook her. Her eyes still refuse to meet mine until I'm directly in front of her. She looks up, but there's a crease between her brows.

"I called in our room service," I stammer out, "but they didn't have ice cream. Who doesn't have ice cream? Don't they know everyone likes ice cream? It would be their bestseller. Obviously." I roll my eyes dramatically. Her lips crack into a reserved smile. "I was actually thinking of running out to grab some from a gas station or something. That was why I, uh, ran into you...the way I did."

Her eyes widen in alarm, and she draws her lip between her teeth. I reach out, cupping her face gently and using the pad of my thumb to encourage her to release her death grip on her now-swollen lip. As her mouth opens in surprise, I let my finger trail along the length of it once before dropping my hand.

I can't believe I just did that, but she isn't running for the hills. Maybe this attraction goes more than one way. I step a little further into her space. She fidgets, rocking side to side, eyes bouncing like she's unsure where to look. I reach out and squeeze her hand once.

"Please don't be embarrassed. Not with me." I stroke a thumb over her hand, and she shivers.

"Okay," she says in a breathy whisper, leaning in.

We're so close, I need to tilt my chin down to see her, our lips mere inches away. My hand that isn't holding hers finds her waist and snakes around to the small of her back. The movement forces her even closer, and I'm leaning in for a kiss when a knock sounds at the door.

We jump apart. *What the hell?*

Her cheeks are flushed, eyes wide. *Why did someone have to knock* now?

I frown but march toward the door, opening it almost violently—taking out my frustration on the inanimate object so I don't direct it at the human standing behind it.

"Room service," the freckle-speckled teen says.

I move out of the way so he can roll the cart into the room. I peek at Maisie. She's in the same spot across the room, but her hand is at her mouth. She looks dazed, puzzled maybe. I reach into my pocket for my wallet and tip the kid—who seems like he's fourteen—and I wait as he scurries out of the room.

As soon as I shut the door, I loose a breath and turn back toward a still-stunned Maisie.

"Hungry?" I ask.

38

You Mean You Travel Without a Bathing Suit?

Maisie

I'M FROZEN IN PLACE, shock at what almost happened rooting my feet to the room's gray carpet. Connor was going to kiss me, right? There's no other way to interpret what happened, but doubt still sits like a weight at the base of my stomach.

Connor lifts the lid off each dish on the cart with a casual ease I envy. Is it so easy for him to switch from what just happened? Or, I guess, *almost* happened.

He wheels the cart closer to me and waggles his eyebrows. "Can I have a fry?" He pouts pleadingly, then sits down at the edge of the bed, patting the space next to him.

"Yeah—not too many, though," I say on autopilot.

I'll share my food, but if he wanted fries, he should have gotten himself some. A girl can only be so generous. I scooch onto the end of the bed beside him, my feet dangling. Our elbows brush, and my cheeks heat. Images of our naked bodies pressed together filter unbidden through my mind. I wonder what it would feel like...my towel dropping, but this time no clothes hindering our contact.

I suck in a breath and shake my head, reaching for a fry.

He looks at me out of the corner of his eye but doesn't say anything. We eat in silence, and it should feel awkward, but that's the great thing about being with Connor. Whether I'm charged with electricity at his touch or sad or upset, I'm still comfortable. Safe. We're friends first and foremost.

He nudges my arm right as I'm about to put a ketchup-dipped fry into my mouth, the jostle knocking it back onto the plate.

"Hey!" I scold. "Don't come between me and my fries. You'll regret it."

He grabs his stomach with a laugh, then reaches out to wipe away the stray drop of ketchup from my cheek with his thumb. He brings it to his smiling lips. Licks it clean...and winks. WINKS. The electricity beneath my skin returns on a current as strong as the ocean's. I can't help but imagine his tongue *elsewhere*.

He's being bold. Acting outside of his character. He wants me, I think. He was going to kiss me. I need to show I'm interested, too. *I want this*. Yes. Logically, I know this could mess with our friendship, but the logical side of my brain is being fried by the spark racing under my skin, gathering at my core like there's a conductor pulling it there.

I swallow and decide to be bold, too.

"Was your sandwich good?" I ask as I lean in ever so slightly, our sides touching along the full length of our upper bodies now. I let out a soft, contented sound, and he quirks a smile.

"It would have been better with some fries," he says, but adjusts so his arm is around my back, his hand on the bed holding his weight.

I lean my head down slowly until it rests on his broad shoulder. I can feel his heart from here. It's pounding into my ear like it's calling my name.

Suddenly, nerves seize me by the throat, and I sit up abruptly.

He shuffles back, dumbstruck. "What's wrong?" he asks.

"Should we go for a swim? We should probably swim, right?" My voice pitches higher on every word that stumbles out of my mouth.

His eyes widen momentarily but then quickly melt into their softened hazel pools of warmth, crinkling at the edges. "We *obviously* should go for a swim. But, I, uh—" he rubs the back of his head, pushing his thick hair forward "—didn't bring a suit?" He shrugs, looking sheepish.

"You mean you travel without a bathing suit?" I laugh. "I didn't know that was even a thing. What if you had to practice while we were home, or we got stuck from, oh, I don't know, a blizzard?! And had to fly straight to a meet or something?"

As someone who plans for every scenario, I am flabbergasted that a man at his athletic level would travel such a long distance without a bathing suit. I might have more suits than regular outfits packed.

"We can still swim. I'll just go in my underwear. It's late enough we shouldn't run into anyone else in there," he says nonchalantly. Like swimming in his underwear in a public place is a common practice for him.

My confusion must show on my face because he barks out a laugh and grabs my hand, urging me to stand up with him.

"It'll be fine, Betty. I'll grab our key and wait outside. You change into your suit, and then we'll walk down together. The worst that happens is there are people there and you can get in without me for a while, or we can come back to the room, whatever you prefer."

He's always giving me choices. Making it clear that he values what makes me comfortable and happy.

"What do you want to do?" I ask in a rush, the words running together.

"Huh?" One eyebrow bent.

"If we get there and there are people, which would you prefer? Stay and watch me swim, or come back to the room?" I enunciate so he can hear me clearly this time.

"Oh, hmm, I guess watch you swim. There's something sexy about watching your body glide through the water. I usually only get to see it when you're diving. *Not* that I don't love that too—" he holds his hands up placatingly "—but it would be nice to watch you just...be. In the water. Swimming for pleasure, not having to perform."

My mouth drops open, and I shut it so fast my teeth click. Sexy? He thinks I'm sexy? And he wants to watch me swim? My head suddenly swirls, feeling like it could float away, and I stagger back a step.

"Whoa, you okay?" He lunges to steady me, his massive hands wrapped around each of my biceps.

"Ha, yeah, sorry—I don't know what that was. I'll get changed and meet you outside."

He eyes me warily for a moment, like he's afraid I might pass out the moment he walks through that door, but finally relents, swiping the key off the bedside table and sauntering toward the door.

"Connor?" I call out before it closes behind him.

He turns expectantly toward me.

"I really hope there isn't anyone else at the pool."

His eyes darken and glide over my body with such intent that it feels like he's physically touching me.

I hold my breath, worried that if I so much as allow my ribs to expand, this moment will vanish.

He slowly, so slowly, retreats backward through the door, his eyes never leaving me. He lets go of the handle, the door closing and forming an unwelcome divider between us.

I rush to change.

39

Drag Suit Practice

Connor

MY MOUTH GOES DRY as Maisie exits our shared hotel room. She opted for no cover-up, so as she turns to catch the door before it slams shut, I'm greeted with an uninhibited view of her backside. I stifle a groan. It's not uncommon for that part to be curvy and muscular on divers, but Maize takes the cake.

I'm distracted by the way her red suit hugs her and the depraved thought of her thighs wrapped around me when she turns to face me. I lift my gaze, but when my eyes meet hers, her nose crinkles like she knows what I was doing. I blush.

The pool is only down the hall, but I gather her hand in mine so she doesn't have any question about where I want to be. Touching her. Holding her. Talking to her. All of it. With her. And *only* her. Not just friends.

I'm still pissed that our kiss was interrupted by room service, but I know her too well. Even with an imminent kiss, she wouldn't want anything to come before food, so we ate. The next available chance, though...

We reach the glass door unceremoniously labeled "Pool," and I open the door for her to precede me. She collects her hair into a ponytail, back muscles stretching taut and exposing the slope of her kissable neck. Too distracted, I completely miss the family of five wading in the shallow end. My eyes must bug out because one of the kids flinches away.

My awareness surges back toward Maisie as she tugs gently at my forearm, guiding us to the opposite side of the pool where there are some empty chairs. I don't think I make a coherent phrase, mostly grumbling in response. She giggles but leads the way, never dropping the point of contact between us. At that, I smile. I love this carefree version of her.

Don't get me wrong—I love her when she's anxious too, nail biting and all—but this moment has a soft glow.

I'm falling in love with my best friend.

I squeeze her hand as my smile grows.

She doesn't seem to mind being trapped here with me, and I daresay it might even relax her. My chest fills with pride at the thought. I want to be her safe place to land, the person she can be her full self with and know there is nothing she could do that would change the way I feel about her. These are big feelings, though, ones I know she's not ready to hear, and that's okay. For now, Operation Kiss My Best Friend is a go. I just need to get this family to leave.

We don't have anything with us other than our key card, so when we reach the chairs, we casually plop down. She looks at me in a way that says *what now?* I'm about to tell her to get in when I hear the dad of the family announce it's time to get out of the pool. It's bedtime. The kids all whine, but he shoots them a look even I would be a little afraid of. One by one, like little ducklings, they make their way up the steps and out of the pool, dripping as they go but quickly enveloped in a toweled hug by the mom.

A pang shoots through my chest. We were a happy family unit once, until my dad ruined everything.

My face must show my inner turmoil because Maisie reaches over to squeeze my arm. *I'm here*, she seems to say.

The corner of my mouth tips up. How did I get so lucky?

We wait a moment until the family is through the glass door. I can still hear their shouting down the hall, and I cringe for the people trying to sleep in those rooms.

As soon as I know we're alone, my skin prickles in anticipation.

Abruptly standing, I bow and hold out my hand to her. "My Queen," I say in a dorky British accent.

She takes my hand and is working on standing when I bend and scoop her up. She squeals—half in terror, half in delight.

"What are you doing!" she shouts, but before either of us can say anything else, I turn and let us crash into the water.

My back takes the brunt of the fall. If hotel pools were lifeguarded, we would for sure have the whistle sounding, but thank goodness they aren't here. It's just me and Maize, and there is literally no place I'd rather be.

We surface, and she releases some water from her mouth, rubbing her eyes to adjust to the chlorine, which is definitely too high for this size pool based on the smell in here. She laughs as I wipe the water from my own eyes and take the single stroke needed to crowd her space. Her laugh cuts out as she tugs at the corner of her bottom lip with her teeth. My eyes track the movement, and when I look back up, her expression is dark...longing, even. Her soft yet slanted eyes meet mine, her lips curved in a subtle smile.

I wade an arm through the water until it rounds her back and pull her into me. She instinctively wraps her legs around my middle and gasps at what she finds there. Her fingers dig into each of my shoulders, and I tighten my grip. Her eyes meet mine, and there is nothing unsure in her gaze. I take that as my green light.

Slowly—so, so fucking slowly—I tilt my head and close what little distance is left between our lips, giving her every chance to pull away. Instead, she crashes her mouth into mine. I nearly lose my footing, but I quickly recover and back her up against the wall of the pool. She tastes like chlorine and sunshine.

I've stared at her soft lips more times than I can count, and now, the feel of them is better than I could have ever imagined. I can't get enough. Part of my brain acknowledges that if someone walked into this very public place right now, that would not be good. My protective instincts flare. No one should get to see her like this. But the other part is chanting *Maisie Maisie Maisie,* and I focus entirely on her.

Absorbing every bit of sunshine that she offers me, I deepen the kiss. She opens for me without hesitation, our tongues tangling. When she lets out a moan, my knees buckle. I envelop the side of her head with my hand, and when my fingers caress her ear, she sucks in a breath and kisses me with even more fervor. With her legs still wrapped around me, I start to nudge my hips, feeling her center even through our clothes.

I should have taken the time to remove them, but I can't bring myself to regret the spontaneous decision that brought us to this point. Her arm is closed tightly around my neck and she's clawing at my chest. This is heaven. I never want it to stop, but before I can think better of it, I pull back, panting.

I drop my forehead to hers and ask breathlessly, "Are you sure this is okay?"

"Yes," she says, but disentangles her legs from me. I'm about to protest when she gracefully pulls herself out of the pool. I zero in on her peaked nipples visible through her suit as she walks casually to the basket of towels not far from the chairs we claimed.

I'm still dumbstruck when she says, "Coming? Or are you planning to get a drag suit practice in?"

I choke out a laugh. Drag suit practice, when we have to swim in our clothes, is one of my least favorites. I sweep myself over the edge and out of the pool as quickly as I can. Not as graceful, but just as fast as her.

She hands me a towel, smirking. "Good choice," she says with a wink. As soon as she dries herself and wraps the towel around her middle, she takes my hand and pulls me toward the glass doors. As if I wouldn't go willingly.

I blow out a relieved breath. This is really happening.

40
Only for Me

Maisie

WATER DRIPS DOWN MY back from my still-soaking hair as we make it to room 108. My stomach swirls in anticipation. That kiss was…unimaginable. My hand shakes as I bring our key card to the device above the handle. It clicks, and we step inside. Connor doesn't waste any time. His lips find mine, and the electric shock from his kiss fizzles over my whole body. I didn't know a kiss could feel like this. It didn't with Karsen. It makes me want more. Want *all* of him.

I hungrily lift the base of his shirt, and he rips the soaking fabric over his head. I stop for a moment to appreciate his body. I've seen him shirtless countless times at practice, but here, in this hotel room together—it's different. I take my time gazing down his arm, at the angry vein popped around his muscled bicep and snaked down his strong forearm. My eyes continue to his torso and to the V that descends further. Swimmer abs are common. But combined with Connor's height, his smile, his kindness? Nothing feels common about the attraction bubbling inside me as I look my fill.

His chest rises and falls quickly. When my eyes finally lock back on his, I'm met with an expressive mix of agony and determination. His desire for me is palpable. It invigorates me. I've never felt so wanted, and we haven't done anything more than kiss yet.

His oversized hand reaches out to cup my cheek, thumb brushing against where I would put blush if I were wearing makeup.

"You're so beautiful, you know that?" He takes a step closer, and I fumble back into the wall.

His other hand reaches out to steady me, lingering on my hip. His finger slides under the edge of my suit, tracing delicate patterns that make my skin tingle in the most delicious way. My chest and cheeks grow hot. He never takes his eyes off me as he continues his slow torture.

Beautiful. Did I know? Karsen had called me hot regularly. I'd gotten attention from other boys in the past, but beautiful? It had so many implications other than the body I was born into and had toned through my sport. My heart pumps faster as the idea twirls through my brain.

"Tell me what you want," he says while resting his forehead against mine. "Tell me what you need, and I swear, Maize, I'll do it."

Him. I need him.

I thread my fingers through his thick hair and tug gently, encouraging his lips down to my own. It's like a switch is flipped. The next thing I know, my legs are wrapped around him, the same way they were in the pool, but this time his strength is on display. His tongue meets mine stroke for stroke. Sounds I've never made before escape me. It feels like a thousand tiny pinpricks flutter along my skin, and when he adjusts so our centers collide through cold, wet fabric, a lightning bolt shoots from my core up to the crown of my head.

I melt into him. Luxuriating in the feeling of being held, cherished, *devoured.*

"Connor." His name slips through my lips like smoke rising from a roaring fire.

"Maisie," he responds, and then glides back into my mouth.

His hands are busy supporting my weight, but mine are roaming anywhere I can get a hold of. His hair, neck, shoulders, back. Each part is warm and perfect to touch. Every part of him elevates my desire higher and higher, like being stuck in an elevator going to the hundredth floor. I'm both nervous and exhilarated to find out what the top level holds.

We're moving, and the next thing I know, my back is supported by a layer of clouds. Or at least that's what it feels like strewn across the hotel bed.

"Tell me what you want, Maize. I refuse to mess this up. You mean too much to me. If you wanna keep going, I won't hesitate. I want you so bad." He looks down pointedly, and my eyes follow to see the evidence of his desire. His arm muscles tense as he leans over me. Feeling caged in should scare me, but I squirm in anticipation, not fear. "But if you want to stop, you say the word. I mean it. You don't owe me *anything*. Do you understand?"

That phrase halts my wriggling immediately. Tears prick at my eyes, and his widen in alarm. It's the exact opposite of my last interaction with Karsen. Things had been better with him at the beginning. What if Connor and I do this now, and then it changes down the road? If he stops liking me, valuing me, or tires of being patient with me?

No. Connor is not Karsen.

I rise to rest on my elbows so my mouth can trail down the column of his throat. Pausing at his clavicle, I let my tongue swirl in the hollow space. His whole body shudders. I feel powerful, desirable. I want this; I want *him*.

"I understand," I say on a breath. "Please, Connor."

His mouth comes to my neck, and my eyes close, rolling back in pleasure. He lets some of his weight rest along the length of my body, and I relish the pressure. I wrap my legs around his middle to pull him closer, and he lets out a guttural groan. He reaches for the strap of my suit and slowly slides it down my shoulder. It's tight, and I'm not sure there is a sexy way to remove it.

"Let me," I say, and he nods his head slowly in approval. He lifts his weight to make room for me to roll off the bed and stand. He sits up, on high alert. I chance a look down at his tented sweatpants.

"Take those off," I demand. "You're soaking the bed."

He chuckles but does as I say. He leaves his black briefs on, even though they're wet, too. The bit of covering leaves little to the imagination.

I swallow.

He moves so he's sitting up, legs dangling over the side of our bed, eyes hungry and body buzzing as he waits.

My gaze still flicking between his burning stare and his body, I finish sliding the strap he had started and allow it to tuck under me fully. I reach for the next one and fight my wave of uncertainty. He's looking at me like he's never seen anything better, and it's intoxicating. Emboldened by his visual encouragement, I slip the entire suit down to my ankles, bending over in the process. When I stand and step out of it, I'm fully exposed to him.

His eyes can't decide where to look, bouncing all over my body. I feel naturally inclined toward embarrassment, but something about his reaction keeps it from setting in.

"Can I touch you?" His voice drops to a low rumble.

I shiver. "Please."

Before I know it, my back is cushioned by the bed again. This time, he's braced on one hand, and the other is *everywhere*—cupping my breasts, gliding down the side of my stomach, reaching into my hair—all while kissing me like the snowstorm outside means we won't have a tomorrow. It's a sensation feast. My open legs bend, feet still on the bed, and he settles between them.

I'm fully revealed to him, a representation of how my heart feels right now. On display. But I trust him.

His kisses begin trailing down my neck and continue to my chest while his free hand simultaneously draws lower and lower. He gently slides a finger to where I need him most, and I gasp. His smile turns wicked. It's an expression I've never seen on his handsome face, but in the heat of this moment, it sends its own wave of pleasure down my spine.

He teases me with achingly slow circles. Practically not touching me at all. The contrast of him taking my entire nipple into his mouth is confusing. I pant, but it's not enough.

"I need more," I say. Because I know I can tell him anything.

"Good girl, telling me what you need."

His words are a caress over my whole body. I had no idea praise could do that.

He uses two fingers to apply more pressure, increasing the speed of his circles. It's exactly right. My hand flies to the side, fisting the sheets.

"Yes," I let out. "Please, right there. Don't stop."

"I wouldn't dream of it," he says before lowering his mouth once again to my neck, his hand gathering mine.

We're holding hands. He's telling me I'm a good girl and bringing me to orgasm and still letting me know he's here. I've never felt so cared for in my entire life.

With that, I fly over the edge, crying out so loud, our neighbors can probably hear me, but I can't make myself care.

He coaxes me through several aftershocks, my legs trembling, until I can't take any more. I push his hand away. He carefully removes it, eyes finding mine, and places both fingers into his mouth, sucking them clean.

My jaw drops. That might be the hottest thing I've ever seen. Aren't first sexual interactions supposed to be awkward? This was anything but.

He shifts to lie on his side, facing me. I'm staring at him, dumbfounded, and I realize I should probably take care of him too. I reach for his boxers, but he catches my wrist, bringing it to his lips for a sweet kiss.

"Not tonight, Betty. I want this one to be only for you."

Only for me. The concept is foreign, but I sink into the idea. It's nice. Not to feel any sort of obligation. Not that I feel that way with Connor, but sex always felt like I have to give in order to receive. And, more often than not, pleasure was tilted pretty far in Karsen's favor, so this is new.

I sigh and shift so my leg is wrapped over his. "Thank you," I say.

"Thank *you*," he says with a wink, his arm coming to wrap around me, drawing me impossibly closer to him. He kisses the crown of my head.

I never want this feeling to leave.

41

A Million Miles

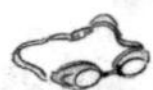

Connor

A BUZZING SOUND KNOCKS into my head like a mini jackhammer, and I stir awake. Maisie nestles further into me for a moment, and I inhale her lavender scent, enjoying the feel of her pressed against me.

Last night was amazing. I'm honestly having trouble believing it was real. The girl of my dreams, my best friend. Wanted me. Let me kiss her, touch her. I can't wrap my head around it. And then after? We cleaned up, changed into warm PJs, and watched a Marvel movie. It's a balance I never would have dared to dream for myself.

The buzzing stops and immediately starts again. I frown and gently reach across a still-sleeping Maisie to check her phone. "Mom," it reads. It must be important if she is calling twice in a row, so I decide I need to wake Maize.

I kiss up her arm, stopping at her shoulder, whispering, "Wake up, sleepy-head."

"Mmmmmm," she mumbles and scoots even closer to me. My cock jumps in excitement at the movement, but this is not the time.

"Maize, your mom is calling. I think it's important. You need to wake up."

She stirs again but still doesn't wake to coherence. I kiss her cheek. I don't want our bubble to pop. I want to spend all day in this bed with her, cuddled up, away from the distractions of the world.

The world apparently has other plans, though. The buzzing starts once more. "Dad" flashes across the screen this time. I gulp down nerves of what could be wrong and shake her.

"Maize, seriously, wake up. Now your dad's calling."

She stretches out like a starfish but slowly makes her way to sitting, her giant sleep shirt hanging off her and her hair wild in the most adorable way. She holds her hand out for the phone, and I place it in her palm.

"Dad?" she answers, her words garbling around a yawn. She's quiet while he talks on the other end.

"Oh!" she says, and I can't quite tell what to make of her tone. She's clearly surprised, but I can't tell if it's good or bad.

"Sure, yeah. We'll get on the road as soon as possible. Yep, see you soon. Love you." She ends the call and slumps back into the sea of stacked pillows. "The storm never actually hit," she says casually. "I guess we're free to head home." She looks at her phone, and her eyes bulge. "Shit! Connor, it's almost eleven—we're going to miss check-out. We need to move!"

The next fifteen minutes are a chaotic whirlwind of haphazard packing of clothes, taking turns to quickly pee and brush our teeth, and getting all our luggage into the hall. I exit our room with the last bag just in time for housekeeping to show up. I give the woman a sheepish grin and turn to hightail it toward the front desk with Maize.

"Check out for Thatcher, Room 108," I say to the man at the counter, blissfully not the same gentleman who checked us in yesterday.

"Sure thing, sir. Did you enjoy your stay?"

"Very much." And I can't help the smile that beams across my face. I turn to look at Maisie, but she's staring down at her phone like it holds the mysteries of the world. Her shoulders are slumped, and her cuticle is between her teeth again. *What happened between the room and here?*

"Here's your receipt, sir. Thank you, and I hope you have a lovely rest of your day."

I manage to grab the receipt and then reach for Maisie's hand, but she startles and retracts her hand from mine, feigning the need for both to pull her suitcase.

My stomach twists. *Did last night not mean the same to her as it did to me?* No, our intentions were clear. Right? This wasn't just some hook-up. This was *us*. If we were going to take that to the next level, it implied more than a hook-up and certainly more than being just friends. Didn't it?

I rush to catch up to Maisie, who's already through the sliding glass doors and a few steps into the parking lot. A car slams to a halt beside her and beeps. She barely spares them a glance. I wave them off and join her side.

"Maize, are you okay?" I ask, concern bubbling.

"Oh, yeah, sorry," she says, but she might as well be a million miles away.

We finish the short walk to the car in silence. I load everything into the trunk as she takes her spot in the passenger's seat. I think I might be sick. I can't lose her. I've barely even had her. What the heck happened?

I climb into the driver's seat and start the car. I sneak a peek over to her, but she's staring out the window, so I can't see her face. Her body tells me she doesn't want to talk. I put on the radio, and Taylor Swift comes through the speakers. My eyes light up, hopeful her favorite artist will be enough to cheer her up, but she doesn't move.

"It's good you'll be home in plenty of time for Thanksgiving," I say, trying anything to break the tension that pulses through the car.

"Yeah," is all she says.

My palms are sweating, and my ears are hot, but I pull out of our parking spot and start the next leg of our car journey. I pray whatever is happening is not what I think it is, and we'll be back to normal soon. Well, our *new* normal.

42

My Queen

Maisie

MY SKIN ITCHES, AND I shift uncomfortably in the car seat. The seat belt is suffocating, and the world is spinning by too quickly. Is it hot in here? I reach for the air on instinct and blast it. It's freezing outside. Connor looks at me with furrowed brows but doesn't protest.

Why did he have to text me? *Karsen.* Why couldn't he just leave me alone? Hasn't he done enough damage?

I was on cloud nine after everything that happened last night. Connor, his words, his lips on mine, the pleasure he elicited from my body. I had known I wanted him, but it was exhilarating experiencing the evidence of him truly wanting me. He called me beautiful. He made me feel safe and cherished and desired in a way I've never experienced. And now...now, I'm reminded that I'm broken.

I lost myself with Karsen, and I don't know if I can get her back. Connor deserves better. I stare down at my phone again, *his* text mocking me from the screen.

> **Karsen:** I know you said we're done, but you know you're never really done with me. Your mom invited me for Thanksgiving and I can't turn down Madeline's pumpkin pie ;) Plus I miss our old hookup spot in the basement. Nothing quite like having my cock sucked

> in front of a wood-burning fireplace. See you soon, babe.

It was like hot iron had been pressed to my gut, branding me in shame and defeat. The world around me fell away, and my hands shook as another text came in.

> **Mom:** By the way sweetie, I invited Karsen for Thanksgiving tomorrow. I know you've had some disagreements, but this is a time to be with loved ones. Drive safe! XOXO

Can she truly not understand?

A tear pulls at the corner of my eye, and I am helpless to stop it from running down my cheek and plopping unceremoniously onto my phone. Thankfully, I didn't have time to put makeup on in our rush out of the hotel or I'd truly be making a mess.

I feel something warm on my left hand. *Connor.* He's being his usual sweet self. As much as I want to tell him exactly what is going on and let him fix it, I can't. I yank my hand away, and the absence of his comfort is like plunging into a cold pool. Ice drips through my veins, holding my heart in a vise.

My breathing shallows, but somehow I'm not going into a full-blown panic attack.

Connor speaks up. "Maize, I don't know what's going on, and I won't touch you if you don't want me to, but I'm here. Whatever you need. I promise." He deserves so much more. I should tell him, but I can't think past this feeling right now.

My tears fall in earnest as I let out a sound not dissimilar to a dying animal. I tuck myself into a ball on my side, as tight as I can go, and slam my eyes shut. I focus on my breathing, the way Connor taught me. I can hear his breathing deepen beside me. I'm still focusing on my breath when, slowly, my head calms, and the next thing I know, the world fades away as sleep claims me.

I wake to the sound of muted squeals. Sitting up faster than is probably smart, I take in my surroundings. Home. We're at my parents' house. Lauren is running for my side of the car. She knocks on my window with a gloved hand. "Open up!" Her voice is muffled through the glass.

I look over at Connor, who gives me a too-tentative smile. All of our car time. It's gone. I don't know what to say to him, so all I say is, "Thanks for the ride."

"Anytime, Betty," he responds, but there is a hollowness to his tone.

Before I can think to say anything more, Lauren rips open the door and pulls me into a crushing hug. The chill from the wind whips at me, and I shiver even in her embrace. As I make my way out of the car, it still feels a little like I'm wading through mud, everything harder at the moment. Connor is already around back, trunk popped, bags waiting on the ground.

When I round the car to meet him, he's holding my coat out for me, ready to help me into it. The ache in my chest is back. I step into the coat, my arms sliding through awkwardly. As soon as I'm settled, he takes a pointed step back, giving me space. *I would too if I were him.*

Lauren grabs my hand. "Let's get inside, it's freezing out here!" she says. "Thanks for giving her a ride, Connor! *I*, personally, really appreciate it. Seeing as I haven't seen MaiMai in nearly five months now!"

"MaiMai?" he says, and I catch a glimpse of a genuine smile from him.

"Don't make fun," I say with a half-hearted groan. "It's what she's called me since we were little."

"I wouldn't dare make fun. It's cute. And who am I to judge, my Queen?" he says with an eyebrow waggle.

He's being goofy. Maybe everything is okay? Maybe last night was just a hook-up for him and he's fine going back to being friends. I'll explain my silence next time we talk, and everything will go back to normal. Probably for the best. I don't have anything more to offer. So why does it sting?

"*My QUEEN?!*" Lauren says on a gasp. "I'll need to hear all about how that nickname came about."

The three of us share a soft laugh, and then Connor's eyes lock onto mine.

"Happy Thanksgiving, Maisie," he says.

"Happy Thanksgiving, Connor. See you in a few days?"

"See you then." He tips his head.

Lauren guides me toward the front door as Connor settles back into the driver's seat. He gives one last wave through the windshield, and then he's gone.

"He's cute," Lauren says from beside me.

"I know," is all I can manage to say in reply. I loop my arm fully through hers, and we head inside.

43

Chilly Chats

Maisie

LAUREN DOESN'T LEAVE MY side as we make our way through the elaborate chandelier-topped foyer, snake through the formal dining room—already set extravagantly for tomorrow's festivities—or enter the kitchen and run into the first family member.

Dad.

We've barely spoken since that day in the hallway after my first meet—well, other than details about coming home or checking that I did, in fact, take the back three and a half off my competition list.

Sometimes I wish he would back off a little. I realize that since getting to college, the space has done me good. I'm starting to see how suffocating all his ideals for me truly are. But still, I let him wrap me in a hug, and I rest my head on his chest, his cheek coming to rest atop it, like we've done my whole life. He may be intense sometimes, but he's still my dad.

"Hiya, Bean," he whispers into my hair, using the nickname he's had for me since I was "the size of a bean." "It's so good to have you home." He punctuates the sentiment with a kiss to the top of my head before pulling away. I sigh. He looks back and forth between Lauren and me. "What are you two going to do today?"

"I'm planning to kidnap her for a few hours. See what she's been up to. It's been too long," Lauren says, resting the back of her hand on her forehead, feigning deep dramatics.

"Well, don't keep her away too long, or your Aunt Madeline will throw a fit. Honestly, I might too," he says with a laugh.

"There's plenty of me to go around," I say, patting both of them on the shoulder.

Dad rolls his eyes, and Lauren barks out a laugh before grabbing my wrist and dragging me to the next part of the house. We find Aunt Kaity in Dad's study, her feet propped up against his expansive walnut desk.

When we enter, she throws her hands up in excitement, shouting, "My babies! Oh, Maisie, sweet girl, how are you?"

She rushes me, arms outstretched, and we practically topple over. She sways me side to side, her cushioned body and familiar scent causing me to melt into her comfort. I've always loved Aunt Kaity. In some ways, I feel closer to her than to my own mother.

"I'm good, I'm good—oof," I get out as she squeezes me a little too hard.

"Sorry about that." She pulls back, grinning. "Sometimes I feel like I could just squeeze you 'til you pop, I love you so much."

All three of our smiles widen. The air of laughter, comfort, and joy is infectious in this stuffy room.

"Where's Aunt Madeline?" Lauren asks her mom. "Wasn't she with you when I went to check on Maize's arrival?"

"Yes, yes, she was." Aunt Kaity sounds less than enthused. "I think she said something about a phone call. I'd try the den or her room."

"Aye aye, Captain." Lauren salutes and grabs my wrist again, leading me through my own house like I haven't been here before. God, I've missed her.

We navigate down a small set of steps to check the den, but no luck. Instead of going back the way we came, however, Lauren slides open the door to the patio and pulls me out behind her. It's furnished with wrought-iron benches and chairs, all circling an unfortunately covered firepit. I stare at it as if I could will a blaze into existence and wrap my arms around myself for warmth.

"What are we doing out here?" I question Lauren, teeth already chattering.

"I wanna know what's really going on with you without anyone hearing." Lauren taps her foot, waiting for a response, apparently unaffected by the cold.

"About what?" I ask, shivering.

She pinches her eyes together and spikes a brow, like I'm the one being ridiculous when *she's* the one who dragged us out here and isn't telling me exactly what she wants to know.

"What happened between you and Connor on your little road trip? Your little *overnight* road trip?" She crosses her arms, waiting for my reply.

My body suddenly goes hot, a flaming contrast to the cold all around us. "Well, for starters, there was only one room left with...one bed."

She squeals and claps her hands. "And how was that?" she prods.

"It was...amazing." I blow out a breath, and the chilled air forms a cloud. "Everything is so comfortable with him, and we sort of hooked up a little?"

I jump back at more squealing from Lauren. Someone is going to come looking for us if she keeps this up.

"But," I interrupt her excitement, "I don't think we can be together like that. I feel...broken, Lo. Karsen really did a number on me."

She all but growls at the mention of Karsen. "That piece of shit doesn't deserve to live on the same planet as you."

"Yeah, well, I was with that piece of shit for two years, so what does that say about me?"

Her eyes soften. "It says you wanted to be loved. Like we all do. It's his fault that he chose not to give it the way you deserve. Not yours. And young love is confusing at the best of times. Please don't blame yourself for his actions." She scoops me into her arms for a hug, and I nuzzle in like I've done since we were little.

"And I'm sorry you feel broken. I'm not invalidating that. I just wish you could see yourself through my eyes, MaiMai. And I'm willing to bet Connor sees you in a pretty damn good light too." The unexpected wetness in my eyes trickles down the slope of my cheek.

I squeeze her back as hard as I can, and now it's her turn to let out the *oof*. "Sorry," I say, but I'm not really. I don't know where I'd be without her. I'm so glad we're finally together in person. "We'll see. I'm still afraid he's gonna bolt again. I don't think I can handle losing him as a friend. I don't want this to ruin us. We'll talk when he comes to pick me up, but I'm not holding my breath."

She's about to say something else when we both turn at the sound of the sliding glass door opening.

Mom says, "What are you girls doing out here? It's freezing!"

We share a knowing look and smile before heading inside together.

44

Fourth of July? Sure.

Connor

A s soon as I'm back on the highway after leaving Maisie's house, I call Hunter.

"Hey, bro, you home yet?" Hunter says upon answering.

"Almost. I'm about an hour out," I reply.

He's silent for a moment. He can tell I need to get something off my chest. He's known me too long.

"Anything else you care to share?" he finally asks.

A whoosh of air leaves my lungs, but it does nothing to loosen the tension in my shoulders. I scrub a hand down my face and realize it must have been a few days since I've shaved. My scruff is overgrown. I've been distracted.

"It's Maize," I say.

"What about her?"

I'm not sure where to begin.

Before I can respond, Hunter says, "Are you going to make me pull this out of you?"

"Possibly." I chuckle. "Fine, we hooked up."

"Maybe I'm still missing something. Is that a bad thing somehow?"

A long-suffering sigh escapes me before I say, "No, it's not a bad thing. Or I didn't think it was. Fuck, it was the best night of my life. I felt like the luckiest guy in the world. And after, we still watched our movie and hung out. It was amazing, and I got to wake up with her in my arms." I grip the steering wheel a little harder than necessary. "But then this morning, it was like a switch flipped, and I don't know why. I don't know what she's thinking, and fuck, Hunter, I can't lose her when I just got her." Although doubt has crept in about whether I ever had her at all. "I won't survive it."

He hums on the other end of the line, clearly trying to think his way through this one. "You got consent, right?" he asks, voice stern.

"Of course I did!" I practically yell.

"All right, all right, I have to check. I don't care that you're my best friend in the whole world; I'd kick your ass to Saturn if you laid hands on a woman who didn't want that."

"I know you would, and I honestly respect the shit out of that. You know me."

"I do." I can hear his smile even though I can't see it. "Explain to me what you mean by a switch flipped."

"She zombied out as we were leaving the hotel. Wouldn't speak to me or even look at me when we got to the car. Then she cried and passed out for the rest of the trip." A steady ache has been pounding in my chest since then.

"But nothing happened?" he asked incredulously. "What was she doing? What were *you* doing? I need more details, man."

"I was paying for the room, and when I looked over, she was staring at her phone. That was when I first noticed the change."

"Do you think she saw something on her phone that got to her?" he interrupts.

My stomach drops out as the gravity of that line of thought sinks in. Fuck, maybe she did.

He keeps prodding: "Do you know of anyone or anything in her life that would make her react like that?"

My teeth grind together involuntarily. *Yeah, I do.* "Her ex, Karsen. You know...the guy I punched? He probably fucking texted her. Hunter, that's gotta be what happened. I swear I don't know what the dick said to her, but when I find out—" I let the threat hang. Defensiveness bubbles under my skin, looking for a way out. Instead of boiling over, I make a point to breathe. I count to ten in my head and rub my hand along the seat of my car, noticing how it feels, what I can smell.

Hunter pops through my meditative bubble by saying, "We don't actually *know* that he said anything to her. Take a chill pill, my guy. Keep doing those breathing exercises I hear."

"I'm calm, I promise." Though that's not entirely true. "That guy in particular just grinds my gears. He never deserved her, and if he's still harassing her, I don't know how to help." My shoulders shake with the feeling of helplessness.

Shit—Maize had frozen for a second last night. Did he do something to her?

I grind my teeth. I swear to god I'll lose it.

Hunter breaks through my thoughts. "Just support her. Don't worry about him and what he's doing or not doing. Focus on *her*." Hunter always seems to have wisdom beyond his years.

I exhale, giving his words a moment to sink in. "Yeah, I guess you're right." Protectiveness still courses through me, but I know what he's saying is true. "Thanks, buddy."

"Anytime. Now, anything else I can help with, or can I get back to making these pies for tomorrow?" He's clearly put me on speakerphone, and I think I hear a rolling pin.

"Nah, that's it. Are you making me any blueberry?" I ask, hopeful.

"I am, but I still stand by that is a weird-ass pie for Thanksgiving. Fourth of July? Sure. Thanksgiving? Just wrong."

"It's my favorite. I can't help what I like," I say.

"I know, and I somehow love you anyway," he jokes back.

I can hear the rolling pin still working away, and I know I should let him go. "Thanks again, Hunter," I say sincerely. "See you tomorrow?"

"See you tomorrow. I'll be the one dressed the best and carrying a whole cooler of pies."

"My man," I say, genuinely laughing now.

We both hang up, and I focus back on the drive. I take another few deep breaths, concentrating this time on releasing the tension at each part of my body individually the way Donny taught me.

In some ways, I feel better; in others, it still feels like a bear is clawing at my chest. I want to know what's going on with Maize, but most importantly, I want to know if she's okay. I want to make sure I didn't do anything that made her uncomfortable, and that she knows she can talk to me about anything.

I had hoped we would talk it out on the car ride. I wasn't expecting her to sleep the *entire* rest of the way home. I couldn't very well wake her, but I sure as hell was tempted.

I finish the rest of the drive, drowning out all my thoughts in a Miles Davis album. I'll try calling tomorrow.

45

Comics & 5Ks

Maisie

WE ORDERED PIZZA LAST night and watched a movie as a family. It was nice, and I nearly forgot about what my mom had done, and what Karsen had texted. I tried to tell Mom again that I didn't want Karsen around, but she said it would be rude to uninvite him at this point. I didn't agree, but it's her house; I guess she can invite whoever she wants.

The caterers arrived early—6:00 AM, maybe? All I know is I was sleeping, and I was startled awake to the sound of dishes scraping together. Or at least I think that's what it was.

I lie in bed for a long time, looking up at the canopy of my four-poster. I was tired. Not just physically, but mentally too. My muscles are sore, and a tension headache has plagued me since the car ride.

This break for Thanksgiving is nice, but there's still school to contend with, and diving, of course. And I truly don't have it in me to face Karsen today. It's like someone vacuumed the willpower right out of me. I wish my mom understood what she was doing. Maybe I should try harder to explain to her who he is and how he has treated me. But after so many unsuccessful attempts, I don't know if it would do anything.

Eventually, I get up, take a shower, and put on a brown sweater dress and tan leggings. I curl my hair, tie one section back with a clip, and apply minimal makeup, opting to skip shoes for now, since I'm not planning to leave the house.

My phone buzzes on the bedside table. Who would be texting this early?

> **Connor:** Happy Thanksgiving, Betty. Hope you have a good day with your family.

The text is sweet. Just like Connor. It makes my heart ache all the more. I set my phone back on the table, screen facing down. I don't know what to say to him after ignoring him yesterday. We should probably just talk in person when he comes to get me. Maybe he's regretting what we did. He's probably regretting what we did. For all I know, he's regretting being my friend at all. *No, Connor isn't like that.* I shake my head free of the traitorous thoughts.

I open my bedroom door and peek out into the long hallway. No other doors are open, but that doesn't mean no one else is awake. Mom always makes us keep our doors closed, so it looks nicer if guests wander up here.

I leave the safety of my room and slowly make my way down the main staircase. Luckily, the marble doesn't make a noise, so no one should be able to hear me descend in my stocking feet. I pass by a series of employees speeding between the kitchen and formal dining room. I hear the chef bellowing orders. I'm sure these people wish they were home with their families today, but instead they're here. Working for a paycheck. I guess money can buy almost anything.

Mom's party-planning voice comes out of nowhere. "Can you confirm the first course will be served promptly at 12 PM?"

"Yes, ma'am, that won't be a problem," a petite woman with ebony hair slicked into a severe ponytail replies.

"Excellent. Thanks, Patrice."

Patrice—apparently—heads toward the kitchen, and Mom turns to see me standing there awkwardly.

"Maisie! Perfect. I love that outfit on you. Are you planning to put on a little more makeup before the others arrive? You are looking a bit pale."

She wouldn't be my mother if she didn't say something.

"I wasn't planning on it," I say blandly.

I don't feel like dealing with her shit today, and I'm proud of myself for not giving in and doing whatever she asks.

"Your choice," she says with a half-hearted smile.

Thankfully, before Mom has a chance to say anything else about my appearance, Lauren bounds down the stairs, still dressed in sweats from her alma mater and hair tied up loosely in a messy bun. "Morning! What time are we expecting people, Aunt Madeline?"

"Guests will start arriving at eleven, dear. You might want to get ready soon. Unfortunately, the staff has overtaken the kitchen, but if you ask, I am sure they will whip you something up for breakfast. You can eat in the nook," Mom explains.

"Sounds good." Lauren stretches her arms above her head with a yawn. "Did you eat yet, Maize?" She looks at me expectantly, like she knows I need an out of this conversation with Mom.

I don't think I can eat a thing—I'm sick to my stomach at the thought of today—but what I say is, "Nope. Let's go."

We're about to make our way into the kitchen together when Dad appears from the left. Probably coming from his office.

"Maize. Lauren. Morning," he says as he reaches for today's paper stuffed under his arm. He hands me a section. "Did you want to read the comics?"

It's such a thoughtful gesture. Even though he thinks comics are frivolous, he knows I love them. I nod, silently taking it.

"Well, see you all later. I'm off to my pre-meal 5K," he says. He doesn't mean a Turkey Trot or anything like that. Every year, he just walks—specifically 3.1 miles—around the neighborhood. One year, I asked why he doesn't sign up for a local race. He said that it would be silly to pay to walk with strangers when he can easily configure a course himself. I rolled my eyes at the time, but the older I get, the more I'm beginning to understand that he simply does what he wants. It's so different from how he is with me. But maybe since he does so, he might eventually accept what I want without...pressuring me so much? I won't get my hopes up.

We watch as Dad makes his way out the front door. Lauren and I are walking toward the breakfast nook when Mom stops us.

"I love you both very much. I hope you know that."

It's a little out of left field, but my jaw muscles relax as she says it.

"We know," Lauren says.

"Love you too," I echo.

She gives us both a watery smile and stalks off in the other direction.

46

Beak Noses & Bubbly

Maisie

ELEVEN ROLLS AROUND MUCH faster than I would like. The scent of nutmeg, cloves, and rosemary wafts through the house—but when the doorbell rings, the smell sours, and my feet shift backward without my permission. Like they know what's about to happen and are yelling "run!"

A small breath of relief escapes as Mom opens the door. It's her friends from the club, Julie and Stew Fowler. I remember thinking their last name was funny when I was younger because Mrs. Fowler's nose has a beak-like quality to it.

"Julie! Stew! Come in, come in."

Mom ushers them out of the cold. Snowflakes have been swirling all morning, but none have stuck. *Thank goodness.* I can't imagine being trapped in this house any longer than necessary with the current guest list.

Not a moment after the Fowlers hand their coats off, the doorbell rings again. My throat closes, and my heart rate doubles. There's only one other person we're expecting.

The door swings open forcefully. Bleach-blond hair and a smirking face greet me above my mom's head. It's like I forgot how tall he was. I used to love it, but now it makes a chill run down my spine. His presence is foreboding.

"Oh, Karsen, sweetie, hurry up and get in here. You will catch a chill," my mom says before wrapping him in a big hug.

He nuzzles into her neck, and I flinch back. He used to always make crude jokes about how hot my mom was, saying he knew what he was getting down the line. How did I not realize how gross he was for so long?

He makes his way toward me, and my brain is still shouting "run," but my body has turned into a frozen traitor.

"Babe, I've missed you." He reaches for my waist, but before his fingers can graze me, Lauren shoves his arm out of the way, blocking his path with her own body.

"Oops," she says sarcastically. Then she lowers her voice, crowding his space, and says, "Leave her alone, asshole. You've done enough damage. Just because Aunt Madeline invited you here doesn't mean you're welcome. Got it?"

His dark laugh of amusement scrapes against my ears. "Sure, Lauren. I knew you never liked me, but damn. It's Thanksgiving; where's your giving spirit? I know I'm hoping Maisie is in a giving mood later." He winks in my direction before his eyes darken.

Bile rises to my throat, and I look away. I regret every touch with him.

"Ow! What the hell!" Karsen shouts.

I turn back toward him and Lauren to find Karsen balancing on one leg, reaching for his other foot.

Lauren loops her arm with mine, guiding us away. She laughs through closed lips. "I wore heels specifically hoping he'd give me a reason to stomp on his toes."

I look back over my shoulder. He's trying to compose himself as the Fowlers walk past him toward the dining room, confusion lining their faces. I turn back and let out a giggle.

"You're diabolical," I say to Lauren.

"Thank you." Her smile is full-blown now. She steers us toward the den. When we enter, she closes the door and says, "Figured we could hide here for a while."

We're all seated by place cards, which, of course, put me right next to Karsen and across the table from Lauren. Dad is at the head, standing to carve the turkey. Once he cuts a ceremonial slice, he hands it back to the staff to finish in the kitchen. The first course, a small pear and candied pecan salad, is distributed, one dish in front of each of us.

Dad clears his throat. "Let's pray." He bows his head, and we all follow suit. Karsen reaches for my hand, but I smack it away under the table. Dad begins in his projected bass tone, "Good Lord, thank you for your abundance and grace. Thank you for those who prepared this food. Thank you for those around this table. And we take this time to remember and honor our dear Richard. We thank you for continuing to care for his wife and child, and we look forward to seeing him again one day. Amen."

When I open my eyes, I see tears reflected in Lauren's. I know that after all this time, the holidays don't get any easier for her. I feel even worse that today is stained with bad company. I shoot Karsen a death glare, but he doesn't see it. He's already grabbing too many rolls for his plate.

"A toast." Aunt Kaity stands at her place next to Lauren, raising the glass of champagne we all have next to our water goblets. "To moving on in life," she says. She sits down and winks in my direction.

Everyone joins in hesitantly: "To moving on."

"This is a delicious salad, Madeline," Mrs. Fowler mentions casually.

"Thank you," Mom says as if she had a hand in making it. Mom then pivots to ask, "Karsen, how are classes?"

He wipes his mouth on the cloth napkin in his lap as if he's a perfect gentleman. "Pretty good. All except Science 101. That one tends to get people in trouble," he says and shifts to look at me. I narrow my eyes in response, heart rate kicking up.

"Oh, I see," my mom responds, oblivious to my turmoil. "How so?"

"Well—" he starts.

"Will there be mashed potatoes, Aunt Madeline?" Lauren interjects.

"Of course, dear, but it is rude to interrupt." Mom gives her the "disappointed" look. "You were saying?" she prompts Karsen.

I kick him under the table, but his face gives nothing away. He continues, "Maisie didn't tell you? Her little friend punched me out of nowhere after class one day. Completely unprovoked. I had to get stitches!" he says, really milking the attention for all it's worth.

It feels like someone is stabbing me in the chest with a thousand tiny knives. My anxiety fuses with my overwhelming anger, chased by shame.

My mom's eyes bulge so wide, I'm worried blood vessels will start popping. "Maisie's friend? Is he talking about that Connor kid?" She directs her stern tone at me. "The one you rode home with?"

My leg bounces like a car over a rumble strip.

Karsen reaches for my knee, a look of concern plastered on his fake-ass face.

My anger burns red-hot, and I shove my chair back, shaking off his hand. "That's not what happened!" I shout.

"Maisie, sit down!" Mom bellows.

"No! You invited him here even after I asked you not to! Yes, Connor punched him, but it was after Karsen was saying vile things about me. Connor was *defending* me, Mom. Don't believe a word this jerk says." I stare daggers at Karsen, wishing they could form metaphysically and actually puncture his skin. I hate him.

Mom nervously looks between me and the other guests. "Well, this is all a bit of excitement, but Maisie, why don't you just—"

"I think you ought to leave," Dad chimes in. His voice is low and authoritative. He doesn't need to shout. His point is made perfectly clear.

Karsen's eyes bounce wildly between everyone at the table, but he doesn't move.

Dad stands, fists clenched. "Out!"

Karsen scoots back so fast, his chair almost falls in his haste to stand. He quickly makes it to the other end of the table from where Dad is seated and must regain an ounce of his bravado because he stops and says, "Your bitch of a daughter isn't worth it anyway."

Dad lunges, but Karsen runs like the coward he is right out the front door.

Tears spill down my face in a tidal wave. "Excuse me," I say as I quickly move away from the table and toward the staircase, intent on escaping to my room.

I make it to the top of the stairs and see, out of the corner of my eye, Lauren and my mom entering the foyer below. It looks like Mom is the one coming to talk to me, and I can't say I'm happy about that decision.

When I reach my room down the long hallway, I lock the door behind me, like I'm still thirteen. I sink to the floor, the door at my back. My head is in my hands, knees curled to my chest, and I don't hold back, letting out all the anger, sadness, and hurt I feel. For a moment, all I want to do is call Connor, and that makes me cry harder.

A minute or two later, there's a soft knock at the door.

"Maisie, sweetie? It's Mom."

"Go away!" I shout. God, I really am acting like a petulant teenager, but I can't make myself care.

"Please open up. I want to apologize."

I think on it for a bit, but eventually stand and unlock the door. She slowly opens it. I stand off to the side, arms crossed, and I'm sure my face is puffier than a winter jacket.

"My sweet girl," she says and pulls me in for a hug. "I am so sorry."

I don't hug her back, but I don't push her away either. She takes my hand and leads us to sit on my bed. She sighs, still holding my hand in both of hers, gently rubbing each knuckle. I have to admit it's soothing.

"I know I got carried away pushing you toward Karsen. You could call it a mother's desire for her daughter to be with someone from a good family. Someone talented and whom I know would provide you a life where you wouldn't have to worry. But I am afraid it is more than that." She takes a deep breath, and I scrunch my eyes, waiting for what she'll have to say.

"Did I ever tell you about my high-school boyfriend?" she asks.

"I don't think so," I say, shaking my head.

Her eyes turn glassy. "His name was Hugh Jacobs, and we were madly in love." She sighs and looks away slightly, as if she can see him standing behind me.

"Okay," I say, filling the space. "What happened?"

"The day after our senior prom—" She pauses a moment to compose herself. "He was in a car accident. A drunk driver swerved and hit the passenger's side. He was dead on impact." A single tear falls down her delicate cheek.

"Oh," I say, softening a little. "Sorry, Mom. That sounds awful." I can't imagine losing someone that close to me so suddenly.

"It truly was. It is still the hardest thing I have endured in this life. And do not get me wrong, I am very glad I married your dad and had you. I do not regret that for a second, but I still think about Hugh often. What his life would have been like had he lived."

"That makes sense. It sounds really traumatic," I say.

"It was, and I think the trauma of that incident has infected me as a mother."

"What? What do you mean?"

She cups my cheek. "Karsen looks a lot like Hugh did," she says.

Understanding dawns, and my hand comes up to wrap around hers. "Oh," I say.

"Yeah, *oh*." She laughs, but there isn't any joy in it. "I got so wrapped up in you playing out the love that was stolen from me that I did not listen to you when you were trying to tell me Karsen was not good for you. Hugh was taken from me. I did not have a choice, but you…you chose to leave Karsen, and after today, I would say for good reason." She tucks a strand of hair behind my ear. "That was not fair of me. To put that on you. To want you two to work out because it did not for me. It was selfish, and I am sorry, Maisie. I should have listened to you first and foremost. *You* are what matters to me. Not who you date. I am so, so sorry."

Bitterness still clings to my edges, but it's giving way to forgiveness. I didn't know any of this about Mom, and it helps to understand how she could act the way she has, specifically regarding Karsen. But I'm not ready to fully forgive her.

She watches the emotions play out on my face.

"I'm glad you told me," I say. "And I'm sorry that happened to you. I can see how that has affected your actions, but I'm not quite ready to forgive you. I have a lot of hurt to work through myself."

Her mouth wrinkles, eyes tight, but she nods in understanding. "Of course, sweetie. Take all the time you need." At that, she stands, patting my knee. "Do you want me to send Lauren up with a plate?" she asks.

"That's okay. I'll be down in a bit."

"Okay. Call if you need anything. I love you," she says and walks toward the door. She gives me one last soft smile before closing the door behind her.

I roll onto my side and pick up my phone from my bedside table. I probably shouldn't do this—it could make me even more emotional—but I shove down the doubt and call Connor.

47

Broken Time Machines

Connor

Brock: Happy Thanksgiving to my best bros!

Hunter: Happy Thanksgiving guys! Hope you're all resting up and enjoying the time with family.

Me: I will once you get your ass over here with my pie

Hunter: Dude I'll literally be there in 15 mins. Chill

Tyler: Happy Thanksgiving.

Brock: He speaks! You too, buddy!

Me: Hey guys…

Hunter: yea?

Me: Love you weirdos

Brock: Hell yeah! That's some man love right here!

Brock: Hunter, your sister gonna be there bro? Tell her I miss her

Hunter: Stay the hell away from my sister!!

Me: Come on, man. You know better than that

Brock: Debatable

*Tyler emphasizes Brock's text

Me: See you all in a few days. Try to stay out of trouble

Brock: No promises

Maisie never responded to my text this morning, so I decided to leave my phone in my room during Thanksgiving lunch with the fam. They don't need to see how pathetic I am, checking it every five seconds. Plus, I've missed them. Even Liam, who is currently holding his finger an inch from my face, saying, "I'm not touching you." I want to be annoyed, but part of me is glad when he acts like a little boy. It means he had a better childhood than the rest of us. Didn't have to grow up so quickly.

Hunter, his moms, and his little sister Ariella arrived an hour ago, but he went straight to the kitchen to help my mom with preparations. A heavenly mix of cinnamon, sage, and sugar has been wafting through the house ever since, making my mouth water.

When we finally sit down all together, I look around the table and smile. We're not a conventional family, but I wouldn't have it any other way. In a way, I'm glad Dad left. We are better off without him. We've crawled our way back from a hellish situation, and I'm proud of who we've become. The thought of him spikes my anxiety nonetheless. I hope he doesn't try to contact any of us today.

My thoughts are interrupted by Mom saying, "Well, dig in!"

My brothers don't hesitate. They start slopping huge helpings of mashed potatoes and stuffing onto their plates and fighting over the basket of crescent rolls. All it takes is one lifted brow from Mom, however, and they all drop it, feigning civility for the sake of a nice time.

My chest expands. It's good to be home.

"Save room for dessert!" Hunter says over the clanking of dishes.

"Duh," Oliver says.

"Don't eat too much or you'll puke during touch football," Robert says with a grin.

It's tradition. Every year, we all play, even our moms.

The mention of a sport, however, draws my mind back to Maisie. I wish she would talk to me. Maybe I should just check that she hasn't tried to get ahold of me. I excuse myself.

Hunter gives me a concerned look, but his attention is quickly drawn away by something Ariella is saying. He adores his little sister, and I know he's missed her.

I'm almost to my room when I hear a faint buzzing sound. I book it the rest of the way, fumbling to my nightstand. *Maisie.* She's calling. I pick up haphazardly, nearly dropping the phone in my attempt to get it to my ear.

"Hello?" I say, trying to catch my breath.

"Connor." Her voice sounds small. It gnaws at my gut.

"Maize, what's wrong? Talk to me."

"It was awful," she says, and I hear her sniffle. Is she crying?

"What was, Betty? What happened?" I say, and I must sound desperate because she rushes to get out the next part.

"Karsen was here. Mom invited him. He was saying awful things about you, and then my dad kicked him out. Apparently, Karsen looks like my mom's high-school boyfriend, and that's why she's been so freaking weird about him. And now I'm in my room, and everything kind of sucks, and you always know how to make it better. So can you? Make it better?" She sniffles again.

My mind spins with all of this information, and my jaw works when I think about Karsen anywhere near Maisie. Thank god Mr. Thatcher kicked him out, but he never should have been there in the first place.

Maisie doesn't need angry Connor right now, though; she needs her goofy friend to make her laugh, make her forget the pain of the day—so that's what I do.

"Did you know that the Avengers were an actual group after World War II? They were Jewish assassins who hunted Nazi war criminals."[1]

"Wait, are you serious?" she asks.

"I am," I say with the confidence of someone who has read way too many World War II history books.

"Why do you know that?" she asks. She doesn't sound like she's crying anymore.

"From one of my super cool books on the aftermath of World War II." It was something Grandpa got me hooked on. After he was done reading, he'd pass books on to me.

"So, you're telling me one of your hobbies is reading about WWII? Sometimes I swear you're eighty years old!" she says, laughing now, and the sound is music to my ears. I know she loves all of my old-school habits, which makes me feel loved. Like the hole my broken family has left can be filled.

"You didn't know? I'm actually eighty." I keep the jovial tone going. "I'm a time traveler stuck in an eighteen-year-old's body."

"Where's your time machine?" she asks, playing along.

"In my mom's garage. It needs maintenance. Your time doesn't have the parts I need yet."

"How long are you going to have to wait?" she asks.

"Well, you see, there's someone here who's caught my eye, so I don't think I ever have any intention of leaving." I hold my breath after the nuanced admission.

There's a pause, but then she says, "I'm glad to hear that. I wouldn't want to lose you to a future time."

The smile that overtakes my face would be embarrassing if anyone were here to see it. I hear a knock on her end of the line.

"Connor, I'm sorry, I have to go. Lauren's here. But...thank you for talking to me. You really helped."

I gulp. "Anything for you, Betty. See you in two days."

"Two days," she says. "Bye, Connor."

"My Queen." I bow even though she can't see it, then she hangs up.

There's a knock at my own door. It's Hunter.

"Come on, ya sad sack, the party's out here," he says, leaning casually against the doorframe. "Hope Maisie is having a good Thanksgiving."

The fact that he knows the only person I would leave Thanksgiving with my family for is Maisie says it all. I don't want to betray her trust by telling Hunter what happened, so I say, "She's had better."

"Well, I'm sure you helped cheer her up. Now come on, I can't save you a roll for much longer." He motions with his head for me to follow.

"I'm coming, I'm coming," I say with a half-hearted laugh. I pocket my phone *just in case* and follow Hunter back to the festivities.

48

New Luggage

Maisie

THE NEXT TWO DAYS fly by. Lauren and I went out to breakfast the morning after Thanksgiving, and it was nice to get out of the house and away from everyone for a bit. It was a little bittersweet, seeing as I don't get to see my family much since going to college, but the alone time with Lauren was much needed. Later that day, Mom, Aunt Kaity, Lauren, and I went shopping for Black Friday. I got a new pair of sweatpants and some sneakers. My mom tried to convince me to buy something other than athletic wear. It was all very familiar. As we continued on, however, the anger that I held close to my chest started releasing.

The day after, we went to a local Christmas tree farm and cut down this year's tree. Afterward, we went out to dinner, and it felt like a breath of fresh air. I wasn't angry with my mom anymore, and even some of my Karsen turmoil seemed to dissipate. Some of that may be from the fact that Connor and I have been texting nonstop. Although we haven't addressed what happened in the hotel yet.

It's late Saturday afternoon, and he'll be here in an hour. I'm packed and everything is ready by the door. I don't know what to do with myself, and I realize I must have been picking at my cuticles again because one is bleeding. I navigate to the half bath on the main level for a Band-Aid. After wrapping it up, I step back into the foyer and find Dad inspecting my luggage.

"Can I help you?" I say in my best customer-service voice.

He startles a bit but recovers quickly. "You need new luggage," he says. "I'll have a new set for you when you come home next."

My chest swells. He's always taken such good care of me.

"And, uh, Bean, I wanted to talk to you before you leave."

A weight drops in my stomach. What could this be about?

"Okay," I say tentatively, crossing my arms and worrying my bottom lip between my teeth. "About what?" I pinch my arm a little in anticipation.

He takes a step toward me, and I tense. His brows crease, and he retreats the step. "I..." He trails off and pinches the bridge of his nose. It's more emotion than I'm used to seeing Dad show. "I know I'm hard on you," he starts. "And I know I was harsh at your meet."

"It's okay, Dad," I say, but I can't seem to infuse truth into the words.

"It's not." His tone is stern.

My eyes fall even though I know it's not me he's mad at.

"I was scared," he whispers.

My brows shoot up in surprise. "You were?" I ask tentatively.

"Of course I was, Bean. You have no idea what it's like having your heart walk around outside your body. You. You are my heart, and my heart was being pulled out of the water by a lifeguard. I'm sorry for the way I reacted afterward. I'll try to be better," he says, giving one terse nod.

"Oh...okay, Dad. I appreciate that. Really, I do. Thank you." I drop my arms and step forward for a hug. I think we could both use one.

"Of course. And have a safe trip back. I promise we'll come pick you up next time," he says while giving me a firm squeeze.

I step away, looking up into his deep brown eyes. Eyes I always thought of as fierce. Eyes that can stare down an opponent in court or pierce through my teenage soul—but also eyes that shine with affection for the things he loves: golf, walking on a beach, and his wife and daughter. I sigh. He may be complicated at times, but he always has my back.

"Thanks, Dad. But I'm happy riding with Connor. Doesn't make sense for you guys to have to do the trip twice when you don't need to." The corner of my lip tips in a smile.

He grumbles but acquiesces by lifting his hands in surrender. "Fine, fine. Let some boy drive you across the country instead of your dear old dad."

"Dad!" I squeal with laughter.

"I'm just kidding," he says, meeting me with a smile of his own. "I like that Connor kid. Better than Karsen, that's for sure." A shadow passes over his eyes like he's reliving Thanksgiving day. "He better hope our paths never cross again. What he said was unacceptable. I hope you know that was no reflection on you. Boys like that are just that. Boys. They are small both in mind and spirit, and they try to take down anyone who shines brighter than them. And you are the brightest light in the sky, Bean."

My eyes water involuntarily, lips quivering. "Thanks, Dad," I manage to say. "I love you so much."

"Love you too," he says and then walks away, squeezing my arm on his way past.

I'm about to turn for the kitchen to grab a last-minute snack when I'm attacked from behind.

"Don't leeeeeaaaavvveeee," Lauren whines, clinging to my back.

"Get off, ya weirdo," I say, but grab hold of her legs at my sides and spin her around.

"Let me down, I'm gonna be sick," she says, and I laugh.

I set her back on her feet. "Serves you right for sneaking up on me like that," I scold playfully.

She fixes the hair that flew into her face. "Sue me for being sad. I won't see you for god knows how long after this."

I smirk. "My dad's a lawyer; that can be arranged."

"Uncle Alan is my lawyer, too. That might be a conflict of interest." She moves to poke my stomach, and I dodge, smacking her hand away and pulling her in for a hug.

"I'm really going to miss you too, LoLo."

She nuzzles deeper into the hug. "I hate only getting to see each other a few times a year. It royally sucks."

"Totally sucks," I agree.

"And I won't even get to see you at Christmas," she complains.

"Well, that isn't *my* fault," I clap back.

"I know. I know. Jameson *had* to book us flights to go visit his extended family in the UK. It was obviously rude of him."

"So rude," I play along.

Jameson is her boyfriend of six months. He moved to the States when he was thirteen and still has lots of family back home. They were close friends in college, both having been in the engineering department, but didn't start dating until recently. She seems extremely happy with him, and that makes me happy.

"Promise to call more?" she says wistfully.

I slowly peel away from our hug. "Pinky promise," I say, presenting my pinky, so she can connect hers, and then we kiss our thumbs to seal the deal.

There's a knock at the door, and we both jump. Connor must be early.

49

That Was Practically a Love Declaration

Connor

I'M EARLY. I COULDN'T help it. The moment I woke up this morning, I was buzzing with energy. I couldn't wait another second to be in Maisie's presence again. I'm glad we've been texting and that our friendship seems to be intact, but I'll be damned if we go another car ride without actually talking about what this thing is between us. And what I want it to be, for that matter.

"Connor!" Maisie greets me as she swings open the house's heavy front door. I can't tell if she's worried or excited. Maybe a little of both. Honestly, same, so I get it.

She shuffles to grab the bags at her feet, and as I move to help her, I see Lauren standing behind her with her arms crossed, smirking. She mouths "good luck" to me over Maize's bent shoulder. I let out an involuntary snort. I wonder what Maisie's told her.

"Weren't planning to leave without saying goodbye, were you?" Mr. Thatcher appears at Maisie's other side.

She drops the bags and blushes. "No?" she says *super convincingly.*

"Madeline, darling, our girl is leaving!" he calls out to Maisie's mom, who comes through a set of swinging double doors on the opposite side of the expansive foyer. She's moving quickly, clearly not wanting to miss her daughter's departure, but is doing everything in her power not to seem rushed.

They both crowd her in a bruising hug, and it feels like someone stuck a needle in my heart.

I ease out a deep breath. I'm happy for how much they love her, but it never gets easier seeing a family that hasn't been ripped to shreds.

I finish gathering her bags by the time they release her from the hug and turn to head toward the car—then Mr. Thatcher says, "Get my girl home safe."

I turn, meeting his steely gaze, and nod, saying, "Maisie is always safe with me, sir."

He nods his head once in return, and this time, as I turn to go, Maisie is right by my side, a smile curling at her lips.

"What?" I say, bumping into her playfully.

"Nothing. That was just practically a love declaration from my father."

A full laugh escapes me. "What do you mean?"

She bumps me back with her shoulder. I'm happy to see the easy physical affection has not dissipated from a few days apart. "I meannnn," she emphasizes, "that my dad likes you—and that makes me happy." She tacks the last part on like it's no big deal.

While I've been working on my feelings regarding my own father and the *lack* of needing his approval, I'm happy to hear Maisie's dad likes me. Makes the plans I have for our future all the easier. Not that I would let something like parent disapproval stop me from loving Maisie. A hurricane couldn't stop my love.

Love.

I've known I've loved her for a while now, but the clearness of the thought causes me to trip a step.

"You okay?" she asks, brows furrowing slightly in concern.

"All good," I say.

I love you, is what I think.

I know without a shadow of a doubt she isn't ready to hear that yet. We'll start with how she felt about the other night first.

Once everything is loaded and we're settled into our seats, I hand her the car's auxiliary cord, and her smile beams. Car DJ, her favorite. I watch as her eyes find the snacks and drinks in the cup holders.

"Cool Ranch Doritos and root beer?" Her smile somehow doubles in size, eyebrows high on her forehead.

"Only the best for my Queen," I say, dipping my gaze in deference.

Her laugh sounds through the space like chimes in the wind, and I'm struck once again by how beautiful she is. Not just physically, but her soul. Her spirit. Her light.

I quietly sigh, reaching for my seat belt. She's everything.

Backing out of the driveway, I look over my shoulder, hand behind her headrest, and I catch her watching me out of the corner of my eye.

"What?" I ask. "Do I have something on my face?" That wrings another laugh from her, which I tuck into my heart for safekeeping.

"No, I was just, um, admiring the view," she says.

"What view?" I ask, incredulous.

"Haven't you ever read a smutty book? This is like a woman's crack."

I nearly slam on the brakes but force myself to keep going until we're facing forward.

As I drive out of her neighborhood, sun blasting through the windshield, I chance a quick peek over at her, only to find she's biting her lip. I tuck my chin in a smile and reach over to take her hand, dragging our joined hands up to place a kiss on her knuckles.

"Maize," I say, my voice hoarse.

"Mmm?" she responds.

"I think we should talk about the other night..." I swallow, ready to lay myself bare, when she interrupts.

"I'm not ready for a relationship," she blurts. "I don't know if that's what you were hoping for or not..." She trails off.

It was. It *is*. But now that she has stated her piece, I scramble for what to say. "I want..." I pause. "I want whatever you have to give me, Maize. I can't lie to you, though, and say that it wouldn't be torturous not to be able to kiss you. To go back to being just friends after everything." I blow out a breath. "But I mean it. I won't lose you, so if that means being only friends, then that's what we'll do."

She's quiet. I would worry she fell asleep on me again if I couldn't feel her rapid pulse through our joined hands. Or maybe that's my own heart. Hard to tell.

Thankfully, she puts me out of my misery and starts to speak. "I—" She shifts nervously and gently picks at her leggings. "I can't lose you as a friend."

My heart plummets out of my chest and hits the car floor. I blink a little too quickly but remain focused on the road and wait for what she might say next.

When nothing comes, I decide to push, just a little. "You felt it too, right? How amazing we were together?" I wait a beat, wishing I could close my eyes as I say, "*Can be* together?"

"I've never felt how I felt the other night in the hotel," she says in a whisper, like she's ashamed at the admission. I squeeze her hand, letting her know I'm here. She can tell me anything. "And I don't want to stop doing what we did...but Connor—"

"So don't. Let me show you all the ways I care about you. Physically, sure, but also so much more. All the ways we can be together." I didn't mean to interrupt her, but I want her to hear it. Need her to know this is more than sex for me.

She starts biting at her cuticle and says through her teeth, "What Karsen and I had...I thought it was love. I spent two whole years with him and found out I never really knew him. Well, he never really knew me. I was a means to an end for him. And I *stayed with him*. What does that say about me? He didn't treat me with respect. He didn't listen to what I wanted. It was always about him. It took him literally trying to force me to pleasure him for me to do something about it, and then—"

So he *did* do something to her. *Fuck.*

"—and then hearing what he said about me?"

Rage burns through my body at hearing he tried to force himself on her, and I hate that I ever had to tell her what that dick said. Tears well in her eyes and my chest constricts, but I don't dare interrupt her this time.

"I know you're different, believe me, I do." She wipes away the tears, and I squeeze her hand again, feeling helpless to comfort her the way she needs while driving. "But I'm rubbed raw. I don't trust myself, my choices. I feel like damaged goods. I don't want to hurt you, Connor, but I don't know when or if I'll be ready for a relationship, and I can't lose you as a friend."

It's the second time she's said it. I know the feeling. I can't lose her either. I wish I could punch Karsen all over again for what he did to her—for how he has fucked with her head—but I take a calming breath. Once again, she doesn't need my anger right now.

I roll around what she's said in my head. It sounds like she wants to explore physically, even after what Karsen did, but she's scared to commit to anything more and can't guarantee that would ever change. I'm a relationship guy and I'm all in with Maisie, so what she's offering feels akin to being strapped into a torture machine—but I also am honored to be her safe place to land after going through something like that. I want to be that for her.

"I'm sorry he hurt you. I wish I could take away that pain, but I know it's something you need to work through in your own time." Wow. Therapy must really be sinking in. "But know, just because you think something doesn't make it true. You aren't damaged goods. You didn't deserve to be treated the way you were. And it is never okay for anyone to force anything.

"You deserve the world, Maize. The whole fucking world. And I'll be here, holding your hand, whether you're ready to explore or not. And if that means physically for now, means you want more of what we did the other night without any expectations attached, then I promise you won't lose me as a friend. You're safe with me." And I mean it. I'd wait forever for her. For her to see her worth. I'll endeavor to show her every day.

Even though I'm still focused on the road, I can see her eyeing me with wary hope.

"Promise?" she warbles.

"Pinky promise," I say, and I bring our hands to my lips once again. This time, kissing only her pinky.

50

Naked Room

Maisie

WE'RE NEARING THE END of the semester, and I'm no closer to understanding or *liking* my chemistry class. Honestly, biology hasn't been great either. I don't think I'm a big fan of learning about plants or having to look through a microscope for anything. Especially for long periods of time. First-year seminar has been fine, but it's meant to be. It's a freebie, really. A way to integrate students into college and provide support. Creative writing has been...fun. Yesterday, we were supposed to pretend we were writing from the perspective of insects that took a trip to the beach. My praying mantis, Galentina, got a terrible sunburn. Quite the predicament.

I'm currently hunched over in chemistry lab, trying to at least pretend like I know what I'm doing, all the while leaning way too heavily on my lab partner, Bridgette. Bridgette wants to be a chemical engineer, so this is a breeze for *her*. Whereas I'm thinking, for what feels like the hundredth time, *What am I doing here?* Sure, chemistry is an occupational therapy school prerequisite, but I can't even seem to make myself care about becoming an occupational therapist lately, either. *Or did I ever really?*

Maybe Lauren was onto something. Maybe it's okay to not know what I want to do. To think of college as an exploratory time. To...change my mind. The concept is scary and foreign, and my body initially tenses, rejecting the idea.

That is not what my father taught me, but does that make it true? Maybe, maybe not.

I'm slowly releasing the remaining tension, dropping my shoulders, taking a deep breath, when the professor calls out, "That's it for today's session. I don't care if you're finished with the lab or not. I need to get home to let my dog out. If you still have work in order to write your report, schedule time during my office hours."

I guess that means me, unless Bridgette gets real cool with sharing real fast. I peer over at where she is cleaning some beakers in the sink, and she meets my gaze, shaking her head. I practically flinch. She probably hates having me as a lab partner. Shame swirls in my chest, and my cheeks flush. I hate letting people down.

I rush out of there as fast as possible and head back to the dorm to grab my gear for practice.

When I enter our room, Angie is battling with a bathing suit halfway up her body. "Shut the door!" she squeaks as she tugs with all her might at the suit.

"What on earth are you doing?" I ask, not sure exactly what I'm witnessing here.

"My parents shipped a box of stuff from my room. I guess they are cleaning it out to make space for their 'naked room.'" She visibly shudders, and honestly, I try to shake the mental picture too.

"That suit looks like it last fit you when you were eight," I deadpan.

"I was able to wear it freshman year of high school! I don't..." she tugs, "know..." I swear I see it ripping at the seams, "—why it won't fit me." She huffs. "Now!"

I gently grab her arm to stop her from tugging at the material. It should be awkward since she's practically naked, but a) we're roommates, and b) we're both in water sports, so we are completely unfazed by this fact.

"Ang," I start gently. "Bodies change. It's fine that the suit doesn't fit you anymore. You have lots that do, and you look amazing in them."

She looses a weathered sigh. "You don't get it. I grew up with a coach who was always telling me I could stand to lose a few pounds. That real swimmers needed to be as slender as possible to glide through the water. I know that's bullshit, but it really messed with my head. And apparently still does sometimes." She shrugs casually but starts pulling the tiny suit back down her body.

"We can donate it. Some girl, not a *woman*, will really like that suit. Same as you did when you had a *girl's* body. I know there is a lot of shit out there and people feel entitled to comment on our bodies, but *they're* wrong—not you. Your body is beautiful, and more importantly, it's strong and it does amazing things for you." I squeeze her shoulder. "Say it with me: 'Thank you body for all that you do.'"

She exposes a quirk of a smile and repeats, "Thank you body for all that you do."

"Good," I say. "Now, should we circle back to the naked-room thing?"

"God, please no." She laughs, and with her cackle, I know my job here is done.

"Wanna grab a snack at the kiosk on the way to practice?" I ask, hopeful.

She smiles. "Yeah, for sure. Gotta fuel up."

"Hell yeah!" I shout, and we high-five before she finishes changing. Then we scoop up our bags and leave for practice together.

Practice is a bit of a shit show. Dublin and Finn look like they've never been synchro partners a day in their lives. Janique has consistently smacked on every reverse two and a half she's attempted. Lola hasn't ripped a single entry—absolutely out of character for her. Jamey twisted an ankle and has to sit out. And I have balked—started a hurdle or back approach and chickened out before actually going for the dive—so many times, Coach Megan told me for every balk from here on out, I'm doing twenty-five sit-ups.

So here I am, on the mat, doing sit-ups. It's not going well, so why do I think today is a good day to try the back three and a half on ten-meter? God only knows. But I do. I've been scared since the incident at the first meet, and my dad's orders afterward didn't help. But I've been working hard in the gym, and I set this arbitrary date as the day I would try—so, dammit, I'm going to.

I gingerly approach Coach Megan, ignoring the screams coming from my abs. "Coach, I want to try the back three and a half."

She scoffs, then realizes I'm serious. "Are you crazy, Thatcher?"

"Maybe a little, Coach, but I've been putting in the work. I know my body can do it. I just need to get my mind on board."

She sighs, dropping her clipboard to her side. "Okay, fine. You have my approval. I've seen the work you've been putting in. But I don't give a crap that this is a hard dive for you mentally. If you balk, you're doing sit-ups. Understood?"

"Yes, ma'am." I salute like she's a drill sergeant instead of my diving coach.

I make my way up the tower, verbally telling myself *I've got this.* I pass Lola on the five-meter, and she nods before taking off backward, long red braid whipping along behind her. She's the definition of a diver. I don't think she knows what it's like for the rest of us.

Finally at the top, I walk out to the edge. I toss my shammy down first, then turn around to take my position.

What was I thinking?! Today is the absolute wrong day to be trying something like this. My head isn't on straight. Why did I have to hold myself to this arbitrary date? I could have picked another one, like a normal person! But I didn't want my anxiety to get the best of me. I wanted to prove that I could do this.

I swing my arms once but don't take off.

Coach Megan's voice is far away but clear: "That's twenty-five! You wanna go for fifty? Get down here, Thatcher!"

My abs are going to be beyond sore after today.

Okay, I tell myself. *You got this. You got this. You...got this.* That last one wasn't so convincing, but before I can think any more about it or give Coach an opportunity to dish out more punishment, I'm leaving the platform. I'd say I'm relying on muscle memory, but I've never reached that point with this dive. I think I'm doing okay, when...*smack!*

The deep bone ache is immediate, but I haven't lost my breath this time. My head swirls slightly as I manage to paddle upward. As I surface and the shame of not being able to make any progress on this dive bubbles inside, I feel the pinch of tears. I swim to the stairs, and Coach is waiting there, arms crossed.

"I don't think that one's for you, kid." That's all she says before she walks away.

My head lightens. *Not for me.* It's a necessary dive to compete at this level, but it's *not for me.* So, does that mean being here, being a part of this team, is *not for me?*

The tears fall in earnest now, and I rip my shammy from the ground. I hear Lola calling after me, but I don't stop until I make it to the locker room. I fumble to undo the latch on my locker and grab my phone as quickly as possible. I dial the one person other than Lauren who has ever been able to calm me down on the brink of a panic attack. *Connor.*

51

December in North Carolina

Connor

I'M THANKFUL THAT THE men's team had practice earlier today, or else I would have been swimming when Maisie needed me. She was crying through the phone, and it absolutely tore my heart to shreds. I hate that she feels like she isn't good enough. I let her vent, guided her in some breathing exercises, and told her to go stand under a cold shower to help reset her nervous system. She called back when she was done, and I told her to come over. No one is here, and I don't want her to be alone.

A knock sounds at the door, and I'm buzzing with anxious energy. I'm not sure why. We've been good since the car ride home. Since actually talking about everything. But we haven't done any more than hold hands. I'm letting her take the lead for whatever she is comfortable with, but I don't know if I can refrain from kissing her much longer. Every time we're in the same room, it feels like I'm being drawn to her by a magnetic force.

I open the door and find a still-wet-haired Maisie sniffling. Her normally tan skin looks pale, and she shivers as if she's freezing even though it is a comfortable fifty-five degrees out. I can't say I'm mad about December in North Carolina. I instinctively pull her inside and into my arms. I breathe in the scent of lavender and chlorine and something that is distinctly Maisie.

She nuzzles further into my chest, and my arms tighten, letting her know I'm here. We stand like that for a moment, my shirt now wet from her hair, until she pulls back and looks up at me. I'm captivated by her emerald eyes, so sad and devastatingly gorgeous.

"Take me to your room," she says, and then after a beat adds, "please."

"Sure," I say, but my heart ratchets up to double its usual rhythm. I take her hand and lead her up the stairs. She's quiet as we enter my room and I close the door. "No one's home," I assure her. "What did you want in my room?"

"You," she breathes and takes a tentative step closer to where I'm leaning against the door.

"Can you be more specific, Betty? I need some guidance here."

Her eyes spark with something I can't quite identify, but then they avert from my gaze. "I want to forget about this shitty day. About all the ways I'm failing. I want to feel like I did that night in the hotel. Away from everything and everyone and consumed with only you."

When I don't immediately respond, she shifts on her feet. "Is that still okay? You meant your promise in the car?"

"Yes," I whoosh out. "I meant it, Maize. I'll never lie to you."

And I *did* mean it. My body aches for her, and I won't deny her what she wants, what she *needs* right now. There is a pinch in my chest, though, that she only wants this—wants me—so she can forget, but I won't go back on my promise. And more than that, I'd give her anything. Any part of me. At any time. Some might call that weak, but I call it love. And if I can't tell her, I'm going to have to keep showing her until she knows it without a doubt.

"Come here," I say, and she takes a few more steps toward me. She had wandered closer to my bed, but I don't want to rush this. I want to savor it; savor *her*.

I take her hand and pull her into me, so her hips are crushed against mine. So she can feel the evidence of my desire for her. I don't want her to ever question it with me. She sucks in a surprised breath but waits for further instruction. I glide my hand through her hair and angle her face close to mine. Her hands draw up, resting on my chest. Another half an inch and our lips would be touching.

"I'm going to make you feel good, Maize. Going to make you forget this shitty day. But I need you to know one thing. You're it for me. And I know you're not ready for anything serious. But know I'll wait for you, and this is always going to be more than just sex for me."

Her eyes go wide, and I'm scared she might bolt at the admission. But then she closes them, blocking me from the mesmerizing green I see even in my dreams. I hold my breath, waiting to see what she'll do. When she opens them, they're pierced with determination.

She nods. "I want you."

And she crushes her lips to mine.

At first, our kiss is hurried, but I slow down our pace, interlocking our lips languidly and pulling back in a kind of dance. I bring my other hand up, so that I am fully framing her face with my hands, and I guide her head to every angle I want it, eventually dipping in my tongue to taste her. When I do, a shockwave reverberates down my spine, and it takes everything in me to keep things slow.

Her fingers trail down my chest; it would tickle if my body weren't on fire for her. Her hand continues its path down, and she gingerly cups me through my shorts. I groan and pull away, shifting to lift her so her legs are wrapped around my hips to carry her to my bed.

"Not yet," I tell her as I carefully place her at the edge of the bed.

She smiles up at me, and her eyes are so trusting, I almost don't feel worthy.

I swallow, regaining my composure. "May I?" I hold the base of her shirt and wait for her approval.

"Please," she says, and her willingness and blatant desire make me the luckiest guy on this whole planet.

I slowly remove her shirt. When I toss it away, I notice a piece of wet hair stuck to her face. I gently remove it, tucking it behind her dainty ear.

"Are you sure about this?" I ask and search her face for any indication she's changed her mind.

"Connor, please," she whispers.

The *please* snaps something in me, and I move to press lingering kisses along her neck, up to her ear, where I whisper, "Take off your pants, Maisie."

She shuffles to remove them and looks up at me in only her sports bra and panties. My tongue goes dry. My cock is at full attention now, and I watch as her eyes track down my body and land at my arousal. She reaches out again, but I grab her wrist.

"You first." There's an edge to my voice that I didn't wholly mean to be there, but her eyes snap back to mine and a wicked smile curls her lips. She likes this. A lot.

I sink to my knees in front of her and pull her in for a bruising kiss. Her hands go to my hair this time, twisting and pulling every which way. My heated skin flames in response. I cup her through her bra, then glide my fingertip along its edge, teasing her.

She huffs in annoyance and demands, "Touch me."

My heart pounds with excitement.

I tug the strap to the side and lick her collarbone. Her legs come around my torso, and in one swift motion, I stand, taking her with me. I claim her mouth, plunging my tongue against hers, then retreat to bite at her lip. All the while, my hand skates up her side, finding the edge of her sports bra. Lifting it over her head as I continue peppering her with kisses. Once it's off, she wiggles, trying to reach down between us to remove my shirt. I *tsk* and toss her on the bed, and as I crawl over her, I scrunch the fabric on my back and yank forward. Her eyes track the movement with hunger, which only adds fuel to my flames.

As soon as my chest is exposed, she pulls me down to her. Our naked skin connects, igniting firecrackers along my body, anchoring in the place that craves her touch the most. I prop myself up on my elbows and kiss her until she's writhing beneath me, asking for more with her body. I'm more than happy to oblige. I reach between us and draw one line along the inside of her underwear before sitting back on my ankles to shimmy them fully down her legs and toss them to the floor with her other clothes.

I take my time looking at her, taking in every inch. *She's breathtaking.*

After a bit, she squirms, and I know I can't let her wait any longer. I dip a finger through her slit to find her dripping for me. Her head falls back on a sigh, and my chest pulses in pride at being the source of her pleasure. I slowly circle her clit the way I learned she likes from our night in the hotel—but this time, I dip my head, replacing my fingers with my tongue.

Her back arches, bowing off the bed, but it's quickly followed by a tightened "Connor!"

I stop only long enough to look up and see her eyes wide with panic. I retreat onto my heels, so she has room to move, and meet her eyes with concern.

"What's wrong?" I ask.

"Nothing's wrong," she says, but she closes her legs, blocking my view. "You just don't have to do that."

"What do you mean?" I question, confused by her reaction.

"No one...I mean, um, well, Karsen...he told me no guy actually enjoys doing that. He said it was too much work."

She covers her chest too, and I hate how she's retreated. My nostrils flare. I hate *him* for being the cause of it even more. My chest is tight, so I take a few intentional breaths, wanting to ensure I'm calm and Maize feels safe. I don't want her to think any of my frustration is with her.

I tenderly move my hands up and down her legs, and she shivers. "Maisie, I'm not him. And he was feeding you bullshit about what guys want. I *want* to go down on you. It's not too much work. It's an honor and a privilege, and I really fucking want to, but I won't do it if it makes you uncomfortable." I squeeze her calf to punctuate the statement.

"You do?" She shifts on my sheets.

I watch her as I gently reach for one of her arms, pulling it away from her body to kiss the inside of her wrist.

"I really do," I say and move my lips along her arm, pressing another kiss to the inside of her elbow, all the while watching her for consent.

Her shoulders drop, and she slowly releases the other arm that was blocking her breast, her body relaxing and leaning into my touch. I shift to swirl my tongue around her nipple, which draws a moan from her. My cock stirs in response, but this is about her right now. Showing her she's worth this and so much more.

I flick my tongue until her nipple is fully peaked, then draw her into my mouth one last time before working my way down her body, kissing and licking as I go until I'm back right where I want to be. I grab each thigh, spreading her legs apart, and use my new access to lick a long strip up her center. She lets out a low, buzzed *hmmm*, and I smile. *That's my girl.*

I start in earnest then, and as I feel her climbing higher, I taste the evidence of her arousal. I take her hand and place it on my head, looking up her body into her eyes. She seems to catch my meaning because she grabs on tightly to my hair and angles open even more, working her hips against my mouth. I suck in a sharp breath through my nose at the sensation of it and can't help but nudge my hips into the mattress, desperate for any friction. She watches as I work her tirelessly, showing her that her pleasure is my number one priority and that it is never a burden. Her eyelids begin to flutter, and I growl into her sensitive skin.

The wordless command communicates because her eyes lock with mine again. I want to see her when she falls apart. She's panting now, making all kinds of sounds I tuck away for later as I wring every drop of pleasure from her body. She's close, I can feel it. I suck her entire clit into my mouth and slowly insert a finger inside her, curling to the sensitive spot I know is there. Her eyes go wide but quickly close, lost in the sensation of it all, and a scream of pleasure rips from her throat.

"Fuuuuuuuck," she shouts, but I don't stop until she's so sensitive, she shoves my head away.

I chuckle, removing my finger from inside her too, and while she's catching her breath, I lick my finger clean and plop down behind her on the bed, pulling her into me.

She wiggles until our bodies are perfectly aligned, her back to my front. She doesn't seem to mind the feel of my still-hard cock against her ass because she takes a deep breath, saying on the exhale, "That was...amazing."

"You're amazing," I say, kissing her head.

"I want you to feel like that too," she says.

"Getting you off is better." *And I mean it. That was incredible.*

I can feel her frown even though I can't see it, so I add, "I'm serious. Watching you release is like... Well, there's nothing better." I wrap my arms even tighter around her naked body, slick with sweat.

A quiet beat passes, and I remember once again why we started this today.

"Do you feel thoroughly *consumed*?" I ask in a low tone, playfully tickling her side.

She peeks over her shoulder, smiling shyly. "Of course I do," she says with a yawn, "but next time, I want to participate too." She drops her head and snuggles impossibly closer to me.

I can't stop the smile that lights my face at hearing she's satisfied. "If you want," I say, "I won't stop you."

Although it will be hard to have her touch me when I can't have her whole heart. I shake the thought away.

After a few minutes, her breathing deepens, and I feel weightless, like we are both about to drift into sleep, when my phone buzzes on the table. I lift my head enough to see over Maisie to the nightstand. I wish I hadn't. "Dad" flashes across the screen. *Why would he be calling?*

I lay my head back down, closing my eyes so tight it hurts, but then I remember the woman in my arms. I let the press of her deep breathing into my chest unwind the tension coursing through my veins. I lift myself to press a kiss to her shoulder, needing the extra assurance that she's here; that she's mine in this moment. Then I lie back and let sleep overtake me.

52

Two Things Can Be True Simultaneously

Connor

"Tell me more about this Maisie," Donny, my therapist, says.

He's resting comfortably in his wingback chair as always. We each have a mug of hot tea in our hands. He keeps all the supplies for tea, coffee, and hot chocolate in his office—but today is the first time I took him up on the offer, so he decided to join me. He takes a sip, awaiting my response.

"She's...my best friend, but also a lot more. She's fun and playful, but she cares deeply about others. About me. She knows me and wants to know me in a way no one else has before. She's brave and beautiful. I want a relationship with her, but she's just getting out of a shitty one." I shift my weight on the couch, ever uncomfortable thinking about Karsen.

"This 'shitty' relationship...it was with the guy you punched?"

"That's the one." I heave a sigh.

"Has that impacted your relationship with her? Have the two of you talked about a committed relationship?" he asks, and it feels like a punch to the gut having to voice this out loud.

"She says she doesn't know if she can trust herself, her judgment." I stop to take a sip of tea. It's just barely cool enough to drink. I take a healthy gulp.

Donny mirrors the action. "That she isn't ready for a relationship. That she doesn't want to ruin our friendship, but she wants..." I eye everything but Donny for a moment. Still not meeting his eyes, I get out, "She wants to be physical, though." I flinch like I'm going to get in trouble.

When my gaze finds Donny's, he's still as neutral as ever. As soon as he's sure I'm not going to add anything else, he inquires, "Do *you* want to be physical without a relationship commitment?"

No. The word blares through my thoughts like a foghorn. *No. No. NO.*

"I'd prefer a relationship, but I won't pressure her."

"You could still be friends. You don't need to have a physical relationship just because she asked for one. If you'd prefer to keep that part separate unless there is a commitment involved, there's nothing wrong with that." He says it so simply. Cuts right to the heart of the thing.

My wants matter too. What a world-rocking statement. Even so, I'd rather have whatever Maisie will give me than go back to being only friends.

"I don't think I could go back to just being friends," I tell him.

"All right. Then I encourage you to be honest with her. Not in an ultimatum way, but let her in. Let her know how important being in a relationship is to you, especially with being physical. You can still acknowledge her desires while expressing yours."

Two things can be true simultaneously. It comes back again. The thought of baring myself like that and being rejected sounds worse than drag suit practice, but now that the idea is in my head, I'm not sure I'll be able to let it go.

"I think you're right, like always." Now to work up the courage to actually tell her.

A smile breaks through as I laugh, and he lets his own mouth tick up an inch. A small sense of pride ripples through that I got him to show emotion.

"How is swimming going?" He sets his mug on the small wooden table to the right of his chair.

"It's...going," I hedge.

"Care to elaborate?" He quirks an eyebrow, which essentially means he's calling me out.

"It's fine. I guess. I show up, I swim, I go home. It's familiar." I scratch at a loose thread in the couch.

He waits a minute again before asking, "Do you like it?"

"Uh, yeah, sure. As much as always. I enjoy seeing my friends. I like getting exercise. I like watching Maisie dive."

He lets out a soft *hmmm.*

"What?" I ask, incredulous. My chest tightens in anger. I take a few calming breaths.

He waits, then says, "What made you angry just now?"

"I'm not angry, I'm just—" I ball my hands up. "I'm just doing what's expected of me. I'm fast and win races. I work hard. It builds character. I don't have to love it."

Again, he waits. I release my balled hands.

His calm voice rings through. "Okay, maybe you don't have to love it. Maybe it's what's expected of you, but is it something that honors what you'd like to do with your time and energy?"

My eyes feel heavy. I let my head fall to the back of the couch. "My dad wouldn't ever talk to me again," I say, feeling disconnected from myself as I do.

The fourteen-year-old boy version is raging, telling Donny, *We can't do it! We can't let that happen. He needs to love us. If we swim, he loves us. Even when he's not there anymore.* Present me, the one who ignores my dad's calls, the one who is working through the anger that lingers in his absence, is quietly saying, *Maybe not swimming isn't such a bad thing. Maybe we shouldn't have to do anything to earn our dad's love.*

"How would that make you feel if your dad stopped talking to you if you quit swimming?" Donny breaks through my thoughts.

Complicated. Which feels—"Shitty," I say out loud.

"Tell me more about that."

"Shitty because I've been doing it for so long. All those years. I can't tell what was for him and what was for me. Shitty because I don't *want* to talk to my dad, but I also don't want to disappoint him. It doesn't make a lot of sense, really." I shrug.

"It makes sense to me," he says. "You have a complex relationship with your father, and it has wound itself around swimming. It makes sense that it's hard to untangle what you want on all fronts. More than one thing can be true at once."

"Thank you." The rest of the tension in my body loosens slightly, and I sit up.

He nods. "You're welcome. Unfortunately, that's all the time we have today. Are we still good for next week?"

"Yep, I'll see you then, Doc. Still a lot to untangle in this web of shenanigans that is my brain." I knock on my head for emphasis.

He chuffs a polite laugh, and I grab my backpack and head out the door. But everything we talked about continues to rattle around in my mind.

Ride or Die

Maisie

"HE DID *WHAT*?" ANGIE's water sprays from her mouth. It's actually a little gross, and now her shirt is sopping wet, but I have to admire her theatrical dedication. She automatically reaches for a new shirt in her dresser drawer.

"He licked his finger clean after," I repeat for her.

She laughs. "I heard you the first time, but dang girl, that's hot." She pulls off the soaked shirt and shimmies into the new one. "And I can't believe you didn't tell me about the first time you hooked up! In a hotel? Did it feel like prom night? I guess not since it was nice and not a shitty motel."

I shiver at the memory of that shitty motel Karsen took me to on our prom night. We found a dead rat in the corner, and he wanted to *stay* there. That should have been my first clue that our values didn't align.

I sigh, shaking the thought of Karsen away, and say, "No, it didn't feel like prom. And I'm sorry I didn't tell you. I wasn't sure anything was going to happen again, and I wasn't sure how I felt about that. I'm still not sure how to handle things. He's my best friend. Except you, of course." I blow her a kiss, and she catches it without looking.

"He can be your guy best friend or whatever, because it's different. I know who your top is, don't worry." She winks.

"Exactly," I confirm.

Because it's true. Connor and I share something special, *obviously*, but nothing will ever be like a girl best friend. She's ride or die, no matter what guys come and go in our lives. Although the thought of Connor *going* is enough to curdle my stomach. He feels like...a hell of a lot more. But that's why we're doing this, right? I can't lose what I don't have and vice versa. What we do *have* is friendship, so we can't lose that. Yeah.

"Earth to Maize." Angie waves a hand in front of my face. "I lost you there for a second."

"Just thinking." I pointedly look away, feigning interest in what could be out the sole window in our dorm room. It is nice out, actually, but when isn't it?

"Don't make me pull it out of you," she says, stepping into my line of sight and blocking the window. Her arms are crossed, and she's giving me *the look*. The one that best friends give when they call you on your bullshit.

"Fine. I was thinking about how Connor feels like...more than a friend. More than a friend with benefits, too... But I still don't know if I'm ready for a *real* relationship. If we take that step, there's no going back. I could lose everything. I could lose *him*." My lips tremble on the last word, and I drop my head, shying from Angie's knowing gaze again.

"I know it's scary, babe. But sometimes things are worth going after, even when they're terrifying. My aunt always used to say, 'You can be scared to do hard things. You just do them scared.'"

I sigh and walk to the mini fridge to get a root beer. Looking down at the drink in my hand, my mind swirls with memories of Connor. A root beer and Doritos ready for me in the car. The first night we watched a Marvel movie.

I smile and say, "Your aunt sounds wise. She sounds like my Aunt Kaity, actually." A pang of homesickness hits, and I remind myself to call Lauren later this week. "But it's not as simple as a saying. I gave my whole heart away for...for a long time. I don't want to make the same mistake twice. I don't want to lose myself and not know my worth. I used to do things just because I thought I should. Not because I wanted to. All in the name of being a girlfriend. I don't want to get lost in the weeds again."

"Those are all wonderful things, Maize. And I'm so proud of you for knowing your worth. Knowing what you want and need *is* the most important thing—but being scared and not moving forward isn't honoring yourself, either." She gently takes my hand, giving it a little squeeze before letting it drop again.

I know she's right. Well, my mind knows she's right, but my heart is a stubborn organ that can't seem to take the hint. It's been hurt, and it's fighting tooth and nail to prevent that from happening again. What Connor and I are doing is working for now. We'll just keep going. There's no reason to fix something that isn't broken.

Clearly seeing that I'm done with this conversation, Angie shifts topics. "So you know how my birthday is next weekend?"

I hold a hand to my chest, while sarcastically quipping, "It *is*?"

"Ha, ha, very funny." She rolls her eyes. "I know I've mentioned it once or twice."

A Cheshire grin stretches across her face, making her freckles spread out like fireflies dancing in the moonlight. Her joy is infectious, and I catch myself smiling and laughing in response. "Of course. Only once or twice," I say with a wink.

"Anyway, I'm thinking it would be fun to have a party!"

My smile drops. A party? In our tiny dorm room? She knows I'm not a partier. Who knows when people would leave? I'd have no place to hide if I got overwhelmed. Plus, the place would be a disaster. I don't want to find used condoms in my shower caddy. I shiver, worrying my bottom lip between my teeth, and she eyes the movement.

"I can see you're stressed at the prospect, but I was actually going to see if you'd ask Connor if we could have it at his place."

My nose scrunches at the thought of invading Brock's space for Angie's party, but a relieved breath also escapes me that she doesn't want it here.

"Sure, I can ask, but you know it's obviously not just his place. Aren't you worried about a certain...other swimmer who lives there?"

"I don't know who you could mean. Hunter is amazing, Tyler keeps to himself, and I could care less about he-who-should-not-be-named." She crosses her arms and sticks her nose in the air to prove her point.

"All riiiight…should I text him now?"

"Please do."

I pull up my text thread with Connor, and my heart gallops at the last thing he wrote.

Connor: Missing you already

I hadn't had a chance to respond, but I guess I'm gonna ignore that now to text him about the party.

Hey

He responds immediately.

Connor: Betty what's up?

So you know how it's Angie's birthday next weekend?

Connor: Haha how could I not? She tells me almost every day at practice

That makes me laugh out loud, and Angie side-eyes me like I better not mess this up for her. I cool my expression and keep typing.

Well she was wondering if maybe her birthday party could be at your apartment? She's here now staring me down so I have my fingers crossed you say yes. In fact I'm not above begging. Pretty please?

Connor: You never have to beg with me Betty

The implications of that text make my stomach somersault.

Connor: Let me just double check with the guys but it's fine by me. That way too if you get overwhelmed at any point we can hide out in my room

A pang of something stabs in my ribs. He knows me so well. The feeling of being known is almost...overwhelming? But I think I could get used to it.

Connor: Luckily everyone was home so I did a quick tally. Brock was the only one who put up a stink but since it was 3 to 1 we decided it's a yes. Did something happen between those two or something?

Your guess is as good as mine

Not a total truth, but I can't break girl code by telling him that.

But great! Tell the guys thanks from me :)

Connor: Will do. Wanna grab dinner together after practice later?

He's always making plans with me—always the one to initiate, but always making me feel like it's my choice. It's something I didn't realize I wanted, but Connor seems to fill in a lot of the cracks in my heart simply by being himself.

Sounds like a plan

Connor: See you then <3

I turn back to Angie, who is smirking at me.

"What?" I ask.

"Nothing. You're just smiling like a little schoolgirl at your phone. If that doesn't give you a clue about how you feel about Connor, I'm not sure what will, babe."

Part of me knows she's right, but like I said, my heart is stubborn. She has walls up. Walls that are there to protect me. Although I think some bricks of those walls have shaken loose, it's going to take a little more time.

"So I guess you don't want to know if they said yes or not?" I taunt her to change the subject again.

"Tell me! Tell me!" She lunges at me in excitement, nearly toppling us both to the ground.

"They said yes." I laugh and shove her off me.

"Yes!" She pulls her fist down in front of her in victory. "Let's start planning!"

54

A Worthy Opponent

Connor

THE DOORBELL RINGS, AND my heart kicks up a notch. I haven't seen much of Maize since we hooked up. Just practice and a few dinners. I puff air into my open palm and take a whiff. Smells fine to me. Hopefully Maisie agrees. I grab the door, and as soon as I see Maize on the other side, my jaw drops. She's wearing a little black dress like the night we met, but this one has a deep V cut in the front and—as she walks inside past my still-gaping mouth—I see it has a twin in the back. It wraps around her thick thighs in a way that makes me jealous of the fabric.

I finally find my words and shake my head, saying, "You are *breathtaking*."

Her cheeks pink, but she rewards me with one of her brightest smiles. "Thanks—you don't look so bad yourself." She rocks side to side with nerves, but her eyes never leave mine.

"Thanks again for hosting!" Angie bursts the all-consuming Maisie bubble I was wrapped in.

"Uh, no problem," I mutter. "Happy birthday, Ang."

"Thanks!" She beams and bounces away into the kitchen. I overhear Hunter greeting her and asking what drink she wants to start with tonight. He even goes so far as to offer to be her personal bartender for the evening.

When I turn back to Maize, she's picking at her cuticle again. I gently take the hand at her mouth and bring it to my own lips, stepping into her space. "Don't worry about tonight. I've got you. Promise." I kiss her fingers where she had just been picking.

Her eyes dart away for a flash, but she returns them quickly. "How do you always know the right thing to say?" she asks.

"I don't. I know you, and I want you to be happy. The rest just happens."

She sighs, and her eyes soften. The way she's looking at me makes me feel like the luckiest bastard in the world. I think, not for the first time, that she reminds me of sunshine. I'm drawn to her light. I know it would never be her intention, but I pray she doesn't burn me. My heart is out on a floating dock, and she's the ocean. It could pitch at any time, and I'd be lost to the deep.

Her smile fades as she takes in whatever expression must be on my face, so I slap on a smile, grab her hand, and pull her into the kitchen currently housing both of our roommates.

It isn't long until more people show up. Plenty from the swim team, but it seems Angie has invited some of the men's hockey team, too. I never get to make it to any games since we're both winter sports. I watch as one guy—I think his name is Caden—dips down to whisper into Angie's ear. Next thing I know, Brock is between them, his back to Angie, facing down the hockey player who has at least fifty pounds on him, but Brock doesn't seem fazed by that. Caden's brows pitch up, but he quickly retreats. Angie crosses her arms, yelling something at Brock. He lifts his hands in exasperation, firing back, but I can't hear what either of them is saying. She storms away.

I turn to Maize to see if she witnessed the event, and by the wide-eyed look I'm met with, I'm assuming she did.

"Brock isn't usually the overprotective type," I say and toss another ping pong ball casually toward the other side of the beer pong setup. We aren't playing a real game right now, just practicing.

"What's he usually like?" She sticks her tongue out in concentration, head tilted to the side as she throws a ball back my way. It lands in one of the empty cups, and she whoops in victory. My little competitor is so cute.

"Obviously I've only known him for a few months, but from what I've seen, he's a one-and-done kind of dude. Not that he doesn't care about women, but I've never seen him be anything close to possessive." I shrug.

Come to think of it, though, I'm not sure I've seen him with a woman in a while. Maybe he calmed down after those first few weeks? I should probably check in with my roommates more often. Not that they'd want me in their business like that, but I make a note to ask him what's up sometime soon.

Maisie's nose scrunches in distaste at my assessment of Brock. Then Tyler walks up to the table.

"Hey, guys." He nods nonchalantly. "You playing?"

"We were just practicing," I answer. "You wanna play?"

I look to Maize for confirmation that I made the right decision. She smiles, one of her genuine smiles that softens her emerald eyes, not her "being polite" smiles, where her eyes remain tight, so I know we're good.

"Sure," Tyler says. "I'll go grab a fourth?"

"Sounds good!" Maisie speaks up this time, and I give her a knowing wink. She's about to get so competitive, and I'm going to revel in every second of it.

When Tyler returns, he brings Lola with him. I didn't even know she was here, but I guess she and Maize are sort of friends, so it makes sense Angie would invite her. Tyler takes my side, and Lola—her red hair in its signature braid falling over a shoulder—sidles up next to Maize.

"Lola!" Maisie shrieks. She hasn't even had anything to drink. "I'm so glad you could make it! You can be on my team! We'll crush these boys." She smirks.

"Thanks for inviting me," Lola responds shyly, fidgeting with her fingers at the end of her braid.

Guess that answers that question. I'm proud of Maize for branching out, making more friends. I peek over at Tyler and catch him watching Lola's fingers with an intensity I haven't seen from him before.

"Everyone know the rules?" I ask, and I'm met with a chorus of "yeps" and nodding heads. "Great! Ladies first." I stretch an arm out and give a deferential bow to the other end of the table.

"You can go first," Maize tells Lola, who looks like a deer caught in headlights. "Or I can go first if you'd prefer?" Maisie backtracks.

"Sure, that's good," Lola says, taking a cursory step back to give Maisie room for her turn.

Maisie goes for the bounce technique, and it lands perfectly in the cup, which means we each need to down one. Tyler silently takes his, and I wink at Maize as I drink mine. Her hands fist up like she wants to shout in excitement, but she keeps herself contained while making room for Lola to take her turn.

Lola puts in a solid effort, but ultimately misses. Tyler does the same, and then I land one straight from the air, no bounce. Lola grabs a cup, and I see Maisie mouth, "Are you sure?" and Lola nods.

Maisie doesn't miss a single shot the entire game, so we're down to the last cup. Angie, Brock, and Hunter surround the table at this point, along with a few other partygoers.

"You got this, babe! Kick their ass!" Angie shouts, to which Brock rolls his eyes.

Hunter eyes her and laughs, tipping his baseball cap at her. Brock glares at Hunter, who doesn't seem to notice, and leaves in a huff. Lola went first for their team but missed, her cheeks red from alcohol and the excitement. Now it's Maisie's turn. If she sinks this, they win. Even though I'm a competitive s.o.b., I want her to win. She's an amazing athlete, even for dumb things like beer pong. Her body is so graceful and strong. It's like every move she makes is intentional. It's mesmerizing.

She launches the ping pong ball, and it's a perfect shot! "Yes!" she shouts and turns to hug a startled Lola.

Tyler decides to down the last cup for our team and then nonchalantly walks away. I rush to Maize, picking her up and swinging her around as she laughs in my arms.

"I took you down, Bocelli!" she says directly into my face, our noses touching. I can't help but smile as I put her back on the ground.

"I'll happily lose to such a worthy opponent," I say, and she blushes.

I realize we're probably being rude. I turn to say congratulations to Lola, but she's gone too. Huh. I guess she and Tyler have that in common.

Next thing I know, Angie is wrapping Maize in a hug. "That's my roommate! Hell yeah! You've made us proud on this, my birthday party!" I think she's had a bit too much to drink, swaying recklessly and slurring her words a bit.

Maisie must notice too, because I hear her tell Angie to drink some water.

"I've got her, don't worry," Hunter interjects. "I won't let anything happen to her."

Maisie beams. "Thanks, Hunter. You're the best."

"What about me?" I joke incredulously.

"You're also the best, *obviously*." She rolls her eyes.

Another guy pushes through the crowd to congratulate her on her win. I don't recognize him. Maybe he came in with the hockey guys? But it has the hairs on my arms standing up. "That was an impressive game," he says, inching as close as he can to Maisie. It takes everything in me not to physically shove her behind me and declare, *Mine*, like a caveman.

"Uh, thanks," Maize says awkwardly, retreating a step.

He closes the space she just created, and that's what does it. Nope, nuh-uh. Can't he see he's making her uncomfortable?

"Step back," I say, tone dripping with authority.

"Whoa, calm down, man. I was just congratulating her."

"You can congratulate her from a normal distance away." I point.

"Ha. What are you? Her bodyguard? I'll do whatever the fuck I want."

I want to shout, *That's my girl, dickwad!* But that's not true, is it? The realization hangs like a weight in my gut, and some of my bravado cools.

"Connor, I want to go to your room," Maisie says, tugging at my arm for me to follow.

The guy adds, "What? You're choosing this loser over me? Fine, be a bitch."

My temper soars, and every instinct in me has me wanting to deck this son of a bitch for ever speaking to her like that, but I fight it. Maize doesn't want me to be violent, and neither do I. She tugs harder on my arm. I know I need to go with her.

Before following her, I crowd the guy's space and seethe, "Get out of my fucking house."

The guy huffs, but then Brock reappears out of nowhere. "You heard the man. Out!" he barks, shoving the guy in the direction of the door.

"Fine, fine." He holds up his hands. "This party was lame anyway."

Angie reappears at Maisie's side, holding her by the waist in silent support. Thankfully, the guy doesn't argue further and leaves. I take a shaking breath and pull freaked-out Maize away from Angie and into my embrace. I whisper into her ear, "Let's go upstairs, Betty. I've got you."

She nods shakily, and we sneak away.

55

Edward - Coded

Maisie

"**S**AY SOMETHING TO DISTRACT me from going after that guy to make sure he never bothers you again." Connor breathes heavily, fists clenched, pacing his room. Maybe his anger should scare me, but it doesn't. I know it's just because he's protective, and I know it's something he's working on in therapy. I also know he would never hurt me.

"I was jealous when Angie talked to you that night at the swim house party," I blurt out. "I didn't understand it then. Well, more like I didn't want to admit why it was impacting me, but I was so worried she was going to try to go home with you."

His brows furrow. "Maize, the only one I would have gone home with that night was you. I only had eyes for you."

I smile, warmth radiating off my cheeks at both our admissions.

He takes my hand, rubbing circles with his thumb. "You wanna know what I thought that night?"

"What?" I ask, curiosity piquing.

"That some day, we'd have a first kiss. I had to hope it was true, even though you were with someone else. Turns out, you beat me to it in the hotel pool, but if I'm going to take second place to anybody, I'm glad it was you."

I suck in a breath, letting his words wash over me.

He reaches up and brushes a misplaced piece of hair behind my ear. He lets his hand linger on my neck, and I close my eyes at the sensation of his massive yet soft hand touching me so intimately.

When my eyes open, he's watching me with a tenderness that breaks me apart. This man is beyond anything I could ever hope or dream for. Plus, his admission means he's had some semblance of feelings for me since that night. I want to say something meaningful back, but the words are stuck in my throat. Instead, I lean forward, pressing my lips to his.

A vibrating hum escapes the back of his throat, only egging me on further. In a slow dance, I shift, so I'm straddling him at the edge of the bed. Our lips meet and pull away. It's slower than we've ever kissed, exploratory, intentional. His fingers skate up my ribs, and I shiver. I grind my hips down and am met with the hard length of him.

I've never seen him fully unclothed, and I decide that tonight I want to—with his permission, of course. I work my hips harder as our kiss intensifies. His fingertips curl into my hips with a delicious pressure. If he leaves bruises, will everyone be able to see when I'm in my suit? Do I care?

He wraps an arm around me and shifts like he's going to move me to my back, so I tense, placing my hands on his chest.

"Wait," I say, and my voice has a rasp to it I don't recognize. "I want to touch you. *Please.*"

His eyes search mine as if looking for something contradicting my words. I stare back, hoping that he sees and feels all my intentions. That he can feel between the lines of what I'm not saying out loud. *I'm yours. I want to be yours forever. But please don't break my heart.*

I shift to standing and slowly lift my dress, letting it glide along every curve of my body in agonizing slowness. When I finally lift it over my head, I step into him, bending down with a curve to my lips.

"Your turn," I command.

His mouth kicks up, too.

"As you wish," he says before quickly removing his shirt and standing to unbutton his shorts.

When we're standing there in only our underwear, inches from one another, I reach my hand out and run a finger along the top of his navy-blue briefs. The skin on his stomach pebbles at my touch, and I allow my hand to sink in until I have a full grip. He groans, and it shoots an electric jolt up my spine.

I've barely touched him, but every line of his body is flexed and taut. I can tell he's fully restraining himself, and having this effect on Connor is intoxicating.

"I want to make you feel good," I breathe.

His lust-filled eyes find mine and pierce through me with so much intensity that I'm worried I've said something wrong.

He runs a finger along the top of my bra, over the curve of my breast. My body leans into him with abandon.

He pulls me in closer by the small of my back before whispering, "I love that you want to make me feel good. Believe me, I really fucking love it, but I need to be clear that you don't owe me anything."

His tenderness, his worry for me, somehow still surprises me, even though it is so him.

"I know," I whisper back and punctuate it with a stroke where I'm still holding him. "I *want* to. The freedom you give me, the lack of pressure, the full and total support—it's everything, Connor. It allows me to step into being a woman, and right now, I want you to let me do that because it's what I want." I stroke my hand once more, and he lets out a garbled sound, a mix of elation and agony.

"Fine, but here's how we're going to do this." He pulls my hand from inside his underwear and bends to remove them altogether.

He springs free, and my eyes nearly fall out. I know I just felt him, but he's huge. I'm small—like, all of me is small: hands, mouth...everything. Nerves swirl, but he takes my hand, calming me instantly.

He kisses me as he unclasps my bra, letting it fall to the floor.

As he begins kneeling in front of me, working my underwear down my legs, he says, "We're both going to make each other feel good. I can't sit idly by while you get me off, but I won't take that away from you either."

I step out of my underwear. He peers up at me, both of us fully bare now, and lifts one of my legs over his shoulder to lick a long stripe straight up my center. I somehow manage to gasp and moan simultaneously. It's not a pretty sound, but it's honest. Connor's tongue can do no wrong as far as I'm concerned.

He continues for a few more seconds before saying, "You're going to sit on my face backwards and you can have full access to my cock to do whatever you like, but if you don't come, neither do I, got it?"

My eyes flutter in surprise at his words. As far as being physical goes, Connor has been one surprise after another, and I am *not* mad about it. The fact that he's still concerned about my pleasure more than his own when I'm all but begging him to let me touch him says so much. Karsen would never. It was always about him; I see that now. And I'm really liking how I feel from this new way of doing things.

I give full control over to Connor as he locks our lips again, shifting us back to the bed. He turns me around so my back is to his chest, slinking a hand between my legs to feel the wetness there, and he groans, the combination keeping me absolutely desperate for him.

In a move I'm convinced only a peak athlete such as Connor could pull off, he lies on his back while picking up my bottom half, pitching me forward on my hands and knees. He wastes *no* time taking me into his mouth, and I rush to gather his hard cock in my hand. The dual sensation of working on each other's pleasure is already sending me close to the edge.

I lean down further, just close enough that I can lick the tip as I continue to stroke him. His responding growl reverberates through my entire pelvis, sending pinpricks of pleasure up my spine and even to my ass. The ass that he has gripped tight, so he can move me any which way he goddamn pleases. I love that he has me, that he wants me, and that he lets me know it.

I let my mouth glide over his length, and this time, I'm the one groaning. I work him with both my hand and mouth, while he physically moves me over his tongue, grinding my hips for me in a pattern I don't think I could have performed myself.

Fire licks up my spine and lingers at the base of my skull as my legs contract. He holds them tighter as I'm sent flying over the edge, a wave of pleasure emanating throughout my entire body, even down to my toes, all while my lips are still wrapped around his cock. It's a sensual gluttony I've never had the honor to experience before.

As I'm riding the waves of aftershocks, Connor quickly lets out, "Gonna come. You don't have to—" His words are lost, but I know I want all of him.

My pleasure doesn't ebb in the slightest as I double down on my efforts. His whole body jerks, and he uses my center as a cover for his scream as he releases into my mouth. There's so much, but I swallow down as much as I can, the rest dribbling out between us. It's filthy, and I smile; I can't help but love everything we just did.

He maneuvers us so we're lying on the bed facing one another. He licks the remaining mess from my lips before finishing with a tender peck, his arms wrapped tightly around me and my leg caught between both of his.

"You're...remarkable," he says, still catching his breath. "Absolutely fucking remarkable. But are you okay? You didn't have to swallow." His lazy gaze turns steely, his concern for me never leaving.

I beam at the praise and press soft kisses to his chest. "I'm perfectly fine. Better than fine, really. I wanted to."

His arms relax, worry abated. He kisses the crown of my head. "Do you want to go back downstairs?"

I sigh, content in a way I never have been before. "No. I don't think I do. Let's stay here as long as we like."

And so we do.

56

One of the Many Reasons

Connor

WINTER BREAK COMES AND goes. The long car rides I share with Maisie are by far the best part. I miss her when we're at our respective families' houses. Thankfully, we text throughout each day and FaceTime almost every night. She virtually shows me around her house and tells me how much she misses Lauren being there. I introduce her to my brothers—briefly, because they are menaces—and send her pictures of some of my favorite coffee shops in town. She hypes me up that one day I'll have the best coffee shop in town, wherever that might be. Her belief in me is one of the many reasons I love her.

I. Love. Her. I want to shout it at the top of my fucking lungs, but instead, we're walking into her dorm room—hand in hand, mind you—but without her knowing how I truly feel.

I'm going to tell her. Today. Donny's voice rings in my head, assuring me that two things can be true simultaneously. I can tell her, and she doesn't have to say anything back. I'll make sure she knows that.

As we shuffle the rest of the way into her room, I log that Angie isn't here yet. That's good.

I drop the suitcase I'm carrying for her and shift to pull Maisie in for a hug. She relaxes into me like being in my arms is the most natural thing in the world. My chest swells, and my throat clogs with emotion that is hard to explain. Every day, I earn more of her trust—trust that Karsen ripped from her. I'm honored to be a part of her healing journey from that bastard.

I don't want to spook her with what I'm going to say, but I need to say it for my own sanity, and that's okay, too.

I take a deep breath. Then another one because this is scary as fuck. But Maisie beats me to talking first.

"I texted Ang. Looks like she's not going to come back until tomorrow. Want to stay here with me tonight?" Her eyes sparkle.

My shoulders slacken, and I can't help but smile at her. She's so goddamn beautiful. "Yeah, that sounds nice," I answer.

She quirks a smile, then snuggles her head into my chest. I pull her even closer. She gives the best hugs. My cock jumps a bit at her proximity, so I disconnect us and back up a step, not trying to start anything tonight. If I'm going to say what I need to say, I need her to know it's not connected to what we do or don't do physically.

She laughs when I step away because I'm sure she could feel the evidence of how much I want her. "Should we take care of that?" she asks, eyeing the now-obvious bulge in my sweatpants.

I laugh and drop my head, rubbing the back of my neck with a tinge of embarrassment before pulling her close again. "I *always* want you. If we 'took care of that' every time, we would never stop. Tonight, though—let's just cuddle, watch a movie. Spend quality time together. I really missed you these past few weeks." I kiss her temple, then rest my cheek on the top of her head as we continue to embrace.

"Mmmm, that sounds so cozy and nice," she says, still nuzzling into me like a cat. "Check the fridge for any leftover snacks, and I'll queue up the next movie."

I'm making my way to her mini fridge when my phone buzzes in my pocket. I pull it out, and it feels like all the heat flees my body, leaving me ice cold. Dad. Again.

Frustration clamps a hand around my throat for a moment, and I want to chuck my phone at the wall. I don't want to talk to him right now. Or ever, for that matter. With shaking hands, I put my phone back in my pocket and take some steadying breaths.

I find ice cream in the mini fridge's freezer section and smile. When I turn back to face Maize, she's eyeing me warily. She can tell something's wrong.

"Was that your dad?" she asks.

My lips flop as I blow out the breath I didn't realize I was holding. "Yeah."

"Do you want to talk about it?" She eyes me with concern but not pity.

I know I could trust her with anything, including how I feel about all of this, but I don't want to let my dad ruin this night we have together.

"All I'll say is he's been calling, and I keep not answering. I have nothing to say to him, and honestly, I don't want to hear what he has to say to me, either."

She takes a careful step closer and reaches out to take my hand. "That's understandable. He's caused a lot of pain, not only to you but to people you love too."

"Yeah, it's complicated, and it's going to keep being complicated, so for tonight, I'd rather we just hang out? Forget he called or even that he exists for a little while?"

She plucks the ice cream carton from my hand. "I can do that. Did you find any snacks for *yourself* in there?" She motions with her eyebrows toward the fridge.

"What, you're not willing to share?" I laugh, fully knowing the answer.

"You can have *one* bite." She holds it out to me, as if by offering me a taste of ice cream, she's cutting off her own arm or something.

A smile curls my lips. I'm so beyond thankful she is here in this moment. That I don't have to face the plethora of feelings that race to my brain whenever my dad calls me while I'm alone. That she cares about me, about what I think and feel. I know I can trust her with how I feel about her, too.

"You can keep it, Betty."

She shakes her butt happily as she spoons some into her luscious mouth. A mouth I fall asleep dreaming about. And her eyes, her hair. Fuck, even her ears. I love all of her, and I need her to know it.

When we're settled onto her bed, laptop open, I wrap my arm around her, pulling her in close. "I need to tell you something, but I promise it doesn't mean you owe me anything. Words, thoughts, anything. Okay?"

I feel her tense beside me, but she gives a tentative, "Okay…"

"I love you." I tilt her chin so she can see me as I say it. "I'm in love with you, and I have been for a while now. You're my best friend, and I refuse to lose that because I love you." She looks like she's about to say something, so I cover her lips with the tips of my fingers. "You don't need to say it back." I shake my head. "You don't need to say anything at all. I just had to say it. Needed you to *know* it. Know that I'm not going anywhere, no matter what." I draw her closer to me. "That you're the first person I think of when I wake up and the last when I fall asleep. That no one has ever understood me the way you do, and I've never laughed so much. I love our Marvel movies together and how we can talk about our pasts and our hopes and dreams for the future. I love how defensive you get over your ice cream. I love that you're a planner and think to bring a swimsuit home on break, that you love the people in your life fiercely, and that you're stepping into who you are. It's beautiful. You're beautiful. And…I love you, Maisie. So. Damn. Much." I rub my thumb along her cheek, tracking her eyes as they bounce around my face, searching for answers, though I don't know what her questions are.

She's quiet, and I feel a pressure in my chest like I've gone too far. Then she sighs. "You're my best friend too, Connor. I do love you as my friend, and that's all I can give you right now." Her eyes slant to the bed beneath us.

It's a punch to the gut, but one I was prepared for. She is still working through all her hurt and trust issues. She doesn't even want to commit to a relationship, let alone process feelings of love. I've thought it through, and I wasn't expecting her to say it back.

"That's more than enough!" I rush to say. "I meant it, Maize. You don't owe me anything. I just had to be true to myself and tell you. It was too painful not to." I brush her hair back from her face and look into those gorgeous green eyes. I can't tell what she's thinking, but I can tell she's not going to say anything more, so I tuck her back under my arm and press *play* on the movie.

She falls asleep halfway through. I stay up for hours after.

57

Without Hesitation ...Right?

Maisie

C ONNOR LOVES ME. HE loves me. His words play over and over in my head. We wake to Angie bursting through the door, giggling over finding us tangled up in my tiny twin-size bed, then politely requesting Connor leave—read: tells him to get the fuck out—so she can, quote, *get naked in her own room*. He obliges.

Angie does, in fact, get naked and take a long shower, then puts on warm jammies to do some yoga. She says it is necessary after being trapped in the car for too many hours. Can't say I blame her. Chatting with her distracts me for an hour or so, but then she leaves to grab lunch, pajamas and all.

And now here I am—pacing, Connor's words washing through me again and again. *I love you. I'm in love with you, and I have been for a while now.* How long is a while?

He seemed to really mean that I didn't have to say it back and that he wouldn't let loving me ruin our friendship. Did I want to say it back?

Yes.

The answer comes to me without any hesitation when it exists in my own mind. It's the thought of letting it out into the world that terrifies me. That would make it real.

What if we get serious and he breaks my heart? What if I break his? What if he changes? We're only eighteen, for fuck's sake. What if he stops talking to me again? I would positively shatter. What if this is just another thing I fail at? My pulse picks up.

I'm ripped from my invasive thoughts by my phone buzzing on the desk. I walk over, my heart plummeting a little when I see it isn't Connor. He's only been gone a few hours, and I already miss him like crazy. But then I feel bad for having that reaction because it's Lauren calling, and I've missed her like crazy, too.

"LoLo! How's life across the pond?" She's still visiting her boyfriend's family in London.

She sighs. "Everyone's lovely, but I can't help feeling a little out of place. I miss home. I miss you."

"I've missed you, too. Christmas wasn't the same without you. Have you had any fun over there?"

She chuckles mirthlessly. "Oh, sure, of course. We've visited the natural history museum and rode the London Eye, and I've eaten my weight in fish and chips. And Jameson's family lives on an estate, so we've taken daily walks in the gardens. That always makes me feel like I'm in *Bridgerton*, taking a turn about the lawn." She says the last bit in an overly exaggerated English accent and laughs for real this time. I can sense the sadness shaking off her the more we talk.

I keep the ball rolling, content to talk about her woes over mine. "Sounds like a bit of an adventure even though I acknowledge it must be hard to be away, to feel out of place." I know Lauren better than I know myself, so I add, "I know Christmas is a hard time for you, too. Do you think that might be more of what's going on, rather than not enjoying London?"

There's a long pause, but then she says, "Yeah, I think you might be right. I always miss Dad more around the holidays. I think not being around my family this year was something I wasn't truly prepared for. I love Jameson, and he feels like home—but being out of my routine, the time change, missing you guys, it all feels like too much." She sniffs, and my heart breaks for her. I miss Uncle Richard so much, but I know it's something that affects her daily life, the marrow of her being.

"I think you should tell Jameson how you're feeling. He loves you, and I'm sure he'll do anything he can to make you feel better."

She chuffs a laugh. "When did you get so wise?"

I rub at my forehead. I certainly don't *feel* wise. Otherwise, wouldn't I know how to handle my own shit? It's so much easier helping Lauren with hers.

"Uh-oh, you went quiet on me. What's wrong?"

"We don't have to talk about it. You have enough on your plate."

"Nuh-uh, that's not how this works. We're always a two-way street. It's my honor and duty to be there for you. Now, spill."

My chest constricts at her words. I think of her the same way, but after all these years, it's still nice to hear it. Nice to know I'm loved. That she's never going anywhere. That she knows every part of me and loves me—not just because we're family, but because we've chosen to love each other.

I give her the breakdown of everything that's happened since Thanksgiving. How I felt like a failure when I couldn't get my back three and a half, how Connor and I hooked up when I went to him for comfort, how he defended me at Angie's party and everything we did after. How he told me he loves me, and that I don't have to say it back, but that I want to and that that thought *terrifies me.* Because so many things could go wrong, and I don't know how to deal with that.

"What if it goes right?"

Lauren's statement is a knife sliced through my chest, ripping me open for all to see.

"What?" I say incredulously.

"What. If. It. Goes. Right?" she enunciates clearly.

"There's no guarantee that it will!" I all but shout.

"No. But there are no guarantees in life. We don't know what cards life is going to deal us. I certainly never thought I'd lose Dad, but that was the hand I was dealt."

My stomach pitches at her blatant words. She's right. Nothing is guaranteed. Losing Uncle Richard at such a young age taught all of us that.

She continues, "We have to decide what to do with what we've got, though. The choices *we* make, what we *can* control. Not on what the outcome will be or what someone else will do because we have no say in that. But we do have control over ourselves, our decisions, how we view life. And that is powerful stuff, MaiMai."

I squeeze the phone, taking a deep breath.

"Plus, look at all the things that *have* gone right for you since getting to college. You're close with your roommate, you stood up for yourself with Karsen, and you *are* healing from that, even if it doesn't always feel like it. You've successfully competed in diving at a level you never thought possible. Even if it doesn't look exactly like how you would want, you're doing it! Plus, you're getting an education; no matter what your major is or what you decide to do after, no one and nothing can take that away from you."

Her words wash over me like the balm they are. Like stepping into a hot shower after being out in the cold. A whole-body soothing. "I love you so much, LoLo." Tears well in my eyes.

She's right. She's so right. And although her bolstered words haven't erased my fears, they have given me the gumption to take a step in their direction. I think about Angie's aunt's words: "You can be scared to do hard things. You just do them scared."

An idea comes like a thief in the night.

"I'm not ready to bare it all, and that is *my* choice that I'm okay with, but your encouragement has given me an idea. I can give at least a part of me. Connor deserves that, and honestly, so do I."

I can hear the smile in her voice as she says, "Go get 'em."

We talk for a few more minutes before saying a drawn-out goodbye with a promise she'll call as soon as she's back in the States.

Riding on the back of her encouragement, I grab my laptop and put "Sock Hop near me" into the search bar. Connor and I can go on a date. A real date. And I don't know what could be better for two old-soul goofballs who like to dance than a real-live sock hop.

I make another call, and she answers on the first ring.

"Mom? I need your help picking out an outfit."

"Oh, sweetie, thank you for calling! I would love to help. What kind of event?"

It feels nice to have something to connect with Mom on. We've slowly been healing since everything with Karsen. Even though I know we won't ever be totally on the same page. We're really different, but it's nice to know she still loves me even if I'm not with him. I know that sounds shitty, but I truly wasn't sure where we would stand. If we would have anything in common. So this is a perfect stepping-stone in the right direction for us.

I laugh. "A sock hop. Have you ever been?"

"I will pretend not to be offended. That was definitely before my time. But oh my goodness, sweetie, you are going to look so cute! Let's switch to FaceTime to see what you have so far. Then you will use your credit card and go shopping on us. Whatever you need!"

Her enthusiasm trickles through my nervous system like water down a rain chain and gathers into a basin of love that I'll use later. Love that helps bolster me to put myself out there. Love to share.

58

Let Them

Connor

"**G**AH! DON'T EAT THEM all!" Brock whines as Hunter grabs the last Antonio's breadstick. We ordered delivery to celebrate surviving our first practice back after break. Sure, we only took two weeks off and were expected to keep up with training during that time, but it still kicked our asses. So much so that I'm on the ground, foam rolling my literal ass.

Hunter and Brock are thumb wrestling for the last breadstick on the couch, and Tyler is sitting quietly on the leather chair in the corner, eating his pasta in peace. I'm so thankful to live with these meatheads. I've heard horror stories about freshman roommates, so the fact that we all get along the way we do—even if we fight over bread and give each other shit—means something. One day, we'll be far apart, doing god knows what. But for right now, we get to be together like this. I don't want to take it for granted.

"I'm thinking about quitting swimming," I blurt before I lose my nerve.

Tyler's fork drops onto his plate, then clatters to the ground. Brock and Hunter stop mid–thumb wrestle and stare at me.

"What?" they say in unison.

I rub my hand over the back of my neck. "I...I've been thinking about it and talking about it with my therapist, and...I don't know. I'm thinking about it."

Tyler speaks first. "We'll support whatever decision you make." A man of few words, but you better believe he makes sure the ones he says count.

I give a tentative half-smile. "Thanks, man."

"Why do you want to quit?" Hunter this time.

"I don't love it. I've been going through the motions for a long time. Plus, it's all tangled up in my shit feelings about my dad." I eye Brock and Tyler, who don't know anything about my dad, but they don't appear judgmental, just waiting to see what else I have to say. "I've had a lot more fun at the meets I've had to sit out. I love cheering you all on. But I gotta admit, I'm scared shitless about what me not swimming would do to our friend group. I don't wanna lose you guys."

Brock barks out a laugh. "Good one. You're stuck with us, big guy. Doesn't matter an inch whether you're in the water with us or not."

Tyler nods in agreement, and Hunter's eyes bore into mine with an intensity before saying, "We all want what's best for you, bro. Plus, I'm sure there would always be a place on the team if you changed your mind." Hunter, always the practical one.

"We'll miss your big-dick energy in our relays, but we'll survive." Brock cackles at his own joke, and even though he's so...him, you can't help but love the guy.

Hunter's voice breaks through the laughter. "What if you tried student coaching?"

My eyes widen, but before I process fully, Brock says, "Yeah! I mean, shit, that would mean you'd be the one telling me to get my ass moving. I might hate you at practice, but don't worry, I'll still love you out of the water." He hits me with an over-exaggerated wink.

"I think you'd be great at that," Tyler adds.

The idea snowballs in my head. "Huh. I think...I'd really like that. You think Coach would go for it?"

Hunter takes a moment to ponder it fully before saying, "I don't see why not. Worth a shot to ask him."

"Yeah, I will. Thanks, man."

"Sure." He shrugs like he didn't just give me life advice that could change the whole trajectory of my future.

My phone buzzes in my pocket, and when I see who it is, a goofy smile spreads across my face. It's been less than a day since I told Maize I love her, but I feel so much better. To have her know, to have those words out there instead of rattling around in my head. And she didn't run away. Didn't tell me to get lost. It hasn't ruined anything. Sure, she didn't say it back, and that stings a little, but I'll keep waiting and praying she comes around the more I prove my trustworthiness.

"What is *that* look for!" Brock berates my smiling face.

"Maize texted, that's all." All the guys know how I generally feel about her, but Hunter is the only one who knows I told her I loved her.

"I think it's nice," Tyler cuts in. "You deserve to be happy." Then he finishes the last bite of pasta, cleans his dish in the sink, and walks away without another word.

"You do deserve to be happy, man," Hunter reiterates.

Brock scoffs. "You all have fun with yourselves and your little girlfriends; I'm going to the bar. Anyone wanna join?"

"Sure, why not?" Hunter shrugs again. He's always such a calm and casual guy. Must be nice not to deal with inner turmoil over loving someone who's allergic to relationships. Plus, the whole my-dad-being-a-prick thing. Maybe I'd be more casual, too, if I grew up the way Hunter did.

I shake the thoughts from my head. Comparison is never good. I learned that from my mom early on.

When they leave and the front door closes, I pull my phone back out to check the message from Maize.

Love: Guess what

What?

Love: We're going to a sock hop!

Seriously?? That sounds amazing. When?

Love: Saturday.

Love: It's going to be our first real date

My heart flutters, picking up pace. She's doing it; she's trying. I'm so damn proud of her and elated for myself all the same.

Love: Let them ;)

Love: Me either :)

59

Your Gravity

Maisie

"YOU LOOK ADORABLE!" ANGIE squeals, her blonde curls bouncing as she jumps and claps enthusiastically.

I found a black-and-white polka-dot poodle skirt at our local thrift store. It felt like kismet. Luckily, Angie had a similar headband to accessorize with. I had a white tank top blouse that passed well enough, and my mom paid for some bobby socks and black and white saddle shoes online. She even paid extra to have them express shipped to make it on time.

"Final touch time! Purse your lips," Angie says through her own pursed lips that I'm to mimic. I laugh but do as she says. Once she's masterfully swiped the red lipstick on and presented me with a tissue to blot, I turn to look at myself in the full-length mirror hanging on the back of the door.

A blush creeps up my cheeks. I look a little ridiculous, like I'm playing dress-up, but I also feel pretty all done up for a date. I know Connor will think it's cute simply because of his "old-person" energy.

As if his ears were burning, a knock sounds at the door. He's here to pick me up like we planned.

When I swing open the door, my jaw nearly drops to the floor. He looks like he just stepped out of the movie *Grease*. He's in nearly black jeans, a perfectly fitted white T-shirt, and a black leather jacket. There's clearly some gel in his hair, and he even has a pair of sunglasses draped along the front of his shirt. I didn't know I had a thing for this look, but he's so handsome.

Maybe it's not the look—maybe it's all him.

"Wow, you look...wow," he says, stepping through the door and closing it behind him, never taking his eyes off me. His pointed perusal is a brand across my skin in all the places it's exposed, but especially where it's not.

My fingers twitch with nervous energy. We're really doing this. Our first date. It's real. While we haven't made any promises to one another, this is a huge step. Particularly for me.

"You don't look so bad yourself," I answer and toe the rounded tip of my shoe into the ground, rocking it side to side, hands clasped behind my back.

"Should we get going?" he asks casually.

"Yes! Let me grab my bag." I race over to my bed to grab the red jeweled clutch I also found at the thrift store. Like I said, kismet. "Okay, ready!" I hold it up triumphantly.

Angie, propped up against her bed, grins from ear to ear. "You two have fun now, ya hear? Don't do anything I wouldn't do!" She waves like a mother seeing her baby off on her first date.

I snort. There isn't much she wouldn't do, so the sentiment is a bit moot.

The GPS tells us we've arrived as we pull up to a series of slightly run-down, white-drenched buildings set back on a grassy lawn. The pebbled driveway that led us here loops in a circle around each structure, but there is a small parking lot off to the left, which I guess is where we're meant to park. Tall trees surround the property on all sides, with iron benches sprinkled along the walkways, yard, and so on. The sign out front of the main building reads "Meadowview Manor" in gaudy, loopy script. Underneath, it features "Caring for you like family."

When I searched for a sock hop, I didn't pay much attention to where it was, just that it existed. Apparently, I should have, though, because we're at a retirement home. Our first date is at a retirement home.

My shoulders fall, embarrassment seeping into my veins like an unwanted drug. I'm about to tell Connor we can just go back to the dorm when he bursts out laughing, shoulders shaking.

"Only us," he says and swiftly exits his side of the car. I'm left dumbfounded as he makes his way around to my side. He extends a hand as he opens my car door. "My Queen?"

A laugh spills out of me, too. "I could get used to this queen treatment," I say with a wink.

"That's the goal," he replies, dead serious.

I gulp. I was joking, but he means it. And I know he does because he *has* treated me like a queen, even in our friendship. Could it be possible he would keep that up if we started dating? No, right? It would stop once we were officially an item. Like all relationships. A small voice in my head says, *Maybe it doesn't have to. Maybe this is what real love looks like.*

Connor waits patiently through my inner turmoil, still holding his hand out gallantly for me. I take it, and electricity filters down my arm at his touch.

When he hauls me and my big skirt from the car, he wraps an arm around my waist and closes my door for me. He leans into my space and whispers in my ear, "We're going to have a great time because you're here. Wherever you are is where I want to be. Whether in the pool, getting ice cream, stuck in a hotel, or at a freaking nursing home, it doesn't matter. You're everything, Maize. I'm just thankful to be pulled into your gravity." He kisses my cheek, and the innocent touch still sends heat throughout my entire body. "Now, let's go dance." He takes my hand and pulls me toward the main building.

And I know the lingering warmth isn't from the temperature outside.

60

Punch and Cookies to Follow

Connor

WE CHECK IN AT the main building, getting a curious look from the guard there. He tells us the sock hop is for residents only, and I fib and say we promised to meet my grandpa here. Grandpa used to tell me all sorts of stories about him wooing Grandma, so I know he would have been okay with the white lie if it meant I got to dance with my girl. *My girl.* I know she isn't technically, but she sure as hell feels like it. Plus, we're here, on a real date. That has to mean something.

I've still got Maize's hand gathered in mine, and it feels so right. She looks up at me with shining emerald eyes. This wasn't what she thought she was getting us into tonight, but I could truly care less. She's beautiful, she's here, and we're going to have the best time no matter what.

When we get to the designated room, there is a sign on the door that says, "Sock Hop 6:30," and underneath, "Punch and Cookies to follow." It's 6:45. We're a little late, mostly from having to check into the facility. I open the door and gesture for Maize to precede me. I was raised a gentleman, after all.

When I follow her in, my face falls. There is a total of three people here: one sitting in a wheelchair—who appears to be asleep—and one couple dancing. Or mildly swaying might be a better description. A few streamers hang from the ceiling and a record player scratches through "Rock Around the Clock." Even for a retirement home, I was expecting a little more than this. I look to Maisie with scrunched brows, but she's covering a laugh with her hand.

"What are you kids doing here?" Our attention is drawn to the man of the couple dancing.

"We came for the sock hop!" Maisie shouts. It echoes in the small room.

"I'm sorry, my hearing aid was turned down." The man tinkers at his ear. "Can you repeat that?"

Maisie takes a few steps toward the man, dragging me by the hand behind her. "I said, we're here for the sock hop." This time, she enunciates each word in a tone he can hopefully hear better. I'm sure the wobbly music isn't helping the matter.

"Oh! Well, isn't that nice. Couple of youngin's wantin' a groove. Do you have a favorite? I'd be happy to play it. I've got all the records. Never sold a one of them. Came in handy since getting her, though, see? I'm Dick, and this here's Doris." He points to his female companion.

Maisie looks to me, and I search her eyes for signs of distress, but she seems...relaxed. "Pick a song," she whispers. "This is in your wheelhouse, not mine."

I drag a hand down my face and let out a coarse laugh, but I suppose we're all in now. "How about 'The Twist'?"

"Oh, my hip can't move like that no more, but I'm happy to watch you two have a crack at it. Doris! 'The Twist'!"

Doris shuffles over to the record player, next to which I notice a little crate set up on a simple table. She slowly filters through several records in the crate before pulling out what I assume to be "The Twist" in triumph. She switches out the record and lets the needle drop.

The familiar sounds of Chubby Checker fill the small space. This was one of Grandpa's favorites. He said this was one he and Grandma liked to dance to when they would go out together, so it only felt fitting to share it with Maisie in this weird, albeit fun situation we've found ourselves in.

I take her hands and start to twist my hips to the rhythm of the song. A belly laugh barrels out of her, and it's music to my ears. She follows suit, twisting her own hips. I spin her around, and I think it catches her off guard because she nearly loses her balance, although maybe it's her new shoes. She's usually so graceful, but here, right now, I can tell she doesn't care how her body is moving; she's just letting it flow, and I'm not sure she's ever been more beautiful.

We finish out the dance, and Dick and Doris clap voraciously for us. The record starts the song over, but Maisie curtsies and says, "Thank you so much for having us, but I think I should get some fries and a milkshake in this one." She points at me while making a funny face. "Don't you guys think?"

The man sleeping in his wheelchair grunts awake and seethes, "Who are these people?" He's clearly agitated, and I don't want to provoke his wrath.

"You don't want to stay for more?" Dick says disappointedly.

"We know you're the superior dancers." I go for charm. "We had our fun, but she's right, I'm starving." I rub my belly to punctuate the point.

The crotchety one chimes in, "Yeah, go on, get!"

"Jim, stop being so rude to our guests. They're good folk," Doris berates him, and he has the good sense to look sheepish.

"Well, stop by anytime!" Dick says with a wave. "Always nice to have young folk to talk to or dance with. Whatever you prefer." He nods his head, and a pang thrums through my sternum.

Grandpa was my favorite person to talk to. Maybe if I quit swimming, I would have time to stop by and talk with some of the residents here on occasion. I can't imagine how hard it must be to have moved from the home you owned into a place designed specifically for those who need extra care due to age. It must be really difficult. Although it was hard to lose Grandpa so suddenly, I'm thankful he went out on his own terms, while he still had his autonomy. Although I think he would have been close friends with Dick had he made it to a home.

"I certainly will, Dick. Thanks for the tunes. Those records really did come in handy."

He beams, and I lead Maisie from the room and close the door behind us. I can barely hear the music on the other side. Now that we're safely in the hall, we both burst out laughing.

"I can't believe that was the sock hop I found online," she says. "How did they even know to advertise it?"

"Must have been the activities coordinator or something. Definitely wasn't Dick, Doris, or Jim in there." I hook a thumb over my shoulder toward the door.

"I was serious about the fries and milkshake," she says.

"Oh, I figured." I bring our intertwined hands to my mouth and drop a kiss on the top of her hand. "My Queen likes her ice cream in many forms. And fried snacks are the perfect accompaniment. Maybe they'll even have root beer floats. That would be the perfect Maisie trifecta." I let go of her hand, but only so I can wrap an arm around her waist as I lead us back through the building toward my car.

"It really would," she sighs. "It really would."

We "split" a root beer float and some fries at a cute soda shoppe near the retirement home. I hold her hand the whole time, and we laugh about anything and everything.

When we get back to her dorm room, it's dark. Maize turns on the light to find a handwritten note from Angie saying she'll be gone for the night.

"She's such a weirdo sometimes." Maisie laughs. "She could have just texted that, but she says sometimes things are better handwritten."

I laugh, but there's a ringing in my ears. I wasn't expecting Angie to be gone. I don't know if I can hook up with Maize again tonight. Now that I've had a taste of her trusting me with her heart, it all feels a bit too painful.

"Are you staying tonight?" she asks, looping her arms around my shoulders and pulling me in for a kiss.

I kiss her back and squeeze her hips. This is agony, but I say, "I had *the* best time with you tonight, Maize. And I want to stay more than you know, but I think I'm going to head back to my place tonight."

She frowns. "Why?"

I rack my brain for the right words, but I come up empty. "You gave me a piece of your heart tonight, and I'm beyond grateful."

I dip my head so we're eye to eye, but her gaze bounces around, not wanting to meet my eyes. I sigh. She might bolt after this, but I have to keep being honest with her. She deserves it, and so do I.

"And I know we've already hooked up and spent the night together, but I think I need to leave tonight what it is. You and me. Our first real date. I know I don't have all of your heart, and I really promise that's okay. I'll wait forever for you, Maize, but it's hard for me to live in this middle ground. For tonight, I need the little bit of separation between matters of the heart and what we do physically. And please don't mistake it; I *love* what we do physically. Any other day, I promise we can make that happen."

I move to wrap her in a hug. She doesn't pull away, but she's practically a rag doll in my arms. Her arms hang loosely at her sides. Maybe I fucked up.

After a moment, she stiffens, her shoulders scrunching, and then she wraps her arms aggressively around my waist, holding me in one of the tightest hugs I've ever received.

"Okay," she says and takes a step back. "I guess I can respect that. I don't really understand it, and I can't lie and say it doesn't hurt my feelings, but I'm glad you told me. I don't want there to be any secrets between us. You're still my best friend."

Friend. I want to be so much more. I honestly always have, but she doesn't know that, and I know for sure she isn't ready to hear it.

So, I say, "You're mine too." I give her one more chaste peck on the lips and head for the door.

Before I leave, she quietly calls out, "Connor?"

"Yeah?"

"I had a really great time with you tonight."

"Me too, Betty, me too. I hope you have a good sleep."

"You too. Good night, Connor."

"Night, Maisie."

As I close the door behind me, I'm left feeling two things: pride for being true to my wants and needs and agony for leaving her alone like this. Two things can be true simultaneously.

I head out of the dorm building into the starry night and walk until I'm too tired to feel anything at all.

61

Failed Exams & Lollipops

Maisie

When Angie returned to our room on Sunday, she was pumped to hear how everything went. While it was fun to tell her about our absolutely outlandish date, I also told her that her leaving was a moot point.

"Why are you holding back?" she'd asked. "You obviously love him. He's only guarding himself because he doesn't want to get hurt either."

"I know. There's still this little fence around a part of my heart. She's holding on for dear life even though a hurricane is raging around her." I'd flopped back on my bed in frustration.

"Is the hurricane you loving Connor?"

"Yes! Keep up, Ang."

"Sorry, sorry. I'd like to remind you that Connor is nothing like Karsen. He has put you first almost every step of the way. Karsen stole little pieces of you over time. With Connor, you're more yourself every day. We don't know what the future has in store, but I think you're hurting yourself and him by prolonging this."

I knew she was right, but I hadn't been in the state of mind to talk about it any further, still raw from the feeling of rejection, even though my brain knew logically that Connor wasn't rejecting me. A girl still had emotions.

So instead of berating, Angie gave me a big hug, said she was sorry, then took me to our favorite ice cream shop, *All Licked Up*. It did a solid job of cheering me up. For a little while, at least.

Now it's 9 AM Monday morning, and I'm staring at my organic chemistry test that the professor just handed back. At the top is a big old "F" for failure. I failed my first organic chemistry exam. As if I weren't already feeling like I'm not good enough, life has to take one more kick. I scrub a hand down my face and thank god I had the good sense not to wear any makeup today.

Tears puddle in the corners of my eyes, but I can't let them fall. Not in front of all these people. I wipe at them and sniff, accidentally catching the attention of the girl beside me. Her brows pinch in judgment. I don't mean to, but I look over at her test. A bright, shiny "A" is stamped at the top. Great. Maybe I'm the only one who failed. While I don't even like this class, I can't be failing things.

Class progresses, and I find myself wishing I could learn through osmosis—that just by being in class, it would stick—but, alas, I barely understand half of what is discussed. Or, rather, I don't care to.

When I pass the professor's desk on my way out of class, he stops me. He discreetly waits as other students pass, but then in a lowered voice says, "Would you mind stopping by my office for a little? Assuming you don't have a class next hour, that is."

My shoulders tense. I hate feeling like I've done something wrong. I'm sure he only wants to talk about my test and make sure I'm doing okay, but still. I'd rather do anything else. Regardless, I nod my assent, and the two of us walk side by side until we reach his office a few doors down the hall.

I settle into a tweed wingback, its twin sitting empty next to me. His office is filled with Marvel Funko Pops and models of various chemical chains. At least we have one thing in common.

"Am I in trouble?" I ask as he situates himself in his own chair behind the desk across from me.

"Of course not," he states matter-of-factly. "I simply wanted to check in and see how you were doing with your other studies. How has the college experience been for you so far? Advising is one of my favorite parts of the job, and while I know I'm not *your* advisor, I have some say about how you should proceed with my class." He reaches into his desk, drawing out a bowl and offering it to me. "Lollipop?"

I shake my head. "No, thank you."

"Suit yourself." He shrugs and leans back, unwrapping one for himself. "So? How are your other studies going?"

"Fine, I suppose. I have calculus, which is going well because I've always been strong in math. History of art, which isn't particularly interesting to me, but isn't overly difficult as far as I can tell. Spanish too. This is the only course I'm struggling in." I roll my eyes, and he chuckles around his lollipop.

"A lot of students struggle in organic chemistry. It is not for the faint of heart. Those who endure either love it or have a strong enough reason to suffer through it, but I don't sense you fall into either of those categories. Am I wrong?"

I huff in annoyance. "It's a prerequisite for occupational therapy school." I say it like he's dumb, but then reel it back. He's only trying to help. Apparently, my fight or flight response chose fight today.

He leans forward, loosely interlocked hands perched on his desk. "And is that what you want to do? Be an occupational therapist?" He raises an appraising eyebrow.

"Yes," I rush out. "Maybe? I'm not really sure."

"It's okay not to know what you want to do. That's what college is for." His eyes soften, crinkling at the corners. He runs a hand through his lightly salted hair. He's definitely on the younger side for a tenured professor, and I should be grateful he cares as much as he does.

"But all the classes I'm taking are geared toward getting into OT school. Wouldn't that be a lot of wasted effort if I changed my mind?" I ask, worrying my bottom lip between my teeth at the prospect. Flutters take root in my chest—not the good kind.

"Hey," he soothes, "you're barely into your second semester of college. Nothing is wasted. At worst, you took a few classes you didn't like. That's good. Finding out what you don't like is just as important as discovering what you do. Now, do you like my class? Do you like any of your other pre-OT classes?"

No. The word is like a foghorn in my head, glaringly obvious, but the actual response feels more complicated. "I struggled in chemistry last semester, too, and I wasn't fond of biology. But it's not like that's what I'll be using when I get to OT school, right?"

"Unfortunately, there will be more classes that align with these concepts. They build. That's why they are pre-reqs. Not that they won't be different, but it might not be the right path for you if you feel disconnected from the coursework now."

A rock sinks in my stomach like an anchor from a ship. This is all too much. My head spins, and I close my eyes against the feeling.

"Are you all right?" he says. I hear the chair squeak and footsteps approaching.

"I'm fine, lightheaded for a minute. It'll pass." I do some of my breathing exercises.

"Well, this all might be a bit too much for today. And that's all right. In the meantime, I want you to think about dropping my class. There's still time, and there is a social psychology class you could pick up instead. It would still be a prerequisite for occupational therapy if you're worried about staying on track with that." He hovers over my chair, nose scrunched in worry.

With everything else on my plate—diving, Connor, my other classes—a psychology class sounds like a breath of fresh air. I could always take organic chemistry another semester, right? Maybe I just need more time to adjust.

"Okay. I can do that. Can you email me a link to the switch form?"

He releases a breath. "I'd be happy to. And I'll reach out to Professor Larpe to give her a heads-up, too."

"Thanks, that's really kind of you," I say.

"All part of the job," he replies.

"If you don't mind, I'll take that lollipop now."

He chuckles and retreats behind his desk so he can offer me the bowl once again.

I unwrap my selection as I stand. Popping it into my mouth, I bid the professor and organic chemistry farewell. In the hall, I realize it's like a weight has been lifted off my chest, and damn, does it feel good. Maybe life isn't dishing out only kicks after all. That is, until I feel an ache in my stomach and pelvis and a gush enters my underwear. The tell-tale sign of my period. Great.

62

Athletes & Heating Pads

Connor

"**C**ONNOR! WHAT CAN I do for you this fine day?" Coach Ken says as I make my way into his poolside office. "You'll be up and running at full capacity soon as can be, just you wait. You'll tear through this conference like it's a stack of paper and you're scissors, you'll see."

I gulp. This was not the best start for what I'm here to talk to him about. Coach Ken was a 1976 Olympic hopeful, but he lost out on his chance to swim because of a skiing accident. I'm in the prime of my life and willingly giving it up. I don't know if he will take too kindly to that.

"Uh, yeah, so, well, the thing is…"

"Spit it out, son."

"Yeah, so I'm here to talk to you about the potential to switch to…student coaching."

His eyes double in size, but he schools his features rather quickly for how big a shock this must be to him. "I'm going to need a good reason, but I'm not saying it's off the table. I have to know: why not swim? You'll be captain by your sophomore year. You'll lead this team. I'd be pretty sore to lose you as a competitor."

My times, my leadership, always winning. He isn't saying anything wrong, but it still feels like a punch to the gut. That's all my dad cares about. I know that isn't where my worth is. I'm slowly learning that in therapy, but this is like jumping into the deep end of wading through that trigger.

"I don't love it, Coach. I haven't for some time." I toe my shoe on the ground, but then stop to meet his eyes. I want him to know how much this means to me. "There's a lot of emotions tied up in swimming for me that I'd rather not get into at the moment, but I will if you need to hear it."

He looks at me with soft eyes. "That's all right, son. While I do care about my swimmers' personal lives—because an athlete is a whole person—you don't owe me anything you're not comfortable sharing." He gestures for me to continue.

Wow, Coach is better than I imagined. I thought he'd barrel into me like he does when we're in the water. But he seems to really care. It makes me even more excited to work alongside him. If he'll have me, that is.

"I still love the sport. I want to be involved with the team. They're like family, even though we're only in our first season together. You said it yourself; I have leadership skills. Let me use them in this capacity. I'll help however you need, Coach. I'm only looking for a chance."

He rubs at the scruff on his face and sighs deeply. "All right. We'll do a thirty-day trial run, and then we'll schedule a formal meeting to check in. Sound good?"

"Sounds great!" I say. I can't believe that worked.

"You can start after the Vimer Invitational next week. You know that means you won't get one last chance to compete before it's over, right?"

A prickling sensation shoots up my spine and into my ears. It is emotional, but I also know this is the right decision. I'm ready. I wouldn't have come to Coach like this if I weren't.

"I know, Coach. Thank you."

"All right, don't get too mushy on me now."

"I won't," I say with a laugh.

When I'm nearly out the door, he adds, "It's important to follow your heart, kid. And seems like that's what yer doin'. I can't fault ya that."

"I appreciate it." I tip my head, and then I'm gone.

When I leave the familiar fog of chlorine and exit the natatorium, I'm met with sunshine. I take a deep breath, letting the nerves that settled in before this meeting fully wash away. I'm making strides to take control of my life, and it feels damn good.

I want to tell Maize, but I hesitate for a second. I'm still not sure how she feels about me after how we left things Saturday. We've texted, but it's been casual.

I won't know unless I try, though, so I pick up the phone to call her. It rings and rings until I get her voicemail. Huh. She isn't in class right now. Wonder what she could be up to. I hope nothing happened.

Probably best if I stop by her room, just in case.

Angie answers the door with a smile on her face. "Your man's here!" she shouts back into the room before scooching past me. "I'll leave you in his capable hands." She eyes me briefly. "And see you after class!"

I hear a low rumble from inside the room, but nothing cohesive. At least Maize is here. I worked myself up for nothing.

As I step in, Angie closes the door behind me. Maize is lying in her bed, curled up like a fetus. She looks pale.

"Are you sick?" I quickly close the space until I'm standing over her, my eyes scanning for signs of harm.

She cracks an eye open, then shuts it. "Hi," she says. "I got my period, and for some reason, it's a really bad one. I've been here since this morning. It'll pass soon, though; it's fine."

I look around like I can fight the offending entity that's causing her body pain, but I know that's illogical. "What can I get you?" I ask as softly as I can, brushing her hair back from her face. "Tell me how to help."

She blinks up at me, but quickly shuts her eyes hard. Her forehead scrunches. Her voice is pained as she says, "Uh, you could grab my heating pad for me. It's in a box in the closet."

"On it." I stalk to her closet and rummage carefully until I find a blue heating pad with a white cord. I plug it into the nearest outlet by her bed and gently place it in her awaiting hands. She shifts to adjust it correctly, and some of the tension from her shoulders falls. Mine do the same. I don't like feeling helpless when the woman I love is in pain. I'll have to make note of her cycle. Get ahead of it next time. Lavish her with snacks and back rubs and whatever else she could need. Maybe she needs two heating pads.

I'm ripped from my thoughts when she says, "I'm happy you're here. I've missed you."

"I've missed you, too, love." It rolls off my tongue before I can take it back. It's the name I saved in my phone the night I told her I loved her, but I haven't dared to say it out loud.

She isn't alarmed, though. Instead, she tugs at my hand. "Will you cuddle me? The pressure helps."

I toe off my shoes and climb into her bed without a second thought, careful not to jostle her too much. I wrap my arm gingerly around her, putting pressure where she directs me. She lets out a contented sigh. I think we're going to be just fine.

63

Show 'Em What You Got

Maisie

I**T'S BEEN A FEW** days since Connor stayed with me during the worst of my period. I didn't know a man could act like that. My dad always pretended periods didn't exist, and Karsen was actively disgusted by it. He also never respected the level of pain that could accompany it. I can't even tell you how many times I asked him not to slap my ass when I had my period, but that didn't lead to any sort of change in behavior.

Connor was sweet, helpful, and attentive. He even snuck out once Angie was back to go get me ice cream. He promised next time he'd have it ready, along with anything else I needed. That I wasn't alone in this. He...really loves me. He shows me all the time. And I love him, too, so I don't know why I can't make myself say it. Maybe because I still don't know why he stopped talking to me for those few weeks? There's something holding me back—whether it's my own shit or his, I can't say. But I guess all there is to do is keep moving forward, see what happens.

I'm walking to class when I have the **urge** to call my dad. I haven't talked to him since winter break. I started my social psychology class yesterday, and I really loved it. I know I need to tell him, but the thought of it makes my stomach flip, which means I need to get it over with.

He picks up on the second ring. "Hi, Bean. Thanks for calling."

"Hi, Dad. How're you and Mom?"

"Oh, we're doing swimmingly." He chuckles. "To what do I owe the pleasure of you calling? Everything going okay with school? Diving?"

His two favorite subjects. At least I actually planned to talk about one of them this time. "Both are good, but I wanted to tell you something."

The silence I'm met with does nothing to soothe my nerves. I snatch my cuticle between my teeth. "I failed my first test, so after talking to the professor, I've dropped organic chemistry, but the good news is I already picked up social psychology, which is also an OT pre-req. And I could always take organic chemistry another semester." The words rush out, and I quickly drag in a breath afterward.

One of my fingers starts to bleed. I wipe it on my leggings as I await his reply.

"That sounds like a solid plan, Bean."

"It *does*?"

"Of course. It sounds like you weighed your options and chose the best path forward for what you're dealing with right now. I don't love to hear you failed, and I'm sure if you had stayed in the course, you could have turned it around—but I think all things considered, you made a good choice. You'll keep your GPA up this way."

"Oh. Yeah. My GPA. Thanks, Dad."

My stomach sours. I thought for a second he was encouraging me that it's okay to want to do something else, but he thinks it's all just a calculated move.

"Did I say something wrong?" He must have noticed the shift in my tone.

"No." *Yes.*

"You can talk to me, Bean. I'm your father."

"I just...I don't know if I want to be an occupational therapist."

"Why not?"

"Well, for starters, I haven't liked any of the classes that are required to get into OT school."

"I see."

"And I want to explore other career paths. Not be boxed into one." Wow. I hadn't even fully formed these thoughts, but they are all spilling out of me.

"What careers?" he asks pragmatically.

"I don't know...and I want to be okay with that."

I wait for the lecture, but instead, he says, "Did I ever tell you Grandpa Thatcher was a long-haul truck driver?"

My mind feels like a record scratch. "What? No."

I never knew Grandpa Thatcher. He was gone before I was born, and Dad rarely talks about him.

"Well, he was. He was gone all the time. He told me to get a job after high school. Didn't support my desire to go to college."

"I'm sorry, Dad. That sounds really hard."

"It was. And everything I have, I had to work for. Hard. Despite what he told me. I scraped for the money to pay my way to college. It was a privilege I fought tooth and nail for." He quiets for a moment, and I picture him running a hand through his hair like he always does when he's passionate about something. "Some of that grit seems to have passed on to you. I see it in the way you fight for grades, dives, everything. I fostered it in you because my dad didn't push me. I do it because I care, but I don't want to push you away. Ever. You're my little girl, and I love you. Understand?"

Tears well in my eyes. He's never told me this, and I can't help but think some things would have been different if he had. He can't begin to understand what his words mean to me. Like a breath of fresh air to scorched lungs.

"I'm thankful for the ways you've pushed me. Truly. I just...also needed to hear you'll love me no matter what. Even if I fail."

"Nothing could stop my love for you, Bean. You're my whole world."

His words wash over me, and I feel tall. Strong. Like I can conquer anything.

"I love you, Dad. So much."

"I love you, Bean. Your invitational is this weekend, isn't it? I thought about flying out, but I didn't want another situation like last time."

"Oh. Yeah. It's okay, Dad. You already apologized for that. You and Mom are welcome any time. Just maybe stick to cheering instead of critiquing?"

"I can do that. I think." He laughs. "Might take a few tries to break the habit, so bear with me." I laugh too. He wouldn't be my dad otherwise. "But hey, kick some serious butt at that invitational, kid. Show 'em what you got."

"I will, Dad. Thanks again. Give Mom a hug from me, too. I'm just walking into class, but I'll talk to you soon. I love you. Bye."

Bolstered by his words, I decide that after this class, I'll head to the gym. I've been putting in the work, and I think it's about time I try my back three and a half in a competition again. I *can* do it. D1 diving *is* for me. That grit my dad passed down is going to go to good use.

As I walk into class, I visualize myself on the ten-meter. And I like what I see.

64

Athletes Everywhere

Maisie

*B*REATHE, I REMIND MYSELF as I work through my stretches on the pool deck. *Inhale, 1, 2, 3, 4. Hold. Release.* I smile at the memory of Connor teaching me that breathing method. While it certainly wasn't fun having a panic attack, it was the first time someone knew how to help without me having to tell them. He's so intuitive.

I focus. Today's the Vimer Invitational, and the pool deck is shrouded in athletes. I tuck my headphones a little tighter and keep working through my warm-up routine. Lola is nearby in her own world, Dublin and Finn are already warming up on the springboard, Jamey is over by the locker room chatting with one of his old high school teammates, and Janique is on the trampoline.

Nerves skitter down my spine. *Breathe.* I scan the stands out of habit. True to my dad's word, my parents aren't here today, but where is Connor? We met up briefly this morning. He brought me tea and a scone, but he only handed them over on the promise that I would eat some protein too. He said he'd been looking into women's health and that apparently protein-rich breakfasts are important. He'd given me a kiss for good luck, and I felt like a balloon about to blow away after.

But now he's not here. Maybe he went to the concession stand? I can't worry about that now. I need to stay focused. I visualize my success, running through each dive on my list in my head. I picture sharp lines and clean entries. I picture *victory*. I haven't let myself even hope to win since starting here. I thought I wasn't meant for diving at this level, but now I'm determined to prove myself wrong. And even if today doesn't go my way, another day will. I won't give up.

Making my way through the throng of people warming up, chatting, or sitting—some not competing until hours from now—I cautiously sidle up to Coach Megan. "Coach, I need to talk to you."

She slowly lifts her gaze. "What is it, Thatcher?"

"Add the back three and a half to my list today...please," I tack on.

Her eyebrows pinch together and her nostrils flare. "You haven't practiced that dive, and the last time you did, it didn't go well."

"I know I can do it. I've been working hard in the gym, visualizing, everything other than physically performing it at practice. I've even been throwing some lead-ups when you weren't looking." That gets her attention, but she lets me continue. "Let me throw it in warm-ups, you'll see. I've got this, I promise." Confidence feels good.

"It's ultimately your decision, but I want it on record that I'm advising against it." She marks something with a pen on her clipboard. I think she's writing in my new dive. I smile. She frowns. "Next time, a little more warning than the day of would be nice." She scoffs.

"Aye aye, Coach!" I salute. "You can count on me. I'm here for the long haul, and I'm ready to prove myself."

She eyes me warily, but then relaxes her face into a clipped smile. "Well, I do love your spunk. Could have used that at the start of the season, but I know it's a difficult task adjusting to college. Glad to hear you're on board. Now go warm up." She walks away without another word.

I wade through the sea of bodies toward the platform ladder. Time to do this.

Warm-ups went…okay. I didn't enter perfectly on any of my back three and a half attempts, but I'm not going to let that stop me. It doesn't have to be perfect; it simply needs to exist.

I scan the crowd again. Still no Connor. Flutters pick up in my chest. Is he okay? Should I go look for him?

Brock passes by, and I grab him by the arm, taking him off course. He slips on the slick deck but rights himself quickly.

"Maisie, what's up? Everything okay? Is Angie all right?"

I quirk a brow. "Have you seen Connor? Every time I look in the stands, he isn't there. I'm kind of worried. I'd go look for him, but my ten-meter competition is about to start."

Brock squeezes my forearm in a friendly, comforting gesture. "I'm sure he's fine. I just saw him in the locker room not that long ago." He points behind him. "He's probably going for a walk or something. You know how long you can be sitting at these things. I know he's planning to be here once you start."

He ducks so we're at eye level. He's being really nice. Not that he's ever been anything else to me, but with the whole Angie thing…you never really know.

I let my head fall back and rub at my eyes. "You're right." I shake my limbs. "He's fine. Everything's fine. I need to focus. Thanks for the pep talk, Brock."

His smile stretches in the most boyish way. "Anytime! Glad I could help."

He beams with pride. It brings a smile to my face, and I head back toward the tower. This time, when my eyes wander toward the stands, they land on the face I want to see most. He's here. Relief floods my veins, and now I feel ready. His steady presence gives me the final push of confidence I need before the competition starts. I blow him a kiss like I did at my first meet. This time, when he catches it, he presses it to his lips and sends one back. I think I could get used to this.

All of my dives have been solid. Not all rips, but solid. I'm hovering in fifth place, which, for how many schools are here to compete today, is a decent showing. I take a quick peek at the crowd. Connor's no longer there. My stomach churns. Where could he be? But I can't think about him right now. I inhale the familiar chlorine air and relax my shoulders. Maybe his mom or brothers called. Maybe he had to go to the bathroom. I'll go find him after. It'll all be fine.

I climb the tower. My legs are jelly, but my heart is strong. Although I appreciate Connor's presence, I don't need it to make this happen. I can do this. I'm meant to be here. I believe in myself.

Before I know it, I'm at the top. Ten meters. Thirty-three and a half feet above the water. Sometimes I think I must be crazy for throwing my body off this thing, but I love it. I can't imagine anything else.

I walk to the end of the platform, toss my shammy, and turn to get into position. We go on three, I remind myself. No matter what happens, I am worthy. No matter what happens, I accomplished something today. I take a final steadying breath, and the natatorium seems to quiet, the world homing in on this moment, holding its breath.

Taking a final deep breath, I close my eyes for a solitary moment. When they flash open, determination strikes like a lightning bolt, and I launch. I'm spinning faster than normal, but I keep my focus. I've got this. When it's time, my legs and arms shoot out with the strength of a torpedo, stopping my rotation at the perfect angle, and I glide through the water like butter. I did it! I fucking did it!

I take a moment at the base of the pool to revel in it, heart pounding. And when I push off the pool floor, I'm smiling as I rise. When I surface, my whole team and even some other teams are cheering for me. I look at the scoreboard. 9. 8. 8.5. 9. 7.

Whoever judged that seven must have had a stick up their butt, but I'm too elated to care. Those scores are amazing. I freaking did it!

Lola meets me at the steps and goes in for a hug, but retreats at the last second. "That was amazing," she says.

I pull her into a hug, and although it takes her a moment, she melts into it. I'm glad to have such supportive teammates, and I really need to make good on our rain check to get dinner. She's awesome.

I release her, but then we're both caught up in Dublin's arms. "You did it!" he shouts. We're a ball of limbs and water, but I'm too happy to care. Then I remember Connor.

I'm about to go search for him when the announcer states, "Maisie Thatcher, National Championship Qualifier."

"Hell yeah!" Dublin chimes in and barrels into Lola and me again. Janique, Jamey, and Finn have made their way over, too. Our little team may be small, but we're mighty. I'm excited that this is who I get to spend the rest of my college career with.

Career. It used to taste like a bad word, but it's true. I've been working toward this my whole life. I've built a résumé of camps, dives, coaches, failures, and successes. And now I get to live it on a bigger stage. That's something to celebrate.

After about ten minutes—and a serious course in self-restraint on my part not to leave immediately—they host the award ceremony. I don't get to stand on the podium, but I place fourth. Fourth and a ticket to Nationals. That's what you can accomplish when you don't let fear and self-doubt win.

But I am still an anxious girly, so the moment awards are over, I sling on my sweats and rush to find Connor. There's something I need to tell him.

65

Quitter

Connor

DAD CALLED AGAIN THIS morning right before I got to Maisie's room with her breakfast treat. I was worried she'd sense my tension, but she answered the door and instantly wrapped me in a hug, melting all my stress away with that one gesture. It seems more and more like she's warming to the idea of being together.

I couldn't wait to support her today, and after this invitational, I get to support the team in my new capacity as student coach. Only my roommates and Maisie—and I'm assuming Angie—know. We're announcing it to everyone at practice on Monday. It feels like the new start I need. The one I want, too.

I get to the natatorium early. Not so early that it's weird, but earlier than your average spectator. Peeking into the locker room, I find it packed to the brim with visiting athletes.

Awkwardly making my way through, I find the guys. "Ready for today? Gonna do me proud?"

"Hell yeah we are!" Brock all but shouts. Then he whispers, "These sorry sacks are going down."

Hunter rolls his eyes. "Might wanna quiet down. Voices carry in here."

"Why would I care about that?" Brock counters. "I'm speakin' facts, nothing less." He cackles and brushes at each shoulder like he's king of the world.

Tyler continues silently stretching, then says, "I'm gonna head out on deck, start listening to my playlist. Anyone else?" He eyes each of us briefly. When none of us move, he saunters toward the door that leads to the pool deck.

"Too bad you can't come on deck, buddy." Hunter playfully punches my arm. "What're we gonna do without your old-man music and jokes?"

"Yeah, it's not gonna slap without you, my guy," Brock adds, but gets distracted by a dude walking by holding a pizza box. I hear him ask, "Got any extra?"

The guy has no shame.

"I'll see you guys after. I think I'll grab something to eat before Maisie's due to start. Pretty sure none of you compete until later anyway, right?"

Hunter, ever the optimist, chimes in, "Yeah, it's gonna be a long day, but at least there's new people to meet."

"Ha, only you would be shacking up with the competition, bro. But hey, kick some serious butt for me, all right?"

"I'll do my best." He salutes and grabs a pizza-less Brock on his way through the swinging doors.

I mosey out to the concession stand and pay for a hot dog. It's nostalgic, and I could use the small bit of comfort. I hate to admit it, but I'm still a bit on edge about my dad calling again this morning. Something feels off. Why would he keep calling when I don't answer? His persistence doesn't make sense when he doesn't care about my life—not really, anyway.

I finish eating and realize I'm cutting it close to Maize's start time. Hopefully I didn't worry her by not being out there already. I quickly find my seat in the stands. Maisie spots me and blows me a kiss, and I send one right back. Some of our teammates are watching, and I'm glad she doesn't care about the public display because I sure as hell want everyone to know how much I care about her. I've wanted to shout to the rooftops how much I love her for so long, but this is a good start for now.

Maisie's up first, and I'm in awe of her strength and grace. She does something few people in the world do, and I hope she knows what a badass that makes her. I'll be sure to remind her every chance I get.

She's about to start her approach when my phone buzzes again.

Dad.

What the hell? I shift in my seat but keep my eyes on her. Eventually, he'll give up, right?

She executes her dive beautifully, and I stand to cheer.

I'm at the edge of my seat the whole competition. I should have brought my foam finger for how loud I've been cheering for Maize. Angie is the only one of our little group who has had a swimming event so far, which she placed second in. Maize is climbing the tower for her last dive when a man steps into my line of sight.

"Excuse me." I shift to look around him.

"Son."

My blood runs cold. It's been a long time since I've heard that voice in person.

"*Dad?* What are you doing here?"

"You weren't answering my calls, so I didn't know how else to get ahold of you."

I look around frantically, like someone will notice my distress and tell him to leave. When I realize that isn't going to happen, I take a deep breath and meet his hazel eyes, the mirrors of my own.

"Please leave, Dad. I don't have anything to say to you."

"Well, I have things to say to you!" he bellows.

I stand and grab his arm to shift us to the lobby, worrying the scene could distract Maisie.

He yanks his arm back but follows quietly. Once we're in the lobby, I turn to face him. His arms are crossed, eyes wide, nostrils flared. He's pissed, and honestly, that pisses *me* off a bit. What does he have to be mad about? That I didn't call him back? Well, he ruined our family. I think we're more than even.

Crossing my arms, I stand as tall as I can and say, "What? What are you doing here? What do you need? In case you didn't get the message from me not picking up your calls, I don't want to talk to you."

"Why the hell aren't you swimming?" He swings an arm toward the door we just came through like he's pointing at the pool that isn't currently visible.

"Not that it's any of your business, but I'm done swimming. Today was the last competition to sit out for my suspension, but I'm not going back after."

"The hell you aren't!" His face is flushed now, fists and jaw clenched. Is this what I look like when I'm angry? I don't want to be anything like this man. Thank god Dr. Fitz mandated therapy. I refuse to turn out like this.

"Lower your voice," I command.

"I'll speak in any tone I so choose. You don't boss me around. *I'm* the parent here!"

"Not from where I'm standing. Parents are there for their kids beyond a few phone calls that only revolve around swimming. Well, I'm not swimming anymore, Dad, so what will you say?"

A crack sounds, and it takes a moment for me to realize what happened. He slapped me. Not overly hard, but he did it. There are two or three other people in here, but it was so quick, I don't think anyone saw it happen.

Anger flares in my chest, so I shut my eyes. I rub my hand along my jeans, letting the texture ground me as I breathe.

"The hell are you doing?" Dad asks.

"Not hitting you back. Even though you fucking deserve it," I grind out.

He pays no mind to the herculean self-control I'm exhibiting and continues to taunt me. "I didn't raise you to be like this. A quitter."

"You quit raising me. If you taught me anything, it *was* to be a quitter, *Dad*."

He grits his teeth but doesn't say anything for a moment. "If you quit, you won't have an apartment."

It feels like a last-ditch effort for control, but I'm realizing he doesn't truly have any power over me. Not anymore. I'm about to tell him I don't want or need his fucking apartment when a silhouette I would recognize anywhere pops into the corner of my vision.

Maisie.

No, I don't want her to see this.

66

Another Moment

Maisie

I STUMBLE INTO THE natatorium's lobby and instantly find Connor. It feels like there is an invisible string between us pulling taut. I'm relieved to see him, but I don't recognize the man he's with. The man looks angry. As I stride quickly toward them, Connor turns to face me with wild eyes. I skid a step.

My senses are on high alert. Something doesn't feel right.

"What's going on?" I ask as soon as I reach the two men.

Now that I'm closer, recognition sparks. They have the same eyes—except where Connor's are warm, this man's are cold and severe—and the same height and build. This must be Connor's dad. *Oh, hell no.*

"This isn't a conversation for your little girlfriend to be a part of. This is about your future!" The man raises his voice, and I instinctively shrink back for a moment before deciding *no*, he doesn't get to talk to Connor like that—or me, for that matter.

I look to Connor. Something fiery yet broken lies in the depths of his eyes. Anger boils inside me, and I glare at his dad.

"You can't talk to him like that!" Defending Connor—the man *I love*, but haven't had a chance to tell yet—is as natural as breathing.

The man swings his disgusted gaze to me, and that snaps Connor into some sort of primal mode. He pulls me behind him before his dad so much as has a chance to say anything. Connor is protecting me from the man who hurt him most in the world. Something lodges in my throat.

"Don't look at her. Don't talk to her. Leave!"

"Is she why you quit? Did you let some woman get into your head and ruin your future?"

I reel back.

Connor's jaw clenches. "She has nothing to do with it, Dad. This was my decision. We're done here."

"The hell we are!"

His dad grabs Connor by the arm, hard. I can see the moment Connor shifts, his fists clenching and his face twisting in rage, and I'm worried he's about to do something he'll regret. I grab his other arm and pull him toward me with all my strength. His eyes whip to my face, and the torment there is anguishing.

"Don't," I whisper.

He twists his arm to extricate himself from his dad's grasp, then follows me toward the doors that lead down to the locker rooms.

"You can't just walk away from me!" Mr. Bocelli shouts, and there is a desperation to his voice that almost makes me feel bad for him, knowing he just lost his last chance with his son.

Connor inhales sharply, but we keep walking until he's out of sight.

We're silent the whole walk, but Connor keeps peeking down at me, like he's making sure I'm okay, even though I'm the one worried about him. He didn't deserve to be treated that way. His dad never should have shown up without permission—and the way he talked to him? I wish I'd said more.

Quiet determination pulses at my temples. By the time we reach a quiet alcove on the main level, I pull him into an embrace. He squeezes me so tight, I'm worried he might dislocate something.

I peel back, but only so I can look him in the eye as I say, "I love you, Connor. I'm sorry for every day I didn't say it out loud. I love you, and I don't want another day, another moment to go by without you knowing it. You deserve so much more than what that asshole gave you. And I'm *so,* so sorry."

A tear slips down my cheek. Connor stops it with the back of his pointer finger.

"Stop apologizing, love."

Then, he's kissing me. But he doesn't just kiss me. He kisses me like I'm the air he breathes. He kisses me like he's been underground and is seeing sunlight for the first time. More tears fall from both of us, the salty taste tangling between our intertwining tongues. He has my back pressed against the wall, and when he moves his knee between my thighs, stars burst behind my closed eyes. I ache for him everywhere, and the heady combination of Connor—his smell, his taste, the feel of him around me—and admitting I love him has my whole body softening, careening toward him in a silent plea for more.

He pulls back, resting his forehead against mine, and the absence leaves my skin hot and scratchy. "I love you so much, and you have no idea what it means to hear you say it too."

"I think I can hazard a guess," I say, dropping another peck to his lips. That spurs him on, and we get caught up for another moment before he pulls back again. A little whine escapes my throat.

"I'm sorry I missed your last dive," he pants. "How did it go?"

This man. He just went through all of that, and he's still thinking about me. About my competition, my goals.

"I did the back three and a half," I say.

He regards me with bent eyebrows. "You did? Why didn't you tell me you were going to?"

Laughing, I say, "I didn't tell anyone. I only told Coach right before warm-ups started. She was pissed, to be honest."

"When isn't she?" He laughs. "I'm so freaking proud of you, love. You're amazing."

Love. He called me that once before, and I secretly loved it. Now that our love is out in the open, I want him to call me that all the time. Although "Betty" and "My Queen" still have a special place in my heart. "And guess what?" I add.

"What?" He tucks me in closer.

"I placed fourth and qualified for the National Championship," I whisper.

Next thing I know, I'm off the ground, flying through the air. He's spinning me around in a hug, like you see in movies. My best friend. My love. My Connor. He's simply the best.

When he lets my feet touch ground again, he still holds tight, saying, "I'm beyond proud of you. I knew you could do it. You can do anything." He kisses me again, and it feels like floating on a cloud.

I love him. I love him. I love him. This is beyond different from everything that happened with Karsen. I can trust him with my heart. And while my heart might remain a little guarded for a while, that's okay. Sometimes scars remain, but that doesn't make me any less healed.

"Come on," he says, taking my hand in his huge one. "This calls for ice cream to celebrate."

A laugh jingles out of my throat, and I can't stop smiling as I let him lead me out of the natatorium.

67

All The More

Connor

WE GRAB A TWO-TOP table at Maisie's favorite ice cream joint. Moose Tracks for her and plain vanilla for me. Although I know I'll need to work through the events of the day—and I will with Donny at our next session, and for a long time after—right now, all I can think about is the fact that Maisie loves me.

I hate to admit it, but I was starting to worry those words may never come. Or, if they did, that it would be much further down the line. But they're here; she said them, and I will treasure them forever. And prove to her each and every day that I am worthy to be trusted with them.

I can finally tell her everything. So, once we're settled in and a scoop of ice cream is hovering at her luscious lips, I say, "I've loved you since move-in day. I saw you from across the parking lot and was taken aback by how beautiful you were, but what really drew me in was your smile. You smile with your whole being, love. And when I saw your eyes, they had a spike of anxiety but also a kindness that reached into my soul. I knew I needed to know you. Then, when fate intervened and you were on the same team as me, I made sure to talk to you. It was like my whole body was naturally pulled toward you."

Her mouth full of ice cream, her eyes widen. She reaches out to take my hand as she rushes to swallow. "Wait. You saw me on move-in day?"

"Yes," I say without hesitation. "Grandpa always said he knew the moment he first laid eyes on Grandma. I always thought it was a load of shit, to be honest, until that moment."

Her eyes gleam.

"And it absolutely *killed* me when I found out you had a boyfriend. I knew he wasn't good enough for you, and watching and waiting for you to realize that was one of the hardest things I've ever done."

She's leaning forward, and I reach out to brush a lock of her hair behind her ear. I don't want it to get in her ice cream.

"I'm sorry I was ever with him," she says melancholily, looking away.

"Hey." I cup her chin and gently turn her back to me. "*You* did nothing wrong. That was on him, and I promise to continue earning your trust every day to prove I'm nothing like him."

She reaches up to wrap a hand around the wrist of my outstretched arm. "I know," she says with a wistful smile. "I really know, and I'm so glad to be with you. I don't even know how to express how glad. How much I love you."

I close my eyes and revel in the words again. Feeling them loop around my heart and squeeze. I won't ever tire of hearing them.

"Can I ask you a question?" she says.

"Anything."

"Why didn't you talk to me for those few weeks?"

I wince. "Oh, love, I'm *so* sorry. That was me being beyond stupid. I was in love with you, and I didn't want to ruin our friendship by telling you how much I liked you. The guys told me to tell you I had a date—it was *always* a *fake* date—to see how you would react. When I told you that night, you didn't seem upset about it, and I thought... Ugh."

I swipe a hand through my hair. I can't believe what an idiot I was to ever lose out on time with her.

"It seemed you only ever thought of me as a friend, and that felt like my heart was being ripped from my chest. I never planned to stay away as long as I did. I only hoped a bit of space would allow me to get over the fact that you didn't like me like that. That I could eventually be okay enough to be only your friend.

Although, in my heart of hearts, I knew I never would be because I've *always* wanted more with you, love."

She bursts out laughing. So hard that the table shakes from where her foot vibrates against it.

"What's so funny?" I ask, not sure how to interpret the reaction.

"So there was never a real date?" She laughs some more.

"Uh...no." What is happening in that beautiful brain of hers?

"First of all, I *did* care. I cared a hell of a lot. I hated the idea of you going on a date with someone else, and I didn't understand why that meant you couldn't talk to me. I was beyond jealous and missed you *so* much. Secondly, I thought you and Veronica were dating. What with the flirting at the pool, and then the coffee shop, and all. But when I went to the Halloween party..." She covers her eyes with her hands, then scrubs them down her face. "I accused Veronica of cheating on you, but she said the guy she was with was her boyfriend. It was so embarrassing, but it didn't help the situation any more because then I figured you went out with someone I didn't even know."

I grab both her hands in mine, squeezing them tenderly. This woman. We could have saved ourselves so much pain and heartache. But I'm thankful. For all of it. Because it got us here, together. And in the end, that's all that matters.

"I'm sorry you ever spent one minute thinking I wanted someone who wasn't you. You *are* my best friend, Maize, but you're so much more. You always have been, and you always will be." I reach across the table to wrap my hand around the back of her neck and pull her into a searing kiss. I don't want her to ever doubt my feelings for her. "Wanna take this to go and head back to my place? I'm sure everyone is still at the pool."

Her eyes light up, and she nods, already excitedly jumping out of her chair. She does, however, bring her ice cream to the front and swiftly ask for a to-go container. Maisie would never leave ice cream behind, not even for the promise of sex. And I love her all the more for it.

We leave hand in hand, and I thank my lucky stars that this woman chose me. And when we get back to my place, I show her just how much. Over and over. All night long.

Epilogue

Connor

WE'RE STANDING IN LINE at the drive-in movie theater's concession stand. Yes, the drive-in, because I couldn't think of a better place for our first Marvel movie premiere together—and we have an "old people" tradition to uphold. We spent the rest of the school year catching me up, and I finally graduated to being able to witness the latest release in real time.

This summer has been a whirlwind. We're both back home, both working, but we take turns driving to each other's houses every weekend, and we meet up halfway during the week sometimes.

I fall more and more in love with her every day, and I still can't believe it sometimes. That I get a best friend and the love of my life all wrapped into one. It was an honor to attend as a student coach when Maisie competed in her first Nationals in the spring. She didn't place, but my girl is ready to work even harder next year. Nothing is going to stop her, and I couldn't be more proud.

I've continued therapy with Donny through the summer. Thank goodness for virtual capabilities because once we opened Pandora's box, there has been a whole hell of a lot to work through. But it's worth it. For myself, and also for my future with Maize.

My savings ran dry after having to pay for the rest of the year's rent on the apartment my dad bailed on, but luckily Coach Ken is going to pay me to student coach next year, and I might even get a side gig at the retirement home as an Assistant Activities Coordinator. Dick said he'd put in a good word for me.

I was able to visit the retirement home about once a month through the end of the school year. It brightens my day to brighten their day. And ever since losing Grandpa, there has been a little corner of my heart that craves wisdom from someone who's been around a lot longer than I have. To interact with someone from a different time and with varying life experiences. It changes you for the better, and I'm honored to have people to spend time with in that regard. Not that anyone will ever replace Grandpa, but I think he'd be happy to know I was participating like this.

Hunter and I decided to share a dorm room next year, and we'll only be one floor up from Maize and Ang. I can't wait to be so close again and get to see my girl every day. Brock and Tyler will be in our building, too. Right next to Angie and Maize's room. I asked them to switch, but Brock refused, which I found odd. But what are you gonna do?

"Cool Ranch Doritos, a root beer and ginger ale, and two ice cream sandwiches, please."

The kid behind the counter enters our order into the computer without a word. God, every time we're somewhere with a high-schooler working, I feel like an eighty-year-old man. I'm probably three or four years older than this kid, but might as well be twenty with how different we are. Price of growing up quick, I suppose.

Maisie bounces on her toes beside me. She's in a dusty blue summery dress with little daisies embroidered along the bottom. A break from being in a pool daily has allowed her hair to grow out a bit, and it caresses the top of her breasts that are poking out of the dress's neckline perfectly. As much as I adore her athletic shorts and tank tops, this dress is doing something to me. But honestly, she could wear a potato sack, and I would say the same thing.

"Come on!" she squeals, and I realize I've been staring at her for a beat longer than is socially acceptable. "I don't want to miss the commercials!"

We arrived early for that very reason, and once we're settled back into the back of the car, the trunk popped and pillow fort made—we took her dad's car so we'd have room to spread out; the Civic wasn't going to cut it—I lean into her space, wrapping her in my arms, and kiss the top of her head, inhaling her familiar lavender scent. This is bliss.·

We end up making out—not an uncommon occurrence for us, even after all these months—until the standing old-timey speaker crackles and the commercials start. She pulls away so fast, I'm almost hurt for a moment. But seeing the excitement in her eyes as she awaits a new installment in her favorite franchise, I can't help but smile. I take her hand, face the screen, and soak up this moment with my love. Thankful I'm right where I'm meant to be.

Acknowledgements

Thank you first and foremost to my amazing husband, Jason. From day one, your encouragement to pursue my dreams of becoming a published author have been unwavering. You've taken care of me and the house, and always ensured I had time to do what I needed to do to keep this train on the track. And here we are, publishing my debut novel. A dream come to fruition. Little Emmy is squealing in joy. And thank you to my Pappaw, who encouraged little Emmy to write books. You saw a path before I did, and it's been one of my best adventures, yet. I love you.

Thank you also to my very first readers and hype ladies, Lillie and Lily. My sister-in-law and dear friend respectively. Your comments not only made my story better, but your excitement also kept me going when continuing felt impossible. Love you both.

And Meredith, my wonderful critique partner/long-distance bestie/sanity keeper/daily encourager/overall wonderful person. This book wouldn't exist without you. Point blank. Definitely not in the time frame in which it is. And if we're being honest, probably not at all. Thank you for every text, every edit and suggestion, every piece of advice. Can't wait to do this with you for a very long time.

Thank you to my amazing editing team: Larissa, Juwi, and Erin. This would have been a very different book without each of your expert eyes.

Thank you to my wonderful beta readers: Ashley, Jade, Vic, Casey, Sophia, and Danielle. You took a chance on a writer's debut and provided invaluable insight. I'm forever grateful. And yes, don't worry, Brock and Angie are getting a book too. Also huge shout-out to my sensitivity reader, Annie. Your expertise is immensely appreciated.

And to my dear friend, Amanda. I called you up out of the blue, my artist friend, asking for help describing my vision of the cover to another artist. Little did I know, you'd throw your own hat in the ring. You didn't have to take on this tiny project, but you did. Working with you is a joy and an honor, and I love getting to create and interact with you.

Thank you to my character artists @conceptsbycanea and @seaborn.studios. You brought Connor, Maisie, and Angie to life before my very eyes. It's a dream to see my characters visually. Also shout out to my Street Team. You all took a chance on me, and I am forever grateful to have you along for the ride.

And to Anna, my hype woman/proofreader: I'm so glad for the fated day we met in Washington. Thank you for your friendship, for every book recommendation, and for being a bad-ass.

Last, but certainly not least, thank you. Yes, you. The one reading this right now. Thank you for taking a chance on an indie author's debut novel. Thank you for hanging out with Connor and Maisie through all their shenanigans. Thank you for supporting me not only by reading my book, but by reviewing and engaging over social media. The book community is a truly special one, and I'm blessed to have found it and get to be a part of it. The connections are real, and I'm thankful for each and every one of you.

About the author

Emmy Lewes writes hot and heartfelt sports romance, where female athletes always shine. When she's not cuddled into the couch typing away on her laptop, she's spending time with friends and family, making any excuse to go to a beach, and narrating audiobooks with her husband. A Pennsylvania native and certified "sporty-girl", she hopes you enjoy her stories as much as she enjoyed writing them. Find her on instagram at @authoremmylewes

References

1 HTTPS://WWW.WEARETHEMIGHTY.COM/MIGHTY-HISTORY/JEWISH-ASSASSINS-AVENGING-THE-HOLOCAUST/